Sticking out of the usual week postal delivery, cream-colored square envelope with no return address and her name spelled out in elegant, formal script. The lettering had been carefully composed by hand with variances in line thickness, a departure from the cold, computer-generated mass mailings she typically pulled from the mailbox at the end of her driveway.

As she returned inside the house, delegating the boring mail to a sloppy stack on an entry hall table, she brought her personalized missive into the kitchen. Before pouring her customary after-work glass of red wine, she tore open the curious envelope, half-expecting a too-clever advertisement.

Instead, she slid out a cardstock invitation to a time machine.

You are cordially invited to
an exclusive trip to reinvent the past
at the request of Mr. Daniel DeCastro
who will unveil the miracle of his
TIME MACHINE
and the Open Horizon of Possibilities

Time Warp

by Brian Pinkerton

All the world's a stage
And all the men and women merely players
They have their exits and their entrances
And one man in his time plays many parts

—William Shakespeare

Prologue

Guns drawn, a crush of police descended on the old warehouse. A man's body rested on its back on the pavement in plain view in the dying sunlight. They cautiously advanced past his lifeless form toward the building's front entrance from which he had emerged.

A long stretch of yellow tape quickly unspooled around the scene as a chorus of sirens announced the arrival of more police and ambulances.

Two officers spoke to the witnesses, sorting through their tangled hysterics against the flashing red and blue lights, while others disappeared into the dilapidated structure, uncertain of what they might find.

In single file, police moved up and down long, dark aisles of mostly empty shelving, shining their flashlights into corners and crevices, scattering rats. Reaching the rear of the building, they discovered a strange labyrinth of brightly lit rooms, a series of living quarters in a maze-like arrangement.

Once the warehouse was properly secured, and there was no discernible threat of further violence, the evidence technicians moved in. One space in particular, an office of sorts, offered a promising collection of clues. This included a thick, handwritten journal found on a drafting table. The item was immediately sealed into an evidence bag. The cover of the spiral-bound notebook displayed a title in black marker. The words were both direct and enigmatic, written in large, confident letters.

TIME TRAVEL LOG

Part One

TRAVEL LOG: REVERSAL 39Y 7M 8D

My hands tremble uncontrollably as I write these words. I am flooded with rich sensations I never expected to recapture in my lifetime. I have returned from an extraordinary journey that defies the limitations of a linear existence.

The first mission has been a total success. It is course correction number one in a history of regret. I re-entered a moment from my past, a reversal of thirty-nine years, seven months, and eight days from my current time and place. I became younger and smaller but equipped with the knowledge of future threats. I acted in ways to create a new outcome. The scene refresh that lay trapped inside my imagination for too long, running on a loop of elusive joy, finally burst free. All of the hard work, determination, and ingenuity poured into this most unorthodox pursuit has paid off.

For the first time since I was a small child, I held my dog.

Reunited with Toby! This was the yellow Labrador retriever I received on my ninth birthday after begging for a pet for so many years. His big, clumsy movements rocked my small bed. I buried my face in the warm softness of his fur. I called out his name. His tail danced in excitement. He licked at my smooth, young face. Everything returned from a long-ago tunnel, distanced by decades but never forgotten: Toby's sweet musty smell, his eager panting, his wet nose, and big, glossy eyes.

I kept my bedroom door firmly shut. Toby stayed with me on the bed, safe and happy in my arms. My newest model airplane kit remained unopened in its box on my bookshelf, alongside my favorite science fiction and fantasy books. These details are crucial because this return to the past was purposefully synchronized to a specific sequence of events that has haunted me deep into adulthood.

Holding Toby, I worried for a moment that perhaps my experiment was only a partial success—maybe I had returned to my childhood surroundings but mistimed the entry. What if my tear-stained childhood diary contained errors? That brittle, fading notebook was my only source for identifying this fateful day. Without it, I was swimming in an uncertain timeline of childhood haze.

Throughout my life, the events of this day had remained vivid, never losing their strength to sting again and again with sorrow. Perhaps even stronger than sorrow was the relentless guilt churned by the ugly truth that I was responsible for Toby's departure.

That's because I was responsible for Toby.

After finally giving in to many years of my pleading for a pet, my father was very firm about the rules: Toby was my dog, and I was accountable for taking care of him. That included walking him, feeding him, preventing him from chewing on the sofa cushions, and ensuring he did not disrupt the order of the household.

If I neglected my duties, the deal was off and Toby would be gone. This stipulation was nonnegotiable. I eagerly accepted those terms.

Toby joined the household, entered my life, and filled a vacancy for companionship. I didn't have many playmates and my older brother Reed was rarely home. I became Toby's care-taker and he became my best friend. I kept him out of trouble, which kept me out of trouble. We were inseparable. He played with me in the backyard. He slept in my bedroom. He waited by the door for me to come home from school.

My parents weren't very social but they did host a back-yard barbecue every summer for my father's carpet distribution business. He was always very tense about the event, bickering with my mother over every detail and obsessing over the invite list to corral the most important clients and would-be clients.

On the day we lost Toby, I was told to keep a watch on him

during the last-minute scurry to get everything in order for the impending guests. My father had left the house to get cases of soda and beer. I was in my bedroom at my desk, assembling a Bachmann Mini-Plane P-51 Mustang, twisting little pieces off the plastic frame of parts and connecting them with small dabs of sweet-smelling rubber cement. Toby lay at my feet, occasionally shifting or stretching. I could hear my mother cleaning in the nearby bathroom.

I should have closed my bedroom door.

I should have closed my bedroom door.

Because Toby silently—paws on thick shag—padded out of the room. I was poring over the instructions for my model, worried about cementing the wrong pieces together, determined to build a perfect aircraft.

So, I didn't realize Toby had slipped away until roughly thirty seconds after I heard my father return from the grocery store.

That's when the explosion began. My father screaming. Toby yelping and scampering away from a beating. My mother's wail of despair. Then both of them yelling my name.

I froze in terror. Even as they called for me, I couldn't budge from my chair.

"DANNY!"

My father burst into my room, eyes blazing and face pinched, crimson red.

"We had a deal!"

Toby had discovered the steaks thawing on the kitchen counter, pulled them down to the floor and devoured them. Then, having gorged himself on uncooked meat, he threw up all over the living room.

"The company will be here in 15 minutes!"

I couldn't speak. I was terrified into paralysis because I recognized the consequences even before they were spoken aloud. It was the constant threat that had been paraded over me ever since Toby joined the family.

"You blew it. That dog is gone. Do you hear me? Gone!"

There was no time for an extended berating. The living room had to be cleaned. New steaks had to be purchased. Toby was jammed into his puppy crate in the garage. He barely fit anymore. He whimpered and peed on himself, but knew better than to bark.

After the party started, I snuck out of my room, where I had been ordered to stay, and visited Toby in the garage. He clawed at his cage, pushing one of his paws through the bars, as if reaching out. His eyes were big and scared. I cried and promised I wouldn't let my parents take him away. I vowed we would stay together.

The next morning, prior to cleaning up the house, my father drove off with Toby. He refused to say where he was going and returned without him.

His only reply to my hysteria was a reminder that it was all my fault. It didn't have to turn out this way. A deal was made, and I failed on my end of the bargain.

Toby was the victim.

"Lesson learned," said my father, giving the entire episode a clinical assessment, like a page from a textbook.

I never forgot Toby's frightened face in that cage. That's what I lived with for exactly thirty-nine years, seven months, and eight days. It was a sentence of shame that has now, finally, come to an end.

When I entered the long, dark passageway and emerged in my childhood bedroom, untouched since that fateful day, I knew I had an opportunity to relieve myself of a burden that had weighed down hard on my shoulders for a very long time.

Today I successfully traveled back in time and created a new reality.

Sitting on the bed with Toby, holding him out of affection and for protection, I heard the sound I had been anxiously waiting to hear.

My father's return from the grocery store.

The door banged open, followed by heavy footsteps and the thud of large cases hitting the floor. Then the door slammed shut.

"I've got the beer and the soda!"

My mother, cleaning the bathroom down the hall, responded, "I'll be down in a few minutes."

"Can you fill the cooler? I'm going to start the steaks."

Then I listened very carefully, irrationally feeling the fear of an impending explosion, and there was none.

I opened my bedroom window. After a while, I could smell the smoky aroma of steaks sizzling on the grill. A little while after that, the doorbell rang. Toby grew anxious, but I kept him secured in my room. The guests were arriving.

The party started and I could hear my father's deep laughter and my mother's cheerful chatter mingling with the other voices.

I was happy to hear my parents so happy. I was happy knowing that Toby was safe and not going anywhere. I was happy I had not failed my duty.

Happy. Ultimately, all this crazy, complicated time travel has just one goal, probably the simplest goal anyone could ask for in life.

To be *happy*.

I am returned now from my excursion, logging the results. As I write these words, I am already looking forward to the next adventure.

I saved Toby from leaving me.

Next I will have an even bigger mission. I will save my mother's life.

Chapter
One

Eyes shut, Danny DeCastro remembered a time in his life when anything was possible.

When he was small and the world was big, the open field behind the schoolyard beckoned to him with a landscape that stretched into forever, limitless. He routinely dashed into its expansive terrain with his eyes closed, arms spread like the wings of a plane, legs pounding the soft matt of grass, air rushing at him in an exhilarating sweep of freedom.

Each year, as Danny grew bigger and wiser, the open field withdrew to a smaller, more realistic scale until one day he found himself in the present, trapped in a box, a cube to be precise, with stifling parameters that didn't give him enough room to stretch his wings without obstruction. He was almost fifty, stubbornly retaining the childhood second syllable in his name, but dragged unwillingly through adulthood nevertheless.

As Danny closed his eyes and tried to recall a sense of freedom and open air, Mack Kosiak entered his tiny space, accompanied by a whiff of dollar-store cologne, and barked at him from up close.

"What? Really? You're napping?"

Danny fumbled for his headset and slapped his mouse to chase away the screensaver, which seemed to function primarily to tattle on idleness.

"You're being outperformed by kids half your age," said Kosiak, loud enough to inform the other cubicles. "They have the drive. You can't survive here without a drive to succeed." He gripped a spreadsheet and gave it a quick wave. "You're not making enough calls. You're not closing on the calls you do make. I hope you haven't forgotten that your pay here is based on commissions."

There was a pause, perhaps to indicate that Danny should respond. He started to, but Kosiak continued on top of him, disinterested in his defense. "I don't need people to warm seats. I can pull bums off the street to do that. Your job is to *sell*. You want to close your eyes, you do it on your own time."

Danny secured the headset and quickly brought his hands to the keyboard to retrieve his next lead.

Arthur Morse, CIO, Vista Enterprises LLC.

A few pokes later, a steady buzz pulsed in his ears and a busy script filled Danny's screen.

Kosiak nodded, gave one more stern wave of the spreadsheet and left to harass the next victim in his cubicle farm.

When a woman's voice answered the line, Danny jumped into his prepared text with a fat tone of confidence and familiarity, both fake.

"Hello again, it's good to hear your voice, dear," he said to the woman. They had never spoken before. "I'm returning a call from Art." According to the notes on his screen, Arthur Morse's closest friends called him Art.

"I'm sorry, who's calling?"

Danny laughed at her memory lapse. "Daniel at Strategy Roundtable. I hope I didn't miss him, he asked us to get back to him right away. The clock is ticking."

Her uncertainty melted away and she fed off Danny's urgency. "He did? I'm so sorry. Listen, he's preparing for a board meeting, but I think I can get his attention—"

"Please do," said Danny. "I've got someone on the other line who wants to take his place, but Art is our number one choice."

"Of course," she said.

Art was on the line within 10 seconds.

"Who is this?"

"I am so grateful we were able to reach you," said Danny. "We almost had to give up your spot."

"What spot?"

"The Strategic Innovation Growth and Profitability Corporate

Leaders Conference. Your leadership team has been a great supporter in the past, and we were so excited to hear you would be an honored guest at this year's exclusive event."

"I'm sorry, I'm not familiar. Who...?"

"Walmart had to send us their regrets. Their Chief Information Officer had to drop out at the last minute for a sudden death in the family, and we have just one spot available—hold on—Nancy, no, it's reserved for Mr. Morse, tell GM we are booked solid. What? No, I don't care if they pay double to get a seat, that's not how we operate." Pause. "Okay, sorry about that, Art. Bit of a madhouse here. I'm trying to protect your reservation at the conference."

"But I never—"

"Bob from New York is so excited you're coming."

"Who?"

"Bob!"

"Bob who?"

"Bob mrphkl-"

"What?"

"We have a great agenda, dozens of attendees from Fortune 500 companies, C-suite executives, potential clients for your business, make that mega clients. I don't want to have to give this opportunity to your competitors, Art. Our surveys show that conference attendees on average see their revenue growth increase 27% and get a boost in brand reputation of up to thirty-three point six. If you're not interested, that's fine, your call. My phone is lit up like a Christmas tree. I just need to hear it from you directly so there are no hard feelings later."

"I don't know what this is all about."

"Don't be embarrassed. I know you're a busy man with a lot on your mind. You've got your board meeting coming up, am I right? Heck, I know half those guys. I see them all the time at our conferences. We're golfing buddies. Anyway, I don't want to take up your time, I know how valuable it is. Just put me on with your secretary and I'll work with her on the scheduling and we'll lock this in and be done with it, so you don't have to worry, sound good?"

"Well, check with Peg on the dates, then if you could send more information..."

"You got it! Thanks so much. Art, always a pleasure talking with you. I appreciate the support and tell the rest of the gang hello for me."

When the secretary returned on the line, Danny jumped into a new set of remarks.

"Peg, we are all good," Danny announced. "Art is all in. Let's invoice this and lock in the reservation."

"When...is this?"

"Next spring. March third through the fifth in beautiful, gorgeous Hawaii."

She sucked in a big breath. After a moment, she let it out. "No, no. That won't work. He's in Europe..."

"I'm sorry, Peg. Did I say third through the fifth? I meant seventeenth through nineteenth. Stupid me. The third through the fifth, that's our CEO World Conference in Paris. That baby is fully booked, no one's getting in there, ha ha. Don't even try."

"Oh. March 17 through 19? Yes, that can work..."

"Excellent. And since Art is an old friend and frequent guest, we are happy to give him our special reduced rate of $45,500. Wow, we don't even break even on that one, so it's not refundable. It's a limited time offer, so we're going to ask for an upfront commitment. Will this be American Express? We have his card on file, but let's hear the numbers just to make sure they still match up."

Danny felt victory in his clutches. Peg was along for the ride. She began reciting the account number. She made it through the first three digits when her voice was abruptly cut off.

Art returned on the line.

"I remember you!" he declared.

"Oh, that's wonderful," said Danny, but he knew the tone was moving toward fury, not affection.

"You guys are one big scam," said Morse. "My CMO just reminded me. You set up bogus conferences for corporate executives, charge them outrageous fees and deliver half-assed, half-empty bullshit events on the cheap."

"I'm sorry...?"

"Every big name you promise mysteriously drops out at the last minute and comes down with the flu. Or else you cancel the whole thing with no refund, just a voucher for some other conference in a lousy hotel in a shitty city with sack lunches and generic presentations of bullshit pulled off Wikipedia."

"I'm so sorry you feel this way," said Danny. "I really believe you have us confused with another organization, Strategic Discourse from Cleveland. They are notorious scammers and it's such a shame, they taint our entire field…"

"No, it's you. I know it's you."

"Well, we have big-name clients from Apple, IBM, Google, and Amazon who would beg to differ."

"I'm going to report you to the Better Business Bureau."

"What if we could offer you a one-time super saver's discount?"

"Give it up. You're pathetic."

And with that, the line disconnected.

Danny remained motionless in his seat, exhausted from his persistent performance, nowhere near ready to dive into it yet again with another cold call.

He pulled the headset down around his neck where it clung like a dog collar. He could hear the lively murmur of other callers in the room dancing through their routines, injecting many of the same familiar phrases and false promises from their scripts.

Danny felt like the air was leaving the room. He was slowly suffocating. How did he get to such a horrible, controlled place? Not just here, this employer, but in life. His everyday existence was squeezed. His words were scripted by others.

He desperately needed to escape. He needed to write his own scripts for a change, starting with, "I quit."

That night, Danny sat at his kitchen table and scribbled two paragraphs of monologue to deliver to Mack Kosiak. He memorized the words until bedtime.

At 8:30 the next morning, he entered Kosiak's office. The office was similar to a cubicle, just a little larger, with real walls instead of fake half-walls, and the addition of a squat window that offered a glimpse of the world beyond the workplace drudgery. The view overlooked the parking lot, which Kosiak boasted about, because it enabled him to observe who was coming and going in his quest to identify employees who were shaving minutes off their nine-to-five obligation.

Danny started to recite the first sentence of his script, but Kosiak interrupted, equipped with his own words, throwing everything off course.

"Oh, hey, I'm glad you're here," said Kosiak. "I've been doing some thinking about yesterday and your performance here and your overall demeanor and all that and anyway, so, yeah, you're fired."

Chapter Two

I have hit a dead end.

Hard as he tried, Danny could not imagine any progress in his future. He sat at his kitchen table facing a blank wall, sipping soup, ears absorbing the loud hiss of a white noise machine he bought online to drown out the unpleasant sounds of the apartments above, below and on either side of him, crushing him with their obnoxious soundtrack: the thud thud thud of hip hop above, the hyper-excitable, yapping golden doodle below, the loud TV blabbing to the right, the screamy kids to the left.

Too often he heard them break past the layer of manufactured white noise, defiant, on a mission to poke him to death with aggravation.

Danny's apartment felt like just another cubicle to trap him, a slow-motion suffocation of dim light and close walls. After finishing his soup, he tossed the bowl in the sink and escaped, which was a joke, because he had no place to escape to. After some aimless driving, Danny decided on the mall. He drove into Racine, Wisconsin, and immersed himself in the big indoor shopping complex, disinterested in shopping, but drawn to the stimulation of bright lights, tall ceilings, and stimulating colors. He touched fabrics in clothing stores. He took in some tastes at the food court. He spent an awkward amount of time standing around in The Soap Box, a small space devoted to scents—handmade soaps, body lotions, and home fragrances in elegant containers and colorful wrappings with ridiculous price tags. The mixed-up smells invigorated him.

"Are you looking for a gift?" asked a pleasant woman in a

cream-colored blouse, "Kim" according to her nametag, a strategy he recognized to immediately place them on a first name basis.

"No."

"Something for yourself?"

Danny's mind went blank. He was unprepared. He wished he had words handy, something to guide him on a path, like the scripts at work.

"No," Danny said simply. It was the wrong answer because it revealed him as someone with nothing to do who was wasting her time, a useless wanderer.

"Let me know if you have any questions," said Kim, and when she turned away, Danny quickly left.

He walked the main corridor a few times, engaged in people watching. He observed fully intact families and other jovial groups making real conversations. He wanted to feed off their happiness and purposeful strides, but it just made him feel more hollow inside.

Danny wandered over to the big fountain that anchored the center of the mall, where people occasionally met others or tossed pennies. He bent down close and became mesmerized by the splashy rhythms and gentle foaming. He inserted his hand into the water and let it consume him up to the wrist.

"Hey!" shouted a nearby security guard. "Don't do that."

Danny retreated.

Back home, in his box, he went to bed early and escaped into a dream. He returned to a reoccurring scene that gave him richer emotions than anything in his waking life.

He sat at the controls of a Boeing 747 and soared.

The jet plane was cruising 500 miles per hour, 30,000 feet above the earth, riding a surface of clouds that swelled and dipped around him like a vast alien landscape. He sat soft and comfortable in his fully adjustable sheepskin pilot chair, experiencing the thrust of the engines and sweep of the wingspan as if they were extensions of his own being, like super powers. The instrument panel sparkled in front of him in a dazzling assortment of controls at his fingertips. Some very special visitors joined him in the cockpit to share their smiles and admiration:

his beautiful wife and a wholesome, loving teenage son.

They crowded around Danny, who wore his snappy pilot uniform: a double-breasted blue blazer, brass buttons, gold sleeve braiding and a white, peaked, naval officer-style cap. With his adoring family at his side, Danny guided the plane gracefully into the sunset. An orange glow filled the cockpit like a divine force, transcending them closer to heaven.

Danny awoke in the dark. He felt refreshed and rejuvenated, rolling in good feelings. Then, far too quickly, the leak began, the return to cold reality, and as much as he wanted to grasp tight and hold on, the sensations left him in a sucking whirl of dissipation. He tried to extend the dream's lingering vibe, but it danced and darted away, elusive once again. He tried to will it back, hopeful for more delusion, but the aircraft had soared on without him. Danny gave up, gave in, and returned to reality.

TRAVEL LOG:
REVERSAL 37Y 2M 2D

On my second trip, I transitioned to darkness under blankets on a cold winter's night. I emerged to see Toby curled up nearby in a swirl of sheets. My bed was my hideout, a sanctuary from the horrible shouts that rattled my bones from another room.

My mother and father had erupted into a heated argument, two days after Christmas.

The familiar words and tone filled the air. But this time my response would be different. Instead of withdrawing, I would step forth. Instead of being a passive accomplice to tragedy, I would take action.

I removed the bedcovers. My childhood bedroom surrounded me with sweet, illuminated nostalgia—the science-fiction posters, the cluttered desk and bulging bookcase, the Radio Shack turntable, the lineup of model kits, the shag rug, the winter-frosted windows.

I stepped closer to my door and listened.

My mother had returned from after-Christmas sales loaded with purchases, a poorly timed venture in my father's eyes, given the huge bills already racked up by the holidays, including, explicitly, my new bike.

Compounding the issue, my mother was drunk, having spent the afternoon with "Betty"—my father spit out both syllables with venom—engaging in cocktails and gossip.

The entire Christmas week had been soured by my parents' bickering, but this was definitely an elevated level, drawing energies from all the other frustrations that peppered the preceding days.

My mother defended Betty and the quality of their conversation. My father brought up a neighborhood party where Betty gossiped about people standing just a few feet away.

My father criticized my mother's drinking, which had become a frequent battleground. He said she sounded drunk, and I listened for it—the way her words smeared together and trailed off.

"What is this stuff? It's a bunch of crap!"

He was poking in her shopping bags.

"It was on sale! I'm being frugal!"

"It's still crap. Overpriced crap!"

She defended her purchases in a loud voice, and he countered in a louder voice. My heart raced. I was reliving one of the worst moments in my life.

Then I heard it. My mother giving in.

"Fine," she said in a brittle tone. "I'll return it. I'll return it all, right now!"

My father said, "You're in no condition to drive."

"I'm fine!" she responded, and I could hear the crinkle as she regathered her bags.

"You better not put a single scratch on that car or we're refunding *all* of Christmas!" hollered my father.

"Just leave me alone," my mother responded.

"Gladly," he said.

I took a deep breath. My time had arrived. I looked back at Toby poking his head out from under the covers.

"I'm going to do it," I told him. I opened my door. I left my bedroom.

I entered the war zone.

I surprised both of them.

My timing was perfect. My mother was still fumbling with the shopping bags. She had not yet picked up her purse from the coffee table.

I snatched it.

They both shouted at me with variations of "what the hell are you doing," a rare moment of unity.

I immediately dug into the purse and pulled out her car keys. They dangled from a leather strap keychain. I had imagined this moment, the touch of the leather, for thirty-seven years, two months, and two days. This was the opportunity I lost, but had now regained, to save my mother's life.

"You can't drive!" I shouted, and I ran back to my bedroom and locked myself in.

My mother and father did not follow. My mother started to object, then stopped. My father grumbled a statement, and I loved his words: "He's right."

They did not pursue me.

I listened from my bedroom, still clutching the keys in my tightest grip.

My mother said she was tired. She said she was going to sleep on the couch. My father said, "Good. I hope you're sober by morning. Find out when the stores open."

His footsteps left her.

I listened to her start to cry.

Her crying did not make me feel sad. It was a relief. She had no idea what I had saved her from. In a split moment, the course of the future had changed. I did not lose my mother.

She did not drive off into the night, muddled by alcohol and rage, speeding on icy roads without a seatbelt.

She did not lose control of the car and slide off the road, striking the big oak tree at the corner of Tenth and Highland.

She did not break her neck and sever major arteries for a near-instant death, flung through the windshield into the pure white snow, soaking it red around her.

There was no funeral, no heavy burden of guilt, shame and regret to weigh down each and every day of my remaining life, no secret desires of self-mutilation, no fruitless searches for a mother surrogate, no self-loathing, no resignation that I could never truly experience complete and pure happiness.

I allowed some time and silence to pass. I hid the keys in a drawer and returned to my mother. She was sprawled on the couch, half awake, eyeshadow streaked, hair a matted mess, limbs in clumsy arrangement.

"I'm sorry," I told her.

I expected a flash of anger, but she produced a heavy, tired smile. "You did the right thing," she said.

And then I told her the words I had never told her before, because now I had my chance. I told her I loved her. Her smile grew and she reached out for me. We hugged awkwardly, with me leaning over the couch. She said she loved me too.

Later, I returned under my bed covers for the journey back to the present and a future of my own design.

Chapter Three

Pushed back into the familiar routine of job searching left Danny unfazed. In a life of hard twists and turns, this was a sturdy constant.

His therapist claimed it was an act of ongoing rebellion against his father. Danny didn't feel it was that clever or calculated. He just didn't care about work and most employers took it with offense.

The original assumption, long ago, was that Danny would join his father's company, DeCastro Carpet Distributors, a mid-sized carpet and rug business serving Chicagoland residential, commercial, and retail customers. "You have to join the company, it's our name on there," George DeCastro stated with simple logic. He began pressuring both of his sons at an early age to follow in his footsteps. Danny's brother Reed dutifully turned his back on a promising baseball scholarship and dreams of playing major league ball to oversee the movement of carpet rolls. Danny himself was talked out of his aviation aspirations to study business management in college and faithfully joined DCD the Monday after graduation.

However, while Reed stuck with the company as the ever-faithful son, Danny left after four years.

"Abandoned me" is how his father described it.

Danny hated the job but it wasn't the only motivating factor. His personal life was in flux as he endured his first divorce. His head and his heart were a mess. He couldn't cope with the emotional demands of sustaining a family business that danced back and forth from being in the black to falling in the red.

His father had expressed ongoing displeasure with Danny's performance on the job and then elevated the criticism after Danny bailed.

As Danny tried other jobs in the business field, his father repeatedly told him, "It's not going to work out."

Danny took those words seriously and they became a self-fulfilling prophecy, as if his father had firmly set the course and Danny was helpless to make a detour.

His next few jobs did not satisfy the employer or the employee, and he began a long journey to find the right fit in a range of diminishing possibilities. His pattern of short tenure sent red flags to recruiters. He began accepting simple jobs to maintain an income. Each lame addition to his resume further narrowed his future potential. He watched the careers of his high school and college colleagues grow to new heights with age. He took the opposite path, withering. Everyone else was writing their life story. He was collecting a book of chapter ones.

When he was fired from an office support role at a realtor, his boss, a tubby man with thick glasses, was blunt with the reason: "I get the impression you just don't care."

"About what?" asked Danny.

"Any of this."

"I do my job."

"You do what we tell you. But you don't bring any of your own thoughts, ideas, or initiative. You don't even pretend like you care."

"I'm not a good actor," said Danny, and since there was nothing left to argue about the conversation came to a mutual end.

In more recent years, single with minimal expenses, Danny accepted gigs that rendered his college diploma irrelevant. He handed out shoes in a bowling alley. He handled phones for "Lawns, Leaves and Gutters," taking appointments and listening to complaints. He waited tables at a multitude of restaurants across a diversity of ethnicities. When his father found out about Danny's inability to land steady work, he responded with a mixture of despair and satisfaction that his predictions for failure had come true.

One thing gave Danny solace. When he spoke with his

brother Reed, who had loyally stayed on with the family business, Reed did not seem any happier.

While Reed had the comfort of predictability, Danny had the freedom of uncertainty. Sometimes Danny imagined himself a pinball projected by others, absorbing life's ricochets. He accepted jobs he knew he wouldn't like. If they were really bad, he would intentionally screw up to get fired so he wouldn't have to go through the ritual of resigning. Surprisingly, some places kept him on no matter how hard he tried to sabotage his own employment. It became a game to see what lever would cut him loose.

As he pushed through his forties, he changed jobs and apartments frequently, wandering like a nomad across stretches of Illinois, Wisconsin, and Indiana. His latest adventures took place in and around Racine, Wisconsin, an area that did not yet bother him.

After leaving the business conference fraudsters, he applied for a job at a local driving school. The interview went well; they liked that he was patient and calm (a byproduct of his indifference). He had a good driving record, no criminal background, acted pleasant and passed a simple written test. His clients started the next day.

They were pimply, nervous teenagers who left sweat on the steering wheel. He set them at ease in ways he wished someone would have soothed him during his tense and awkward teenage years. They respected him as an authority and an adult, one of the better job benefits as of late.

One week in, he was almost enjoying this new job. Even as some of the kids bumped into curbs, braked too hard or panicked at oncoming traffic, Danny felt supremely relaxed himself as if the students had absorbed all of the anxiety inside the car.

Of course, his tranquility couldn't last. On a sunny Friday morning, a tall skinny girl with long dark hair and soulful eyes slipped into the driver's seat next to him, and he experienced a dizzy spell of flutters that pushed him uncomfortably into the past.

She secured her seatbelt, placed her hands at ten and two, turned and smiled with freshness and eager eyes.

In that moment, in a cruel flashback, Danny saw Lisetta.

Chapter Four

In high school, and truthfully beyond, Danny had a huge crush on a girl named Lisetta. As a melancholy teen grasping for a spiritual uplift, Danny became convinced that Lisetta was the solution for all of his yearnings. She was pretty in a natural way, funny and approachable, creative yet grounded.

He liked everything about her. She was tall and gawky, wrote poems and observations in a journal, slipped into long black stockings or knee-high boots, and approached life with a half-smile of amusement and appreciation for the quirky. She wore her hair long and flat, with bangs ending just above her dark, heavy lidded eyes. She could be quiet or talkative, as the mood struck, and sometimes endearingly awkward. She had a long nose and high cheekbones, and when she accented her eyes with shadow and added curls to her thick hair, it transformed her into a sexiness that barely stayed under the radar.

Their first encounter followed when he defended her poem in English class—a poem she wrote and recited with passion, while several students snickered. He later consoled her by the lockers as she fought back tears. He appreciated the deep emotional place that evoked the poem, a place that most of his immature classmates didn't and couldn't understand.

Soon after, Danny and Lisetta became fast friends. In the semesters that followed, they occasionally flirted with becoming something more. But they never quite took the extra step, even when the opportunity presented itself one evening in the front seat of a car...

Danny shook away images of Lisetta as he forced his

attention on his driving student behind the wheel. She had entered traffic, officially beginning the lesson.

"How am I doing?" she asked, turning to look at him with bright eyes and a hopeful smile.

"Watch the road," he responded gently, and it helped lower his anxiety levels to keep her face turned away.

The driving student's name was Clara. She was roughly the same age as Lisetta when the Car Incident—or more accurately, Lack of Incident—took place. He tried hard to focus on the road and her driving, and not the memory that had been released from captivity.

Clara made a series of soft turns, using her signal. She stayed the appropriate length behind the car in front of her. She maneuvered an effective lane change. Her speed hovered between a bit too fast and a bit too slow as she became accustomed to the touch of the gas pedal. He reminded her to check her mirrors and beware of blind spots... all the while studying her profile. She was not quite Lisetta, really, a very different nose and lips—but similar enough to summon the real thing.

Clara's close proximity in the front seat, the hum of the engine and elegance of her bare arms brought back the memory he couldn't hold back. He recalled an autumn night, late and dark, driving Lisetta home from a party. Lisetta was physically close and emotionally closer. She had asked Danny to take her home because she wanted to get away from her boyfriend—a dolt named Martin—who was ignoring her and flirting with other girls.

She was on the verge of crying. She cursed Martin. "He's a jerk. He's a total jerk." Then the words Danny would never forget: "I wish he was more like you."

During the drive, under the steady pulse of passing streetlights, she leaned further in his direction until she was practically cuddling up on him.

When they reached Lisetta's house, he pulled up in the driveway, but she stayed inside the car to talk. He killed the lights and later the engine. Her house was dark, with no sign of spying parents or siblings. They continued talking.

In hindsight, she was waiting for him to make an advance,

inviting it in subtle and not-so-subtle ways. He wanted to and he didn't. True, they got along great, but she had been with Martin for a long time, engaged in a quarrel that was probably temporary, and Danny had no confidence to make a bold move.

Plus, he was scared because he was so crazy about her...

Danny snapped out of the old memories. "Watch the dog," he said, stiffening in his seat. Clara slowed down as an unleashed dog hovered near the curb. She passed it in a wide arc, almost entering the other lane.

"Always take in the big picture," Danny told her.

"I'm sorry," said Clara.

"No, no. You're doing fine."

"I am?"

"You are."

He started talking about other distractions on the side of the road—bicycle! old lady!—mainly to distract himself from thinking about Lisetta.

It didn't matter. After Clara's lesson, on the way home, Lisetta returned to his thoughts from a waiting room, and he knew why the recollections pushed stronger now than at other times. It wasn't all Clara's fault.

Stuffed deep in the back of his mind was the reality that his high school reunion was taking place in exactly one month.

He had not accepted the invitation, but he had peeked at the list of confirmed attendees and Lisetta was on the list.

She was listed solo, although as far as he could tell (via Internet research), she remained married to Martin and living in Eldridge, Iowa.

During a few late-night Google searches, he had drummed up additional background and even a photo—still pretty—trying to walk the fine line between curious and stalker.

Truthfully, Lisetta was his only motivating factor to consider going to the reunion. There was no one else he desired to see. Most of the class would be there to brag about their careers and families, and he had made a mess out of both.

He knew that meeting up again with Lisetta could go one of two ways—a joyful and invigorating re-acquaintance with someone he admired and could engage with...or an awkward and desperate retread doomed to leave him feeling further humiliated.

Online, he checked her status again on the high school reunion website and she remained present, while Martin remained absent. Lisetta's name was not accompanied by the "+1" that footnoted others who were bringing spouses.

He allowed himself to slip into fantasy for a moment. *Okay, let's imagine, for a lark, Lisetta shows up and she's parted ways with Martin, entirely single. What's to say I don't blow it again? After all, that's the story of my life. A string of failures.*

He remembered the lingering hopefulness that followed his missed opportunity in her driveway during high school. He had promptly plotted new turning points to transition the relationship from platonic to romantic.

He had set his sights on Halloween.

One of the boys in their mutual circle of friends was hosting a Halloween costume party in a few weeks and Danny was hopeful that Lisetta's relationship with Martin stayed rocky.

They frequently ate together in the school cafeteria as part of a common group crowded around a long lunch table. The group consisted of an intersection of friends in Danny's and Martin's worlds. Danny always tried to get a seat near Lisetta, and when they shared a conversation, it was always fun, often leading to fits of laughter.

Danny's plan for the Halloween party was to discover Lisetta in a moment of distress over Martin's continued insensitive behavior and then reveal his deeper feelings for her through a kiss in the shadows. The scene played out beautifully in his head, but then reality followed another script.

Danny wore a costume to the party that both spoke to his passions and elevated his handsomeness: a brown leather bomber jacket, scarf, and classic goggles representing a World War II fighter pilot.

Lisetta was a beautiful witch in a pointed hat and short miniskirt. Martin was Jason from *Friday the 13th* with a hockey mask and overalls, wielding a plastic machete. Several times during the night, he smacked Danny with the machete, pretending to be playful but more likely driven, Danny suspected, by a need to show off his superiority in front of Lisetta.

The whacks with the machete didn't hurt him. The real hurt came from seeing Lisetta and Martin making out throughout the evening, many different times in different locations, as if to send a statement that they were indeed a couple and any previous spats were inconsequential.

Danny retreated into friends-only mode and continued to enjoy his time with Lisetta up through the end of high school. His last powerful memory of her was a long, rambling, joyful conversation at a graduation party. They were both tipsy—not drunk—and sharing in the shaky emotions of the day, pushed out of the nest and into the next phase of their lives.

She was still with Martin, they were planning to attend the same college, and Danny had no thoughts of sneaking a kiss or seizing the moment. That train had left the station. After high school, they traded a few letters during freshman year in college, then faded apart.

There was no good reason to see her again, all these decades later, at a silly class reunion, but Danny discovered he couldn't fully let go.

At approximately 11:30 pm, as the neighbors above returned from somewhere with extra pairs of loud footsteps followed by pounding music, a big party without him, the story of his life, Danny bought a ticket to his high school reunion.

The order form asked if he would be bringing a spouse.

He had two, actually, but neither one wanted anything to do with him. Ex-wife number one and ex-wife number two. Long gone.

He placed his order for a single, solo ticket and later showed up on the website's attendee list without a "+1."

Just like Lisetta.

TRAVEL LOG:
REVERSAL 27Y 11M 2D

M y most recent journey to alter my personal history transported me back to my dorm room at Indiana University. I
found myself surrounded by familiar posters of rock stars and
bikini babes, early 90s stereo equipment, fat textbooks in stacks
and scattered piles of clothing. My roommate Elliott was home
for the weekend. I had the space all to myself and Cheryl knew
it.

In the original moment, I was unaware of her true intentions.
But with the insight of hindsight, my second walk through this
snatch of time was far less naïve.

I first met Cheryl when we were paired up to present in class
on a marketing plan for a hypothetical product. We got along
well, shared an A-, and became study partners. I did most of the
work and did not mind one bit: she was cute border-lining pretty,
wavy blonde hair, short but curvy, and a relentless go-getter in
ways that complemented my general lack of aggression. She
played on the tennis team and was a squeezer—grabbing people
for hugs, clutching my arm at scary movies, grasping my hand
tight on walks. Regular physical contact like this was a new experience for me. It was exhilarating. Granted, even the most gentle
brush of her touch got me aroused. My teenage hormones were
in full force.

Enjoying being in the company of her good looks and peppy
personality pushed aside the warning signs that should have
clued me in to the rocky road ahead. First, she always reached
out and grabbed whatever she wanted and wasn't very interested in making compromises or thinking things through. Even

as we deepened our relationship, she didn't let up flirting with other boys, scoping them out and making comments with brazen candor. "Oh my God, that guy without the shirt is so hot."

I ignored the comments and tried to convince myself that the transparency was a healthy thing. She had far more boyfriend experience than I had girlfriend experience. I considered myself lucky for landing her.

Cheryl was very aware of the financial standing of others and curious about mine. "Your dad owns his own business. Will it be yours one day? Is it worth a lot of money?"

I dismissed any family riches, an honest response, but I don't think she ever believed me and I didn't try too hard to correct that part of the attraction. I relished in her interest in me.

In short, we were two immature kids having some fun and should have stayed that way, but Cheryl pushed it one step farther and it changed our lives.

Through the miracle of time travel, I could now relive this pivotal moment. I had new knowledge. I vowed to study her eyes, not her alluring anatomy, to recognize her hidden agenda. She entered my dorm room, dashed away our plans for dinner and a movie, and made quick physical contact. Warm, soft, close. My head swam, my crotch tingled.

"I just want to fuck. I've been thinking about it all day. Ever since Elliott said he was going home. Danny, I am so fucking horny."

The same words as before. We enjoyed each other physically on the bed for several minutes, same as before. I was unbelievably aroused all over again. I momentarily lost the handle on all rational thought. It was entirely possible I would blow it a second time. That would be a cruel twist of fate after all the work that went into mastering the ability to travel back in time to knock my life on a better path.

She was aggressive, even when playful. With a big grin, she straddled my knees and tugged at my belt. Her hair fell forward and her thin blouse was split open. Her round breasts pressed against a lacy black bra. Once the belt had been sprung, she worked the zipper as my hands reached to hike up her skirt and find the elastic band of her panties. We started a rocking rhythm and the headboard tapped at the wall. Her hand snaked into my jeans and between my legs. She bent forward and whispered into my ear.

"Do me."

I reached down and took her hand, interrupting her caress. "Let me get a condom."

"You don't need one. I'm on the pill." She straightened her back and pulled off her blouse. She began to finish the work I had started to pull down the pink panties.

"Are you really?"

She stopped and froze for a moment, the mood changing in an instant. The script had changed. This line was not in the original. It had been added to the remake. She was unprepared.

She attempted to soften her startled reaction. "What? Of course I am." She began to massage my erection, which had me consumed with sensation. I began breathing hard. My mind swirled.

Then she stopped. "Okay. Stick it in."

"But—"

"Come on, I'm wet."

"No."

"What the fuck!"

I said, "I don't believe that you're on the pill."

She removed her hands from me. She looked down from her position on top, losing her sexiness as her face toughened and eyes narrowed. She lowered her weight, sat on my waist, and stared, settling into a position of physical but not mental control.

"What's going on with you?" she asked.

"If we do this, now, you're going to get pregnant."

"I told you—"

"Yes, and when you get pregnant, you're going to tell me it was all a mistake. That you missed taking your pill or the pill didn't work or whatever, but it won't matter because you'll have accomplished your mission. Your grades are no good, your main goal is to leave here with a husband and you've settled on me but two years into the marriage you're going to change your mind and start sleeping around with Barry Cody."

"What the fuck are you talking about? I don't even know a Barry Cody!"

"Not yet."

"Oh my God, you're crazy." She pulled away from me, scowling as the passion of attraction now flowed to repulsion. She stood on the floor in her bare feet and started buttoning her blouse.

"I know these things," I tried to tell her. "I can't explain how, I just do."

"Fuck you," she responded with customary bluntness, hurriedly adjusting her skirt and panties. "We're through. I can't deal with this bullshit. I thought you were normal. You will regret this."

"I'm already over it," I responded, sitting up on the bed, erection receding, all of my proper senses returning.

"You think you can do better? Good luck!" She jammed her feet into her shoes.

"It's not just for me," I called after her, unable to control myself from explaining things she couldn't possibly understand. "It's for our son. He will grow up sad and messed up. Both of us will disappoint him. He'll get into drugs. I can't carry that burden."

"I think *you're* on drugs," she said. "That's the only explanation for this crazy bullshit. *Don't call me.*"

The door slammed and she was gone.

I had successfully removed Cheryl from my life. With it, I lost Adam, too, and relieved him of his sustained misery and my years of guilt for being a terrible father.

I felt relief, but I also felt sickened. I left the bed and turned off the dorm lights with the snap of a switch, introducing darkness, ready to return.

Chapter Five

Once a week, Danny traveled to downtown Milwaukee to see his therapist, Elaine Lundy. Dr. Lundy had been treating him for depression for more than a year when they experienced their first real breakthrough during an exercise of role-playing. Lundy was a small woman with tightly cropped gray curls. She was well-versed in the techniques developed by Jacob Moreno, a Viennese psychologist, who believed in the healing powers of "act vs. talk."

In individual and group sessions, Lundy had her patients reengage with points of conflict in their lives through dramatizations. In group sessions, patients would take turns being the protagonist while the others played key roles in reenactments of unhappy experiences, like little plays. The dramatizations were followed by group discussions to examine new ways to resolve problems that had become sticking points for long-held personal struggles. The patients were able to revisit certain scenes and see them with a fresh perspective, finding therapeutic value in creating new outcomes.

Danny found comfort in these exercises and many of them were simple, one-on-one dialogues with Lundy, who would take on the role of various people in Danny's life, resurfacing arguments and setbacks that Danny outlined in detail.

On a rainy summer afternoon in her seventh-floor office, they engaged in one of the classic frustrations from Danny's childhood—battles with his father over his career aspirations.

"A pilot?" said Lundy, standing before Danny with a firm frown and arms crossed. "Why do you think you have what it takes to be a pilot?"

"It's all I ever wanted to be. I want to fly. I want to sit in the cockpit with all those instruments and fly above the clouds in the open sky."

"Do you know how much training is involved? You fly one of those things, you're responsible for everyone on board."

"I know."

"You can't even take personal responsibility for your own life, let alone a jumbo jet of hundreds of people."

"Why won't you give me a chance?" shouted Danny.

For a moment, Lundy broke character and nodded, urging him to continue with his deep-held outburst.

"You have no confidence in me! You don't even want me to try!" shouted Danny. "Did you ever stop to think maybe I have no confidence because you show me none?"

Lundy continued the arguments of Danny's father. "You're too young to know what you want. Just because you like to read aviator magazines...and build model kits...you're living in a dream."

"So, I can't dream?"

"You're wasting your time."

"This is my passion!" Danny's voice shook and tears welled up in his eyes. He felt fourteen all over again. But he wasn't going to back down. He wouldn't retreat to his bedroom crying.

"I know what this is all about," Danny said to his father.

"What are you saying?" prompted Lundy.

"It's not about being a pilot. That's not the problem."

"So, what's the problem?"

"You don't want me to do anything that doesn't follow in your footsteps."

"What do you mean?"

"Dad, you know what I mean. You want just one thing. You want me to work in your business. Get a business degree, join the family business. You've been very clear about that to me and to Reed since we were little. We can't have any other aspirations. You have it all laid out for us. Why else would you make fun of Reed for wanting to be a baseball player? Nothing can deviate from your master plan."

Lundy took this in. "Maybe you're right," she said. "Is it so wrong for me to want my sons, my own flesh and blood, to be part of the family business? Yes, it's true. And I'll tell you why. Because I don't trust the business to anyone else in the world... except for my sons. No one else is worthy."

Danny hesitated, taking in the comments. Lundy continued. "Danny, your mother is gone. You and Reed...you're all I've got."

Danny crumbled. He broke down and wept. He understood his father a little bit more. He resented him a little less.

"Thank you," he told Lundy at the end of the session.

"We make a little progress every time," she smiled back at him.

"It feels good to argue," he said.

The relief stayed with him as he climbed into his car. Danny hoped the lighter feeling would last. Sometimes it made a difference for a few days but it always dissipated with time.

Danny entered the highway and headed to Kenosha to visit his father. George DeCastro lived in an assisted living facility near the Illinois border. It was a plain, clean building with a staff trained to help Alzheimer victims with their meals, dressing, and bathing. George lived alone in a solo unit on a floor with a dozen other patients of later-phase memory loss.

Opening the door to face his father, Danny never knew what to expect. Sometimes his father recognized him a little. On other occasions he mixed Danny up with his brother, or reacted startled at the presence of a stranger.

Today, his father studied him, seeing a familiar face but unable to place it.

"Ken?"

Danny didn't know who Ken was. "It's Danny, dad." He slipped inside and closed the door behind him.

"Yes. Danny."

"Sit down, Dad. I just came by to see how you are."

"I don't know."

"You don't know how you are?"

"I get by."

"Are you hungry?" Danny stepped into the tiny kitchen. He found a plate of crumbs. The staff had made him lunch.

Danny led his father into the narrow living room. He sunk

into the couch, opposite his father, who sat down in his favorite chair.

"Are you hungry, dad?"

"No."

"Are you feeling good?"

"Feeling good." His dad nodded. Then his dad asked, like an echo, "Are you feeling good?"

Danny nodded, hands clasped. "I feel great," he said in a flat tone.

Danny felt the familiar wave of frustration roll over him. These visits were never good.

"What do you want to talk about?" asked his father.

Danny shrugged. He had no words. He let the room fall into silence.

His father studied him for a long moment. He looked uncomfortable, lost. "Are you new here?"

Danny capped off the day with dinner with Reed at an Italian restaurant halfway between Milwaukee and Chicago.

"It's impossible to have a coherent conversation with him," he told his brother. "He's there, but he's not there."

"Yeah, it was pretty bad last time I saw him. He thought I was Uncle Tim."

"Jesus." Danny took another bread roll from the basket and washed it down with some wine.

"I think it's time," said Reed, "to sell the business."

Danny straightened up. He looked at Reed's expression and right away knew this was a thoughtful, not impulsive, comment. Reed looked tired. He had been gaining weight again. The job had always stressed him out but lately he looked particularly haggard.

"I guess that's your call," said Danny.

"No, it's *our* call," said Reed. "You're a part owner."

"I vote whatever you want," said Danny. "You're the only reason that business is still afloat."

"Sandy really wants me to do it," he sighed.

"Dad will never know."

"True. But it still makes me feel guilty."

Three years earlier, when their father discovered he had Alzheimer's, he formally left the business to his two sons to inherit equally as his descendants. Danny was surprised by the gesture at first, since Reed was the one that worked at DCD, while Danny had avoided the company since leaving at age 26. But financially, Reed reaped most of the rewards anyway. Actively engaged in the business, he drew the good salary and benefits, giving his family financial security. Danny's only compensation was spotty dividends as the company reinvested profits back into the business in an ongoing struggle to grow.

"I ran some numbers," announced Reed after their main entrées were delivered and the wine was replenished. "If we shut down, sell the assets, pay off the debt, we'll be left with maybe $750,000 each."

Danny nearly dropped his silverware. "That's more...than I expected."

"The last 10 years have been hard," said Reed, "but if we liquidate...we'll come away with something. Maybe you can move out of that shitty apartment. Relocate somewhere with a good job market. Go on some dates, have some fun. Travel."

Danny nodded, considering all of these options.

"A sad end to the business," said Reed. "I'm actually glad he's too sick to see this coming."

"He had a good run," said Danny. "You know, he was happy there. That business was his life."

"Yeah, but it also became my life." Reed's mood soured and he poked at his spaghetti. "You know, I still can't watch a baseball game without forever wondering, 'What if?' I had a killer curveball. I had scouts telling me I was a no-brainer for the majors. I had all the tools."

"I saw you play in high school," said Danny. "You were the best."

Reed became wistful, reflecting on the early days with a sad smile. "Another lifetime, bro. That was another lifetime."

TRAVEL LOG:
REVERSAL 22Y 5M 16D

There are so many bright joys to experience along the alternate path I have fostered through time travel. One such key moment is a baseball game on the radio, experienced as I pace circles in my den, in adulthood.

The significance is twofold. My den surrounds me with artifacts from my passionate and blossoming career as an airline pilot. The walls are decorated with framed photographs of aircraft through the eras, a history of aviation that I am now a part of. My flight training certificates and diploma are on proud display. There are photographs of me in my full pilot regalia in a 747 cockpit and group shots with my classmates from aviation school at Purdue University. The most prominent item is an enormous world map that takes up the majority of one wall. The map rests against corkboard and every place I've flown is celebrated with a red pin. A container of red pins sits on my desk as I am continually adding to it with my love for international travel—soaring across long stretches of the globe to take people to new lands and cultures. The pattern of red dots against the map's blue and green colors fascinates me, an illustration of personal freedom.

Spread out across my long oak desk are the latest trade publications—*Flying, Aviator*—and several plastic, assembled model planes from my childhood, a poignant reminder that the boy's dream is now a reality.

But all of this aviation focus is secondary today, overshadowed by the presence in this room of a sports broadcaster's voice coming from my radio speaker. He describes each play as it unfolds in increasingly excited tones.

My brother Reed is pitching a no-hitter.

For good luck, I am wearing a baseball jersey with his name on it and the same model White Sox cap he wears professionally. As I pace, I am clutching the baseball he signed for me after last year's World Series championship.

"To the world's greatest brother, thank you for believing... Reed."

With every ounce of concentration in me, I am wishing for the string of hitless batters to continue uninterrupted. Every strike elates me. When the ball is put into play, I hop nervously until the announcer assures me the runner is out.

This is Reed's fifth season with the Chicago White Sox, his favorite team from boyhood. Growing up on the city's South Side, he favored the Sox over the Cubs and followed every game he could in real time, poring over the box scores religiously each morning. Many teams wooed him in the draft, but he followed his heart and signed with the Sox.

He did not choose the family business. Our father was very, very upset.

But ultimately, he got over it.

A World Series ring will do that. Dad's tone changed as Reed proved himself as a star player and our father's initial disappointment turned to pride. He bragged about Reed to everyone he met and hired somebody else's kids to muddle through the carpet business.

I knew dad was listening to this game because I had called him in the seventh inning, when the prospect of a no-hitter was becoming real.

He laughed. He was already listening to the game with my mother. "We were about to call you!" he declared.

In the bottom of the ninth, Reed faced the biggest sluggers in the New York Yankees lineup.

I paced the den. My hand gripped the baseball tighter.

The first batter grounded out to third base. A routine play. The crowd cheered. The announcer shouted: "Two more to go!"

The second batter worked a three-two count and then popped up. The crowd was going bananas even before the first baseman caught it in foul territory. I had goosebumps.

The third batter of the inning was hitting .347, a lightning-fast baserunner who could beat out a slow roller. The announcer called him "dangerous" and one of the best clutch hitters in the league.

I stopped in the center of the den. I held the baseball with two hands. I closed my eyes tight.

Please please please.

Reed threw a fastball, then a changeup, and quickly took the count to zero and two.

The next pitch was a looooong foul ball in the seats, perhaps ten feet away from being a home run. You could hear the mighty crack of the bat followed by the collective gasp of forty thousand people in the stadium.

As nervous as I was, I knew the no-hitter would stay intact. It had to.

Reed unleashed a vicious curveball and the batter took a monstrous swing and missed as the catcher caught the final out with a solid *whap!*

The crowd erupted.

I erupted, unleashing a joyous yell of victory, dancing around my aviation den, overwhelmed with excitement for my brother.

As his teammates mobbed him on the mound, I popped open a bottle of champagne and took a swig.

I held the bottle up in the air. "To Reed DeCastro, the greatest pitcher in the major leagues!"

Chapter Six

Danny's next appointment with Dr. Lundy concentrated on his first wife, Cheryl, and the scars she left embedded in his psyche.

After an unhappy childhood clouded by his mother's death and father's temperamental and single-minded obsession with his business, Danny was determined to establish a more successful family unit of his own. Despite some misgivings, he married Cheryl the summer after she announced her pregnancy, telling himself that while they weren't a perfect couple, they could certainly grow into one with the right learning and maturing. Their son would be the bond and catalyst to strengthen their sometimes-rocky relationship.

Instead, it all crashed and burned in an uglier mess than he could possibly imagine.

Many years later, he still harbored a knot of angry feelings inside that ate away at him like an evil parasite. He needed to let go, but when so much of his life was spent alone to dwell on things, the revisiting of past experiences couldn't be stopped. Cheryl was more than a rotten couple of years, she was a collision that knocked his life further off track and took him deeper in the wrong direction like an upside-down map.

And he wasn't the only victim. Their son Adam grew up in a broken home with damaged parents, jettisoning any hopes for this next generation of DeCastros to rise above dysfunction.

Danny was well aware that he simply got married—and divorced—and became a father—far too young. He hadn't even sorted out his own life yet.

Lundy told him that much of his unreleased angst was the result of being too young to even know how to react to such obstacles in his life's journey.

"You've held a lot in," Lundy told him.

Danny knew she was right. During his years with Cheryl, no matter how bad it got, he didn't lash out. He feared making things worse. He waited for things to blow over. He hoped that every sour note would be the last. He didn't want to lose his temper, his control, and explode into a red-faced rage. He didn't want to be just like his father.

Lundy believed Danny's passive response may have provoked Cheryl even further to do things to hurt him.

"She was looking for a response," said Lundy. "She wanted to see the passion, good or bad. So, she kept picking away. When you let her get away with something, she tested to see how far it could go."

Lundy talked about kleptomaniacs who made small thefts not for the items they took but for the rush of adrenaline from the act itself. After these kleptomaniacs succeeded at stealing little things, they slowly upped their game to more daring and expensive heists, feeding on the elevation like addicts craving greater intoxication.

Sitting on her soft couch on a dreary, drizzly day, Danny began outlining all the things he wished he had told Cheryl twenty-five years ago.

Lundy stopped him. This was a perfect opportunity for some more role-play therapy.

"I want you to stand over there," she guided him, pointing to an open area on the rug in her office. She stepped over next to him.

"I will be Cheryl," she said.

Danny nodded, shook his arms, and repositioned his feet, readying himself for the routine.

"You will be Danny, young Danny, three years into the marriage. Do you remember the apartment?"

"Of course."

"Put yourself back in that apartment. Adam is asleep. You remember this moment, it's one you've talked about many times before."

"The moment she told me…?"

"Yes."

Danny took in a deep breath. "Okay."

"I want you to be *that* Danny on *that* day," Lundy told him. "And I want you to tell me everything that Cheryl should hear. Don't hold back. You have feelings, Danny. Are you ready?"

He was ready. In previous sessions, Lundy had become other key characters in Danny's life. Genders and ages didn't matter. She found the words and moments to make them real.

"I just got home," said Lundy. "Ask me where I've been."

"Where have you been?" said Danny.

Lundy shook her head. "No, no. You sound like Danny today. Too flat and remote. Say it like Danny then, curious and surprised and suspicious."

"Where have you been?" said Danny with more edge in his voice. Just surfacing the new tone made him feel tension ripple through his body.

Lundy nodded, satisfied. Then she transformed into Cheryl.

"What's it matter to you?" Her voice had a sudden sharpness.

"I want to know. I think I should—"

"Do *I* need to know where *you* are every minute of the day? No, I don't."

"I tell you."

"Good for you."

There was a long silence. They stood in the center of the room staring at one another.

Danny could imagine Cheryl. It made him queasy.

"So that's it?" said Cheryl. "If so, I'm going to lie down. Maybe I'll watch some TV." She made a motion like she was going to move but her feet remained planted.

"No," said Danny. "That's not it."

Cheryl let out a big, exasperated sigh. "Great. Fine. Can this be quick?"

"No," said Danny. Firmly.

Cheryl almost smirked. "What's with the tone, Danny?"

Danny tried hard to come up with words. He struggled. He needed to think…

"Are you just going to stand there? What are you, a plant?"

Phrases moved through his head, half-finished, not right, confused. He had so much to say that everything was a jumble. His heart pounded and his hands grew clammy.

"Do you have something to say to me, Danny?"

Danny nodded.

"Then talk. Share your feelings. Tell me how you feel."

Danny said nothing.

Cheryl stood before him, in their old apartment, a flashback more vivid than any dream.

"If you have something to say, *say it!*" exclaimed Cheryl.

Danny screamed: "*You're a fucking whore!*"

Cheryl's reaction was immediate and disarming. She laughed at him.

He stared at her. He realized he was panting.

"Is that so?" said Cheryl. "Tell me more."

"You...fucked..." Danny started, then stopped.

"I'm sorry, I can't hear you," said Cheryl. "You're mumbling again."

Danny started over. "You...fucked...Barry Cody."

Cheryl studied him for a moment. Her face became a blank, emotionless. She did not show surprise. She was not defensive, not angry, not sad. Nothing.

Then she spoke with a cruel shrug.

"Yeah. So what? I fucked Barry Cody."

Danny felt a wave of fury cover him, like a drenching of hot molten lava. Every molecule inside of him screamed.

"You're right," said Cheryl, almost playfully. "It's true."

Danny couldn't speak, choking on a million possible responses. Cheryl waited and waited, and then raised her voice.

"So," she said. "*What of it?*"

The walls around them swerved madly and then the floor rushed up with a loud slam. Cheryl's eyes began to bug out, tiny veins bulging at the corners, and her mouth grimaced in a crazy, twisted shape. Danny squeezed his hands tightly around Cheryl's throat. He pounded her head hard against the floorboards with repeated thuds, spilling her blonde hair askew in all directions. He squeezed her puffy and purple as she struggled. She stuck her hands up against his face, poking his eye, to push him away. It loosened his grip, allowing her to catch some sudden, deep, gasping breaths, followed by a wild and terrified scream.

Danny rolled off of Elaine Lundy. She erupted into a coughing fit, followed by sobs.

He sat on the floor, hands over his head, eyes shut, lost in time and space, swirling without gravity.

Lundy slowly made her way up off the floor and moved behind her desk. Her neck was red. She fell into her chair, shuddering. She stared at Danny in horror.

"You have to leave," she told him.

He remained seated on the floor. "I'm sorry," he mumbled. "I got...lost."

"You crossed the line. You know the rules about physical contact. You could have killed me."

"I didn't mean it."

"Danny, I'm going to find you somebody else."

"Please don't."

"You scared me. I should call the police."

"It won't happen again."

"I'm ending our sessions. We've gone as far as we can go. I will find you someone better equipped to handle this kind of thing."

"Don't cut me off," said Danny. "I need this."

"You need a different kind of help than I can provide."

Danny slowly rose to his feet. He studied his hands, frightened by their sudden transformation to weapons.

"I never would have started the role-playing if I thought you would get like this," she said. "I think you surprised us both."

In a daze, Danny stepped toward the office's one lone window. He looked out into the colorless sky, watching drizzle fall between the buildings of downtown Milwaukee. The clouds hung low and oppressive.

Lundy allowed him to stand there silently, watching him carefully, hand poised to grab her phone and call security, if necessary.

Finally, Danny left the office without another word.

Chapter Seven

Danny sat in the shadows in his car in an underground parking garage, studying the people who showed up for the high school reunion. The slots around him filled with cars, and individuals and couples walked to the elevators in a steady flow to enter the hotel. Some he recognized a little, many not at all. He wasn't very social in high school and really had only one incentive to be here.

Most everyone was dressed up, hopeful to display confidence and success as they represented the preceding thirty years of their lives. The women wore outfits that, by and large, belonged on much younger frames. The men tucked their paunch inside sports coats that broadened and straightened their shoulders.

Danny wore a basic jacket and tie, classy without being too formal, and a fresh haircut. The gray creeping into his hair was inevitable, and a bald spot was underway, but at least he had hair. A good percentage of the men he observed were bald, heads cleanly shaved in a manner that said, "Hey, I meant to be bald," when in reality there probably wasn't much left to shave anyway.

Danny had arrived early and secured his parking space to get a good look at what the evening would entail. The thought of plunging into the scene cold rattled him. There was too much drama tied to his past and he knew it would twist his emotions into knots. This needed to be a slow entry.

Most importantly, he hoped to glimpse Lisetta before they stumbled upon one another in the ballroom. As the minutes ticked by, he began to wonder if he had missed her or perhaps she had canceled—and the thought relieved him, even though she was the draw that brought him here.

When Lisetta strolled past his window, there was no mistaking that it was her, and he sunk deeper into his seat to avoid being seen. He got a good look as she reached the brighter lighting by the elevators. She was still beautiful, which tortured him. Secretly he had wished she would age into someone else, but Lisetta, unmistakably, was still Lisetta.

She had a youthful spring in her step. Her dark hair continued to flow long, unlike the easy-to-maintain mommy crop worn by most of the other women. She wore knee-high buckled boots, a black skirt, bluish sweater, and dark blazer with sleeves that stopped at her forearms.

She was alone.

In that moment, he weighed whether he should stay or go.

Driving all the way into downtown Chicago simply to glimpse Lisetta in a parking garage was creepy and pathetic, he knew. The only way to redeem it would be as a neurotic precursor to actually attending the event.

And talking to her.

He let fifteen minutes pass to space them apart and opened his car door. He joined the continued trickle of forty-somethings making their way into the hotel.

The reunion was in a ballroom on the twenty-eighth floor. He entered a small logjam in the corridor to hand over his e-ticket and find himself in a table of nametags.

Briefly, he fantasized about taking someone else's nametag and forging a new identity. Greg Burns, Rick Reger…available for the taking.

His stalling caused the female volunteer standing behind the table to gently inform him, "They're alphabetical by last name." As if he was a child all over again.

The woman did not look familiar. She wore a strapless red dress. Her thick mane of bleached hair offered a distraction from a heavily lined face unevenly colored with crusty makeup. She had the misfortune of standing in the harshness of bright light.

Danny flattened his nametag sticker against his sports coat. He entered the ballroom, where the lights were generously dimmed to soften the cruelty of aging and better support cosmetic efforts to roll back time.

The combination of low lights and a loud DJ spinning eighties synth rock made it harder to identify people and hear their voices. Danny smiled and walked casually across the room with fake purpose, when in reality he was wandering aimlessly in discomfort. People strained to look at his nametag to see if he was a long-lost friend.

The room was populated with small round tables where groups gathered to drink, chat, and snack on passing plates of hors d'oeuvres. Each table was decorated with a clump of balloons in school colors. A huge banner welcoming the class filled one wall. The other walls displayed blown-up yearbook and school newspaper photos. People looked for pictures of themselves and posed alongside them for then-and-now selfies. A loud huddle of flabby, reunited football players gathered at an oversized team photo from their glory days. Former cheerleaders rediscovered their youth in black and white. A pair of high school sweethearts found a charming picture of themselves studying together on the floor in front of a bank of lockers.

Danny studied the series of photos for people he remembered. His own presence was absent. He did not exist in this trip to the past.

Bursts of laughter and squeals punched through the loud music as former friends and classmates found one another with loud exclamations and hugs. Danny spotted a swarm around Mark Benedict and Pamela Whittaker, the endlessly admired Prom King and Prom Queen who later married, produced beautiful children, and continued their streak of wholesome perfection. They soaked in the attention, just like the old days. It made him sad and envious all over again.

Danny decided on a destination—the cash bar—even though he wasn't in the mood for a drink. His mother's alcohol-related death had made him a light drinker, and he never got drunk, seeing it as a dance with the devil that killed her. As he reached a layer of people waving for a bartender's attention, someone shouted his name and approached him through the crowd.

"Danny D!" It was a red-haired man who still retained some of his boyhood freckles. "Man, I thought that was you!"

Danny struggled to remember the face, then simply read the name on his chest.

"Kurt!" said Danny. "Good to see you!" Not true, but it sounded like the right thing to say. He barely remembered this person.

Kurt engaged him in five minutes of conversation that made Danny's innards twist and turn from very simple, innocent questions like, "So, what are you doing with yourself these days?"

Danny uttered a lie that at least had some element of truth to it, if you disregarded the shift in timing that kept it in present tense. "I'm a planner for corporate conferences. We put on events around the world for CEOs of Fortune 500 companies."

This impressed Kurt. "You got kids?"

"One."

"Let's swap pics." He pulled out his iPhone and immediately called up a shot of a red-haired, freckled boy in his twenties with more than a passing resemblance to his father.

Danny struggled to find a photo of Adam that showed him in young adulthood and finally had to settle on one that was at least a dozen years old.

"He's young!" said Kurt.

Danny nodded, which was easier than admitting they were estranged. His son had essentially disowned him after he turned seventeen.

"Can I get you a drink?" asked Kurt as they inched closer to the bar.

"No, that's okay, I have to go see somebody," said Danny abruptly. "It was good catching up!"

He wiggled away from the bar crowd as Kurt shouted, "Take it easy!" Danny faked a deliberate path across the room, then returned to aimless wandering. Finally, he slipped out of the ballroom. He entered the men's room down the hall, even though he really didn't have to go.

In the men's room, a collection of guys examined themselves

in mirrors with heightened self-consciousness, playing with their hair and re-tucking their shirts. The muffled thud-thud-thud of the DJ music continued in the background like a heartbeat. Eyes glanced at nametags. Danny wanted to rip his off.

He peed minimally and reentered the ballroom, determined to spot Lisetta from afar. Leaving now would be idiotic. He was here to say hi to her. If he blew this chance, the next reunion wouldn't be for another five or 10 years. His teen years would become even farther out of his reach.

Danny avoided the eyes of others, not interested in another Kurt-like conversation, and scoured the ballroom for Lisetta. He found her as part of a small group of women in an animated conversation. One woman in particular, someone he didn't recognize, did most of the talking. She wore high heels and a long gown, hair lifted to reveal large hoop earrings. Lisetta was listening, smiling, nodding, holding a drink. While everyone around her was trying too hard, Lisetta had remained attractive in a mostly natural way, blessed with a youthful face and figure.

Danny felt himself tighten as if squeezed. His heart accelerated. The reunion experience was turning more unpleasant than he had expected. *Why am I putting myself through this?* he asked himself.

From somewhere deep inside came an answer: *Maybe I'm just here to feel something again after so many years of emptiness. I needed to wake up my heart.*

Danny watched her for a while more, then grew paranoid that someone might be watching him watch her, and he didn't want to be a stalker. He went to the bar, patiently waited his turn, and ordered a 7-Up.

After it was handed toward him, he hesitated, then asked, "Can you add a little vodka?"

Why the hell not? This was a special occasion, and he desperately needed to settle down. Perhaps it would help boost his courage.

The bartender wordlessly turned and poured two quick dashes from a bottle of Smirnoff, filling the glass to the rim.

Danny carefully took it and handed over a bill. "Keep the change."

He protected his drink from the elbows around him and broke away from the bar, headed for a tall window.

The window offered a spectacular view of Chicago's skyline at night. The lights sparkled and he felt invigorated by the panorama. The elevation from the ground made him think of night flying, watching the broad spread of life below.

After a few sips, he began to plot his next move. He needed clever words to say, an introduction. He cursed himself for not rehearsing conversation starters. What he really needed was a script. History had proven he was a poor improviser.

That was the best thing about the corporate conference gig—his words were provided. He just had to become the character written for him.

"Danny, hi!"

Lisetta's voice pulled him out of his thoughts and away from the window.

She stood before him with a big smile. "Oh my God, it's so good to see you!" Her arms opened for a hug, one hand still holding a tall drink.

He had no time to think. He simply entered the moment. He stepped forward and they embraced.

"I saw your name on the table," she said. "I'm so glad you're here."

"I'm not that far," he said. "I live in southern Wisconsin."

"I'm in Iowa."

"Iowa?" he said with fake surprise. He knew where she lived.

"Yeah, oh my God, we have so much to catch up on. You doing good?"

"Yeah, great," he said. What else was he supposed to say? "You look great. You look the same."

She laughed. "Oh, stop it. It's dark in here. I colored my hair. I wish I looked like I did back then!"

"Is your picture on the wall?"

"I don't think so. I wasn't a cheerleader or anything like that. I was more behind the scenes. I worked on the yearbook, but I didn't even put myself in it."

"My yearbook photo is awful."

"Everybody hates their yearbook photo." She turned and

looked back into the room. "Isn't it a rush, seeing all these people again?"

"Total rush," said Danny, searching for something to say. "I ran into Kurt."

"Kurt who?"

Danny had already forgotten Kurt's last name. Desperate to say something else, he blurted, "So where's Martin?"

She absorbed the question with a half-smile, half-shrug. "He didn't want to come." To end her response there, she took a long sip from her drink.

Danny took the moment to drink from his 7-Up and vodka as well. He could already feel a warm buzz coming on and credited it to low tolerance.

A stocky woman with spiky hair and a loud voice slid next to them, holding a fancy camera. Danny had seen her moving around the room before, a professional photographer hired to capture moments.

"Take your picture?" she said.

"Sure!" answered Lisetta, and she repositioned herself alongside Danny, shoulder to shoulder. Danny smiled and a succession of flashes momentarily blinded him.

"What a cute couple," said the photographer. "Which one of you went to Stevens High?"

"We—we both did," stuttered Danny.

"Old friends," said Lisetta.

The photographer moved away to find more subjects.

"So, what have you been up to?" asked Lisetta in a playful tone. "Account for yourself."

"That's a...loaded question," said Danny, uncertain of his response.

"I tried looking for you on Facebook and Twitter..."

"I'm not on those things. I probably should be."

She couldn't hear his response, so he repeated it. Then she said something he couldn't understand.

The DJ had turned up the volume on the music and was encouraging dancing.

"God, it's too loud!" said Lisetta, looking into the ballroom with exasperation.

"I can't hear anything. It's probably part of getting old."

"*What?*" She held a hand up to her ear.

"I said—"

She laughed. "I heard you. I was just joking."

"You were what?"

"I said I was joking—"

"What?"

"Joking!"

Now he smiled. "Me too."

She punched him in his arm with her free hand. "Wise guy."

The physical contact, even a sarcastic punch, made him flush with feeling.

She peered past him, glancing toward the window. She moved closer to the glass and looked straight down. "Hey!" she said in a casual shout. "It's a beautiful night. Want to go down there, by the river? Then we won't have to scream at each other."

"Good idea," he said. "Let's go." He took several healthy chugs from his drink as they crossed the room. In the corridor he left his empty glass on the table with the nametags as they made their way to the elevator.

The elevator took them down to the ground floor and they quickly found side doors that led outside the hotel to a nearby walking path alongside the Chicago River.

The cool air felt refreshing.

"Ah, much better," said Lisetta.

"Now we don't have to compete with Hall and Oates," said Danny.

She laughed, genuine, and it made him feel good.

They walked over to a railing and took in the riverside sights. Towering skyscrapers created a majestic wall across the way, as the city's reflection danced in the waters below. Danny looked up to see tiny lights from planes dazzling the sky like stars.

"I'm sorry I didn't go to the wedding," said Danny, as they stood alongside one another, taking in the view.

"Oh, God, that was so long ago," said Lisetta.

When the invite came to witness Martin and Lisetta's union, Danny was caught up in his own drama. He knew attending their marriage would just rub salt in his wounds, another raw disappointment in his early life.

"I should have stayed in touch," she said. "I lost touch with a lot of people. We moved to Eldridge. Martin got an engineering job, it's in agriculture. We're in a rural area. It's a nice community, but really small. Nothing like this." She gestured to Chicago's skyline.

"Do you still write?" he asked, recalling her passion.

"I do! Sort of—I work for the local newspaper."

"That's cool."

"I write features and news and, well, a little bit of everything. Obits, a lot of obits—it's an older community. It's a small operation."

"But you get to write."

"I'm also writing fiction."

"That's great," said Danny. "What kind?"

"Romantic fantasy." She turned to him. "It's escapism. I love to get lost in my imagination, you know? Right now, the books are self-published. E-books, print on demand. I keep submitting to real publishers. Maybe one day..."

"I'll pick up one of your books," said Danny. "I'd love to read one."

"Thank you," she said, smiling broadly. "I'll send you a link." She studied Danny for a moment and then said, "You know what I'll never forget?"

"What?"

"That day you defended my poem."

Danny smiled. "Oh, yes. I remember."

Her face lit up with the memory. "I wanted so bad to be a writer. I loved creative writing. I wrote that poem and the teacher said I could read it to the class, and I was so excited, and then those assholes—"

"Total assholes."

She nodded vigorously. "Those assholes laughed and later they were making fun."

"I wanted to pound the crap out of them."

"I was crying, and you came over to me, and you talked about the poem, how much you liked it, and I felt so much better. I mean, God, it meant so much to me. I was so insecure back then."

"I meant it," said Danny. "I could tell right away how talented you were. It's a gift."

"Thank you," she said gently.

"So," said Danny, and he couldn't resist, now was as good a time as any, "How's Martin?"

She considered the question thoughtfully and released an ambiguous answer. "Martin? He's...you know... Martin." She said a few more inconsequential words but stopped short, Danny noticed, of saying anything nice about him.

She quickly turned the subject. "Hey, I have to show you a picture of Mindy."

"Mindy?"

"We have a beautiful, talented daughter. She's going to NYU." Lisetta poked at her phone and found a school portrait photo of a young woman with kind eyes, high cheekbones, and long, dark hair cascading on either side of her face.

"Wow," said Danny. "She looks just like you."

"Yeah, she's got my genes. Pretty scary. She's a freshman." She put away the phone. "Enough about me. I want to know about you. Kids?"

"A son, Adam."

"How old?"

"He's twenty-seven."

"Ah, older than Mindy."

"We had him—well, he was born when I was still in college."

"I remember hearing...what was her name, Cheryl?"

"Yeah," said Danny. "She's long gone. We only lasted three years. That's a good thing."

"I'm sorry."

"She cheated on me. We were too young."

A long silence followed and Danny feared he had revealed too much.

Lisetta had the good sense to change the topic, but still entered unpleasant waters. "You work for your dad, right?"

Danny shook his head. "No, that was just—I worked for him a few years after college, but left. I couldn't stand it. My brother stayed with it. The carpet business wasn't for me. My dad was mad I left him."

"Is your dad still around?"

"Not really. He has Alzheimer's. He's there, but not really there, if you know what I mean."

"Did he ever remarry?"

"No. After my mom died, he really poured himself into the business. He dated a little, but nothing serious. I don't think he wanted to get remarried."

"So, what about you? Did you remarry?"

Danny took in a deep breath. More crummy storylines. "Yeah, but it wasn't a good idea. Too fast, too soon. After Cheryl... She took the baby, I was lost. I had friends who fixed me up with a divorced woman named Marci. I guess they thought we were a good match because we were both on the rebound, coming out of bad relationships with bad attitudes, but that's not why you get something started. It wasn't healthy. We got married but we were miserable. It was doomed from the start. Back in those days...I was not a good person to be around."

"You're a good person," said Lisetta. "We all go through bad times."

Just that one, simple statement affected Danny like magic. He felt a lifetime of angst lift off his shoulders, even if it was just for a moment.

"Thank you," he said.

She looked back over the inky waters. "So, enough of the past. Let's talk about today. You work in Wisconsin? What do you do?"

"Conference planning," he responded, and he basically told her the same lie he had told Kurt. It came out easily. The conversation with Kurt had been a good rehearsal.

"Very cool," she said. "You get to rub shoulders with corporate bigwigs."

"No," said Danny. "*They* get to rub shoulders with *me*."

She grinned big and exclaimed, "That's right!"

He wanted to kiss her right then. All the times he had imagined kissing her face culminated in this moment, this new opportunity, but he settled for words over action.

"I had the biggest crush on you," said Danny.

Another lie: the sentence didn't belong in past tense. It belonged in past, present and future.

She cocked her head at him, studying him for a curious moment and then said softly, "Really? I wasn't sure. I could tell you liked me, but didn't know…in that way."

"I was shy. I had no confidence. You were always with Martin or some other boy. I kept it to myself. But I wanted you to know. Full transparency."

"Isn't life funny?" she said. "If you had pursued me…who knows?"

Danny wanted to keep this thread of conversation going but his heart was banging and his head was spinning. If he wasn't careful, he would blurt something stupid.

Which he did anyway.

"Too bad we don't have a time machine!" he said.

With the delicate moment swerving into levity, she followed. "Hey, really! Maybe we all need a time machine. Everybody at this reunion would probably like that!"

"All those football players could grow back their hair!" said Danny, joining in. "And lose their potbellies."

In that moment, Lisetta's phone sounded with electronic tones. She studied it, promptly returning everything to reality.

"It's Martin," she said.

Danny almost said, "Tell him I say hi," an attempt to remain jovial, but the mood had shifted once again.

She grew serious.

"I'm sorry. I should get this. He gets mad when I let it go to voicemail."

"I understand."

She reached out for one more hug. He hugged back, gently.

Then they pulled apart, and she answered the call with a cheery voice. "Hi Sweetie."

Danny didn't want to stick around. The hug was like a farewell hug. The call was the cold slap he needed to scare off stupid fantasies.

As Lisetta talked to her husband, Danny allowed her some privacy. He waved and stepped backward, gesturing to the hotel, indicating he was returning inside.

She waved back, her attention split between him and Martin.

Danny turned and left.

He made his way back to the elevator to take it down to the underground parking garage. As he walked, he peeled off his nametag, rolled it into a crumple and let it drop.

In the elevator, a vaguely familiar face studied him and said, "Hey, are you Danny DeCastro?"

"No," Danny responded. "I'm sorry. I don't know who that is."

Danny hurried to his car, almost hyperventilating as he settled behind the wheel. He waited a few minutes for his head to clear, then backed out of the space and climbed the ramp to the exit. He joined a busy stream of downtown evening traffic, darkness and light, and blended back into anonymity.

TRAVEL LOG:
REVERSAL 32Y 7M 8D

One of the greatest moments of my corrected life took place in a car on a simple autumn evening, engaged in a long and heartfelt conversation punctuated with a heavenly kiss.

By truly expressing myself with courage and confidence that night as a teenager, I set into motion a deepened connection that would resurface years later to blossom into a genuine adult romance.

Young Lisetta sat next to me in the DeCastro family Chevy, distraught over her stupid boyfriend Martin and craving comfort. I had brought her home from a party where Martin alienated her, and when we arrived in her driveway, she did not hop out to retreat to her room for a good cry. Instead she stayed and talked, baring her emotions to me in ways that elevated the general friendship we had developed during the school year to something much closer.

Recognizing this was not a simple drop off, I turned off the headlights and followed it soon after with killing the engine. Her face was soft and sad in the shadows, long hair hanging forward and eyes big and dark. Her lips quivered and I felt struck by how beautiful she looked in sorrow.

She was leaned in my direction and making negative comments about Martin by comparing him with me. "He's a total jerk. I wish he was more like you. You're not a jerk. You know how to treat people with respect. He just has no clue."

When we had pulled into her driveway, she had immediately released her seatbelt, which I took as a cue she was on the verge of exiting the car. But the longer she stayed, the more my perspective changed. I realized she was not unleashed for home but for me.

I casually disengaged my seatbelt as I shifted to better turn to face her as we talked, a movement intended to look practical, not calculated. I had not accomplished this basic but important move in the original enactment of this scene.

As Lisetta poured out her heart to me, I saw tears forming in her eyes. I couldn't bear to watch this sadness roll down the smooth skin of her cheeks. I advanced on her slowly, watching for any signals that I should abort my approach, but her eyes were welcoming, and she moved toward me to meet me half-way. We kissed tenderly. I felt weightless, awash in waves of warmth. I moved my fingers through her hair and she placed her hand on the back of my neck. The kiss graduated beyond the simple pecks of my infrequent dating experiences with other girls to become something far more intimate, arousing, passionate, and real.

When Lisetta left my car, our second take of that critical moment together, she smiled broadly with an extra look back at me.

We had a different kind of bond now, an entry to something bigger, and both of us felt it.

I knew the larger significance of this turning point. I wanted to tell her but kept it to myself. Lovely Lisetta disappeared into her house, leaving a lingering tingle of electricity in the air. I forecast the future privately into the windshield, speaking these words:

"She'll never forget this kiss. It will haunt her relationship with Martin. When he proposes to her after college, she will say no. She will not marry him. She will one day marry an airplane pilot named Daniel DeCastro."

Chapter Eight

Danny surrounded himself in music and danced. He played his favorite 80s compilation CD on the small stereo in his Wisconsin apartment and soaked in the nostalgia of the bright and punchy songs that pulled him back in time. He shut his eyes and became 15 again, a teenager madly in love with Lisetta, looking forward with heart-thumping anticipation to their every little encounter—between classes in the high school corridors, at the designated cafeteria lunch table for rowdy group meals, and weekend roaming and parties with mutual friends.

He wore an adult-sized Stevens High T-shirt in school colors that he bought off a link from the reunion website. Duran Duran filled his ears with a catchy melody he hadn't heard in years. When he opened his eyes, he was purposely facing the wall where he had taped a large photo of an image downloaded from the reunion website's picture gallery and printed on big paper at the local drugstore. Among the highlights captured by the female photographer with the spiky hair was a perfect shot of truly handsome and beautiful Danny and Lisetta, reunited after decades of separation, rediscovering the spark of youthful affection.

If he focused hard, their images shed years and became their younger selves. He transported himself to a mental state of adolescent bliss and felt a small shiver.

His mind game was working, briefly, sort of, and then completely fell apart when the real world persisted and bled through.

His motherfucking neighbors began pounding out their

own music on their much louder stereo, introducing messy, murky bass and drums from their contemporary rock and rap crap into Duran Duran.

His song ruined, Danny turned off the stereo. More noises from the present surfaced to poke at him—impatient car horns on the busy street below, some woman yelling at her kids in the apartment on the other side, a door slam down the hall.

The white noise machine he bought had proven itself to be truly worthless, so his latest method to shut out the world was simple earplugs. They didn't work great either, but at least the aggravations were muffled.

Earplugs snug and wedged deep, Danny hopped on his bed to continue reading from a small stack of books, all written by the same author: Lisetta Madison.

Upon returning home from the reunion, he couldn't resist searching out her book titles online and ordering them all.

They were derivative romantic fantasy, self-published with amateur covers, but destined to reveal insights into Lisetta's passions and frame of mind. Her sales were not good and the sparse reviews on Amazon wavered from obvious friends showering general praise to actual readers who were clearly not impressed.

Danny enjoyed the books, hearing the words delivered in her enchanting voice, finding engagement in the simple plot developments and colorful details of her observations.

He was not a consumer of the romantic fantasy genre, so the clichés did not tire him. Tellingly, all the books featured a heroine trapped in an unhappy relationship finding escapism in a new narrative. The most recent book he had completed, *The Viking's Desire*, centered on a "raven-haired beauty" named Kaylein, wife of Lord Fendrel and carekeeper of their manor in a coastal town in medieval England. Bored and unloved, Kaylein's life took a sudden turn when Norwegian Vikings arrived in warships and raided the village for booty in both definitions of the word—treasures and women. In the second chapter, Kaylein was kidnapped by a Norse warrior named Ivan. As the story unfolded, Ivan turned out to have a heart of gold to go along with his long, golden locks. Kaylein ultimately fell in love with her captor and discovered she had not been enslaved—she had been freed.

The next book he had started was *Whispers in Time*. It featured a depressed suburban housewife who became obsessed with an old photograph of a handsome young World War II soldier. She traveled back in time to romance him, using an experimental time machine developed by a crackpot physicist at the university research lab where she worked.

Future titles in Danny's to-read pile included *Seaside Seduction*, *Prince of Passion* and *Eva and the Island Paradise*.

He was midway through Chapter 7 of *Whispers in Time*, approaching an explicit sex scene in 1940s Europe, when the phone rang with the unwelcome interference of coitus interruptus.

"Yo bro," said the voice on the other end.

"Oh, hey, Reed."

"Listen, I wanted to get some time set up. We need to go on a tour of the company's assets. All of dad's stuff, the carpet inventory, the fleet vehicles, the office furniture, everything we want to sell or liquidate. We'll have to decide if we want to go to auction or maybe work out a deal with Swanson."

"Swanson? Dad's biggest competitor? He'd love that."

"He won't know. It doesn't matter. I mentioned DCD to him the other day, he didn't even know what I was talking about. He said they had good hamburgers."

"I guess it really doesn't matter anymore." Danny sat up on the end of the bed. "Yeah, I'm available whenever. I don't have anything on the calendar."

The whole scenario filled Danny with sadness. The end of his dad's business, passed through the generations, only to die in their hands.

The present day had reared its ugly head, once again.

On a Saturday, ensuring the company's locations would be closed and empty, without soon-to-be-laid-off employees to cope with, Danny and Reed visited the facilities of the family business.

They met at their first stop, a small office in the Pilsen

neighborhood of Chicago, where Reed and his father conducted most of the administrative work. Entering the simple suite, Danny expressed amazement that the space did not look all that different than it did 25 years ago, when Danny was employed there.

"Yeah," said Reed with a small chuckle. "Same old desks and filing cabinets. The chairs might be newer. See anything you want?"

Danny looked around and shook his head. There was still a coffee mug on his father's desk with the company logo, as if his father was still working and active, which made him sad.

"Some of this is going straight to garbage," said Reed. "We're going to have to hire somebody to haul it away."

Danny paused for a moment to look at a framed family picture propped on his father's desk, lightly covered with a layer of dust. It was old and faded, showing Danny, Reed, and their father together with hands on shoulders, pleasant and congenial.

"He didn't cut me out of the picture," mused Danny.

"No," said Reed pointedly. "You cut yourself out of the picture."

"Touché," said Danny, opening a few drawers and finding expected contents—pencils, pens, stapler, sticky notepads.

"I think you were harder on yourself than he was on you," said Reed.

"I'm a basket case," said Danny, poking in a file cabinet, finding more boredom. "That's all there is to it."

"Everybody's fucked up in one way or another," offered Reed. "Mom wasn't exactly all together either."

After picking through the office, they returned to their cars and drove the half-mile to the company warehouse. The old building was long and flat, anchoring the corner of a mostly abandoned industrial park where weeds emerged from cracks in the pavement.

"This place is definitely more dilapidated than I remember," said Danny to his brother after he climbed out of his car.

"The neighborhood's gone to hell," said Reed. "Most of the other companies moved out."

Gang graffiti covered a closed factory nearby. Most of the windows were broken and doors were boarded shut.

Reed pulled out a keyring and found the key for the warehouse entrance. "Dad didn't want to move. You know how he gets stuck in his ways. The rent was good."

They entered and Reed flipped on a bank of lights. As they stepped into the large, open area of carpet storage, Danny started to smile. "Oh man, what a rush. When we were little, remember how much fun we had running around in here?"

"Made for some awesome games of hide and seek."

They strolled up and down the aisles of towering shelving that stored the carpet inventory, most of the rolls tagged in orange, many of them wrapped in clear plastic. Danny ran ahead to a forklift with long tongs. "Ha! I remember driving this thing around like a go kart. I would test it to see how fast it could go, whipping around corners. That was a blast."

Reed's stride shortened and he fell behind his brother's excited pace.

"Wait up," said Reed, and then he stopped for a moment and put his hands on his knees.

Danny circled back to him. "You okay?"

"Out of breath," said Reed in a tone of irritation. "I'm getting old, bro. Fat and old. So much for the athlete of the family."

"I'll slow down."

"It's just a thing. I'm going to the gym again."

"You're doing better than me."

Reed straightened up and looked around with a scowl. "This place really did a number on me. All the tension of keeping it going. Eating fast food every day for lunch and dinner doesn't help either."

"At least you quit smoking."

"Sort of," said Reed.

"Really?"

"Don't tell Sandy. She would be so pissed. All the workers here smoked, I couldn't get away from it. That's another thing I won't miss."

"So, when will you tell the staff about their fate?"

"Monday, probably," said Reed. "A few will be really upset. Mario, Liam. The rest of them—turnover's been bad, we don't keep people anyway."

"Maybe they can go work for Swanson."

"Sure." Reed straightened up and began walking again. "Let's finish this up. So, do you want the fork lift truck? You can drive around Milwaukee in it."

"Yeah, right."

They advanced to an area with racks of square carpet samples, where contractors could make choices and place orders.

"Want to see something cool?" said Reed. He stuck his hand in a layer of carpet samples and pulled one out. "Check it out. Look familiar?"

Danny laughed. It was an orange and brown shag. "That was in my bedroom!"

"Yep."

They advanced into a section of show rooms, carpets laid out with furniture in imaginary domestic settings to accent their colors and sell their practicality.

Reed took in the scene. "Dad never updated his sets. I guess he cornered the market on people looking to go retro."

"Everything that's old becomes new again," said Danny.

"Everybody makes their choices online anyway. We do have a good website. That was my biggest contribution."

Reed led Danny around a back wall and they entered a skinny, dark area of offices.

"We spent most of our time at the other office," said Reed. "It's pretty gross back here. Look out for rats." Reed flicked several lights and entered one of the rooms. He headed over to a long, steel desk. "Hey, I want to show you something." He took out a small key and unlocked a drawer, opening it. "Check this out."

Danny peered into the drawer and saw a handgun.

"Dad had a gun?"

"In recent times, yeah." They both stared down at it. "I told you, this neighborhood was going to shit. Gang bangers. Sometimes we were here late at night, closing up. He told me to use it if anyone got in here that was looking for trouble. I doubt I could even shoot it straight."

"So, who gets the gun?"

Reed shut the drawer and locked it. "You do. Sandy would shit if I brought a gun home."

He walked over to another desk, one covered with books of carpet samples, and pulled open a drawer. He fished out a carton of cigarettes.

Danny smiled. "Aha, so that's where you keep them."

"Yeah," said Reed. He shook one out. "Speaking of Sandy...I hope *you* don't mind."

"I don't care," said Danny. He looked around the room, noting how filthy and cobwebby everything looked. "We can leave. I don't think there's anything here I want. No offense."

"No offense taken." Reed took a puff and savored it, like a dieting man sneaking chocolate. "We can get out of here. Let's check out the garage and call it a day."

They left the warehouse, locking up, and moved next door to a ramshackle building that serviced a lineup of fleet vehicles. The trucks were parked in neat alignment, each one displaying the company logo.

"Want a carpet truck?" asked Reed, still puffing on his cigarette.

"Nope," said Danny without hesitation.

Inside the garage, he found nothing of interest. The fluorescent tube lighting buzzed and flickered, revealing broken down vehicles dissected for parts, surrounded by disorganized engine components and random equipment that had long ago lost its purpose.

They stood inside the doorway, unmotivated to explore further. "Sell it all," Danny finally said.

Reed hesitated before withdrawing from the garage. "Yeah. End of an era."

They walked across the buckled pavement and then stood for a moment outside their cars as Reed finished his cigarette. "I can get a scrap metal guy in here," he said. "It's a lot of junk."

Danny stared into the distance at a large, majestic structure backlit by the descending sun. Reed caught his gaze and followed it. Danny looked away, didn't say anything, but Reed smiled reassuringly. "I know, I know. It's okay. I got used to it."

The White Sox baseball stadium could be glimpsed from the parking lot, a reminder of the path Reed didn't take.

"You can imagine how much fun it was to have that looming

over me every day," said Reed, now puffing bitterly on the remaining stub of his cigarette. "It got to where I would park around back so I didn't have to see it."

"I'm sorry," said Danny, unable to think of anything else to say.

"If I could do it all over, I would. I would've followed my dreams and ignored all the doubters. Dad wasn't the only doubter. There were others. Hell, even me. I doubted myself. After mom died, I was so messed up... I wish I had taken more control. Instead, I gave my life to this place. You did the smart thing, leaving after five years. You escaped."

Danny responded, "Yeah, but escaped to what? More shitty jobs. At least you have Sandy and the girls. What do I have? Two divorces and a son that hates me."

Reed tossed away the remains of his cigarette. "Well, at least we have one thing to look forward to: the money from selling this place. We can do what we want to do. Reset our lives. Better late than never, right, bro?"

"Maybe we can go on a trip together somewhere," said Danny. "Someplace we've always wanted to go, but never been."

"I'm up for that," said Reed. "A guys' weekend. Maybe Vegas or something."

Danny smiled, excited by the idea. "Yes. I haven't been to Vegas in ages. Yes, let's go for it."

Early the next morning, Danny was startled out of his sleep by his phone. He grabbed it from the nightstand, groggy and annoyed.

"Yeah?" he said in lieu of hello.

"Danny? It's Sandy."

"Sandy?" He sat up. She never called him directly about anything.

"It's about Reed," she said immediately.

"Is he okay?"

"Danny, no." Then Sandy started to cry, and she struggled for words. Danny's mind searched madly for what could possibly be wrong. Was he hurt in a car accident?

"Danny, Reed died."

"What?"

"He had a heart attack."

"Heart attack?"

"At the gym."

"No, that's not possible. I was just with him last night. He was fine."

"They tried to do CPR."

"Who did?"

"At the gym."

"Are you sure?" The whole thing felt like an illogical, blurry dream, an extension of his sleep.

"Danny, of course I'm sure! I'm at the hospital. He died.... He died about an hour ago." She began crying again.

Danny felt knives and needles pierce his body. His mind swam and he became disoriented. The walls closed in around him, squeezing his breath. His life had fallen off the tracks yet again.

Sandy blurted, "He had just started going back to the gym. He was dieting. It was that company, that fucking company, it killed him. He should have sold it years ago!"

"He can't be dead," said Danny. Then in a small, lost voice to himself: "We were going to Vegas...."

"Danny," said Sandy, and she erupted into more crying. "I don't know what to do. The girls are back at the house. I haven't told them yet...."

Danny thought of the two teenage daughters receiving news that their father had died, and then he thought about the sudden death of his own mother, plunging him back to a time of terror he could never escape.

Danny dropped the phone. It hit the floor with a thud and he started sobbing.

TRAVEL LOG:
REVERSAL 19Y 7M 13D

Today I experienced my first pangs of fear that I am losing control of my managed narrative. This was going to be another special trip to my alternate history, specifically focused on my brother. I had arrived in my beloved aviation den prepared to sit in my favorite chair and listen to the broadcast of the Major League Baseball All-Star Game, where Reed DeCastro was the starting pitcher for the American League.

As I made my way across the room, I nearly stumbled over a body. It stirred on the floor, and I let out a mighty yell.

I fell back against my desk, gripping its edge and watched in horror as the shape began to rise. It was a hairy man, like a bear, face full of whiskers, eyes glassy and dazed. His stench hit me almost immediately, a rancid aroma released in waves as he moved.

He muttered something confused and garbled. His clothing was tattered and soiled—a ripped felt shirt, crusty jeans and loafers held together with rubber bands.

"Who are you?" I demanded. "How did you get in here?"

He looked away, rather than answer, lost, as if waking from a dream.

I realized he was a homeless man, possibly mentally ill, and he had broken into my residence.

"Get out!" I demanded. When he didn't budge, I took a step toward him. That caused him to take small, shuffling movements toward the door. When I repeated, louder, *"GET OUT,"* he picked up his pace.

After the intruder left the premises, I returned to my den,

my sanctuary, badly shaken. Although the man was gone, his presence lingered like a stain.

Who was he? How did he get in? How long had he been here? What if he refused to leave? What if the encounter turned violent?

With crazy people, you just never know.

Chapter Nine

Danny took Xanax in an attempt to settle the panic and dread he wore like a coat to Reed's wake. He desired a numbing of the senses but the pill's magic seemed to wear away as the room filled with a cast of faces that elevated his anxiety well beyond any hopeful suppression that drugs could offer. Both of his ex-wives showed up, perhaps to genuinely demonstrate compassion and be supportive, but it felt cruel and unhelpful.

Bringing his father had been a monumental chore to begin with, coping with his continuous stream of confusion, irritation, and bizarre comments. There were moments when his dad appeared lucid and seemed to grasp the reality of Reed's death, but they were far outweighed by the instances where he lost himself in the chronology of time and mixed up people, places, and things.

Danny had spent several days writing a eulogy speech, laboring over every word to make it perfect, but he struggled on capsulizing Reed's life story, knowing that Reed himself was not satisfied with it. In the end, he wrote words that others wanted to hear, even if Reed was looking down from the heavens declaring "Bullshit!"

Sandy and the teenage girls engaged in conversations and remembrances with visitors, finding smiles in memories. Sandy had compiled a photo montage on a large board and propped it on a stand. The photos covered Reed's life in a wide arc from baby pictures to recent holiday gatherings. Danny found himself standing at the collection of images, mesmerized by each one's journey to another time and place.

Sandy came over to him.

"These photos are wonderful," said Danny. "Some of the old ones really take me back."

"Reed had a big box of photos that belonged to your dad," said Sandy. "Your dad gave them to him when he moved out of the house. I'll give them to you. You're in a lot of them. There are some of your mom, too."

Danny nodded. "I'd like that. Thank you."

Sandy moved on and Danny continued to stare at the pictures, stuck in a foggy gaze. One old Polaroid in particular drew his attention. It was Reed and Danny, very young, standing in Danny's childhood bedroom. Danny's focus moved past the faces to the details in the room itself: the posters, the bookcase, the wallpaper, the model planes.

He peeled the photo from the board, brought it closer to his face to examine, then stuffed it into the pocket of his suit jacket.

"Danny, I am so, so sorry."

The voice was unmistakable, emphasizing every syllable, louder than necessary.

Danny turned to face Cheryl.

She stood there with Barry, the man she screwed while still married to Danny. Perhaps Cheryl felt that enough years had gone by that bygones could be bygones. But no. Danny still hated him. And her.

He allowed a quick smile, hugged her, shook Barry's hand, and they talked about how sad the whole thing was.

"Too young!" said Cheryl, as if her insight was a revelation. "He was definitely much too young."

"I only met him a couple of times, but I really liked him," said Barry.

I don't care, thought Danny. He didn't say it out loud, but he did express a more nagging thought that had to come out.

"Where's Adam?" asked Danny.

Cheryl cocked her head and gave him a stern look as if he had said something inappropriate.

"Why do you think he would be here?" she asked.

"Because his uncle died."

"I think maybe you should ask yourself that question."

"People are asking me," said Danny. At least four people in the room had inquired about his son, innocently, unaware of the deep wound they were probing. "I don't know how to reach him. You do!"

"He chose to separate himself from you," said Cheryl. "That's between you and him. I am not getting in the middle. He's an adult now, he lives abroad, he makes his own choices."

"You won't even give me his contact information," said Danny, spitting the words out with anger. "You're being fucking ridiculous!"

"Heyyy," spoke up Barry in a drawn-out manner that said *I don't like your tone.*

"He will reach out to you when and if he chooses," said Cheryl.

"But I'm his father!"

"Perhaps if you had been a better father, you wouldn't have this problem."

Barry put his arm around Cheryl. "Honey, let's leave it alone," he told her, trying to act like the voice of reason. Cheryl gave Danny one of her hard, mean looks before turning away. Barry guided her to a nearby table with cookies.

Thanks for coming! Danny wanted to shout at them viciously.

Marci, wife number two, was on the other side of the room. Danny kept his eye on her and regularly adjusted his position to stay a distance away. Still, she caught up with him during a moment his back was turned while listening to a story about Reed from one of Reed's oldest friends.

"I'm so sorry for your loss," said Marci, touching his arm. A perfect, sanitized, greeting card statement. There was nothing more behind it. Danny hadn't seen her in a very long time. She looked like an older, pudgier version of herself, understandably.

"Thanks," he mumbled.

"Where's Adam?" she asked.

"I gotta go."

When the wake service began, and the chatter ended, Danny found some relief. The program followed a paint-by-numbers structure and when the time arrived for Danny to read, he recited the words on his pages without hearing them or seeing his audience. He imagined himself fully automated, programmed to walk and talk through this horrific nightmare.

When it came time for everyone to line up at the casket and pay their last respects, the room grew very quiet, elevating the small sounds of whispers and soft crying.

Danny's father looked into the coffin and said, "Dad." Perplexed, he turned to look at Danny, who was next in line. "You didn't tell me my father died."

"No, that's…." said Danny, and then he stopped himself. Maybe it was better to leave his father confused. Indeed, it made more sense in the sequence of life for the casket to contain a father than a son.

When Danny reached the casket, he looked inside and studied his brother's face one last time. Perhaps it was the Xanax or the emotional overload, but in that moment, Danny experienced a hallucination that took his breath away.

He saw himself in the coffin.

In Reed's face and features, he recognized his own.

"I'm dead," he said softly.

Reeling, Danny moved away from the coffin. He stared at the floor. Dizzy specks danced in his vision. He quickened his pace.

"Hey!"

Danny looked up and saw Uncle Tim approach. "I think your father wet himself," he said.

Danny nodded and turned away. In the seats, for a split second, he saw Adam, only it wasn't Adam, some other boy, and then Danny felt warm tears on his cheeks.

Danny fled the room.

He ran outside, stumbled through the parking lot, and lost himself in an area of brush behind the funeral home. He fell against a tree and pulled out his phone, trembling.

His chest heaved and his breathing came out choppy and pained.

He called Dr. Elaine Lundy. She answered on the fifth ring.

"Danny…." she said in a tone that right away expressed exasperation.

"I need to see you. Please."

"Danny, I told you. I'll help you find somebody new."

"No, I want to…. I need it to be with you."

"We've gone over this…."

"But it's important."

"Have you forgotten you attacked me? Danny, you had your hands around my throat."

"It was an accident."

"Another accident and you might kill me!"

"No, I promise."

"I gave you names and numbers of people who are better equipped to handle your situation. I can have someone call you—"

Danny hung up. He felt the world spin and fell to a seated position in the dirt.

Danny buried his face in his hands and begged God to not let him go crazy.

Chapter
Ten

The next morning, Danny returned to work and picked up his first pupil of the day, a scrawny and pimply teenage boy named Gordon. After grunting a greeting, Gordon settled behind the wheel, secured his seatbelt, checked his mirrors, and very slowly began to roll the vehicle away from the curb and into a lane of mild traffic.

"Easy does it, that's good, you can pick up your speed, not too fast," said Danny in a calm voice. "Parked cars ahead, keep an eye out in case someone throws open a door."

Gordon's eyes nervously shifted between the windshield, his mirrors, and the speedometer.

"You're doing fine," said Danny. "Let's take a right up ahead. Use your blinker."

Gordon turned a corner and entered a main road.

"You can pick up your speed," said Danny.

Gordon looked down at the speedometer.

"Watch the road," said Danny. Gordon snapped his gaze back up.

"You can go faster," said Danny. Gordon applied a little more pressure to the gas pedal, but not much.

"Don't be timid," said Danny.

Gordon flashed Danny a look and scowled. His lips were chapped and flaky.

Cars began passing them with abrupt roars of annoyance.

"Come on, Gordon, live dangerously," said Danny, and he chuckled with forced good-naturedness.

Gordon continued to putter below the speed limit.

"This is no way to go through life," said Danny.

Another car passed them, whizzing by in close proximity, which only made Gordon reduce his speed.

Danny shifted in his seat. He brought his left leg into Gordon's space and pressed his foot down on Gordon's foot.

The car promptly accelerated.

"Hey!" said Gordon, gripping the wheel tighter, alarmed.

"That's better, isn't it?" said Danny, continuing to press.

"Please don't do that, Mr. DeCastro."

"Call me Danny."

"Mr. DeCastro, *stop.*"

Danny pressed down harder. He felt a thrill branch out across his veins.

The car shot forward, advancing five, then 10, and then 15 miles above the speed limit.

"The speed limit is thirty!" said Gordon, tense and braced forward.

"So it is," said Danny. "Are you going to be a rule follower your whole life? Do what others tell you?"

"We're going too fast!"

The car roared down the road, reaching 50. Gordon removed his right hand from the steering wheel and tried to push Danny's leg back across the divider.

"Life goes too fast," said Danny. "Get used to it."

"There are cars up ahead!"

"Obstacles. You either avoid them or you crash and burn. It's in your control, Gordon."

"Please stop!"

The Audi ahead of them rapidly grew closer.

Danny kept his foot pressed down and imagined a big, fiery crash.

Gordon swerved the car at the last minute and zipped past the slower vehicle, close enough to see the full alarm on the other driver's face.

Danny waved, friendly.

Up ahead, the traffic light turned red.

"We have to stop!" shouted Gordon.

"Says who?" demanded Danny.

"Please! You're going to kill us!" Gordon was practically crying as the car shot toward the intersection with no indication of slowing down.

"I'm not going to kill us, Gordon," said Danny, embracing the adrenaline rush racing through his body. "I'm teaching you what it feels like to be *alive*."

When it appeared a massive pileup was all but certain, Danny withdrew his foot from the pedal, settled back in his seat and proclaimed, "Wheeee!"

Gordon's foot leapt onto the brake, slamming it hard. The car skidded and began to slide out of alignment with the road. Other vehicles swerved out of the way to avoid him. Gordon worked the steering wheel furiously, aiming one way and another until he miraculously brought it all under control in time to halt the car inches from the vehicle stopped in front of him.

"Welcome to adulthood," said Danny.

Gordon fought back tears. "I want to go home."

Danny allowed Gordon to return home, without further incident.

After watching Gordon run into his house, Danny drove to the Good Driving Institute and resigned.

He was done with a job that forced him to be a passenger. It was the ultimate cruelty for someone who once dreamed of piloting a 747.

Danny returned to his apartment, played loud 80s music, and plotted his next move.

Destination: Eldridge, Iowa.

TRAVEL LOG:
REVERSAL 27Y 10M 12D

As I conduct my series of time travel trips to rewrite my life story, I have encountered another surprise of strange and unintended consequences, this one even more shocking than the last.

The original purpose of today's journey was to create a pivotal moment the summer after my junior year at Indiana University. On this landmark day, I would receive my acceptance letter admitting me into Purdue University's aviation school to be a flight major and pursue my dream of becoming a professional pilot.

I had secretly applied to switch schools, knowing my father would be upset, but I refused to let that drama hold me back. Three years in, I had confirmed that business school—and a career at DeCastro Carpet Distributors—was not for me. I had broken up with Cheryl, my IU girlfriend. I had saved a good stash of money from summer and campus jobs. I was prepared to take out student loans. The time was right to enter aviation school. I knew I would have my mother's support. I was grateful she was there for me.

The scene was supposed to play out this way: I would call my mother and father into my bedroom, show them the acceptance letter, and announce my firm intentions. A new path would be put into motion.

However, that conversation was put on hold. Before I could trigger this life-altering scenario, I received a surprise phone call.

It was Lisetta.

We had kept in touch regularly since high school graduation, retaining a mutual affection for one another. She was an English major at the University of Iowa, attending the school with her on-again, off-again boyfriend Martin, who was studying engineering. Both were home for the summer.

I almost didn't recognize her voice at first. She was crying.

She said, "Somebody killed Martin."

I staggered, wobbly at the knees, as if struck by a blow. "*What?*"

"He's dead. He was murdered."

"How is that...? How is that possible?" My mind raced. This twist of fate did not make sense. I did not author it.

"They found him stabbed."

"By who?"

"Nobody knows."

"Where did this happen?"

Lisetta told the entire story. Martin had gone into the city with his friends for a night of drinking and merriment. They visited a number of bars and clubs, eventually splintering off in the wee hours to return home. Martin was last seen heading for a train platform.

Police discovered his dead body after sunrise in a Chicago alley, wedged under a dumpster, the victim of multiple stab wounds. There were no suspects.

I was dumbstruck. I didn't know what to say.

Lisetta said, "Can I come over? Please? I don't want to be alone."

"Of course," I told her. "Absolutely. I'm here for you."

I was shaking. This turn of events did not make sense. She was supposed to break up naturally with Martin, years later on my timeline, without any kind of violence. Our intimacy was meant to blossom after I graduated from aviation school and impressed her with a romantic plane ride in a cozy, single-engine Cessna. A dramatic kiss was planned for 10,000 feet. The script was already written.

Some control was lost today, yet for our relationship the intended outcome didn't change. It was simply accelerated. I accepted the plot twist.

Lisetta came over and we held one another for comfort for a long time on my bed. From this day on, we became inseparable. Everything fell into place ahead of plan. Our love grew deep and unbreakable.

Eventually we got married, like a storybook romance, destined to live happily ever after.

Chapter Eleven

Danny sent an email to Lisetta through a link on the "Contact Us" page of the Eldridge Gazette web site, where she was listed as a staff member. He did not know her home email address nor if it was shared with or monitored by her husband, so this was the best channel for outreach. Danny's carefully composed note held his intensity in check, not a trace of desperation, just a light and breezy tone:

"I'm passing through Eldridge next week on my way to Des Moines to scout a location for a corporate conference for insurance executives. I'd love to stop by and see you for lunch, if your schedule permits. Let me know."

After pressing send, he couldn't sit still and left for a long walk, hoping to return to find her response waiting in his inbox like a gift to be unwrapped.

Forty minutes later, he was back at his apartment building. Too impatient for the elevator, he bounded up two flights of steps, threw open his door and pounced on his computer.

The only new arrival was spam and he swore at it before punching the delete button. A few minutes later, as if sensing his presence, her reply appeared. Little spears pierced Danny's heart. He took a deep breath and opened the message.

"That's wonderful. I would love to get together for lunch. Nobody ever visits this Podunk town. I've saved the date on my calendar with a big gold star!"

Danny forced himself to wait 20 minutes before responding. He didn't want Lisetta to think he was hovering over his laptop like a sweaty, overeager adolescent. That kind of behavior was charming at 16 but no doubt creepy at 48.

After precisely 20 minutes had passed, Danny unleashed his reply to her reply. He added a simple sentence at the end he knew would make her feel good.

"P.S.—I read some of your books. They're TERRIFIC."

"OMG, you are so sweet," she wrote back.

On a sunny Tuesday the following week, they met in Eldridge at Harvey's Bar and Grill, a simple restaurant with a hearty menu and gravel parking lot. She was already waiting at the front when he arrived, exactly on time. She wore a pretty, blue blouse, dark skirt, and heels. He wore a new shirt and slacks, purchased the night before. They were both more dressed up than the majority of the restaurant's noontime customers.

She initiated a quick hug, and he immediately tried to read into it—a desire for physical contact or just a symbolic reminder that the relationship was purely platonic?

She chose a booth in the back where they settled in and leaned toward one another. She launched into conversation with a playful confrontation.

"Why'd you disappear at the reunion?"

"I couldn't stay late—I figured you had other people you wanted to see."

"Yeah, but you didn't say goodbye."

"I waved. You were on the phone."

"Admit it, you ditched me."

For the first 15 minutes, she did most of the talking, rambling excitedly as if she had been saving up things to say. She talked about the town and its sleepy charms. She described several news stories she was currently working on, minor dramas from rural life: an old man caught stealing a jar of pickles from the local grocer; a persistent presence of bees menacing the middle school. She talked about her daughter's first semester studying art history at NYU. She asked him about his conference planning trip, and he had no trouble making up lies since most of the job, when he worked there, was built on lies.

They ordered beers to begin and casually neglected the menus. "I can take a long lunch," she said. "If they ask, I'll say I was out researching a story."

"I should have brought your books for you to sign," he said earnestly.

"I can't believe you read them," she said, smiling as sweetly as in high school. The added lines etched into her face could not diminish the smile's effect.

"Of course I read them," he said. To prove it, he talked through each one, pointing out characters and parts of the plot he liked.

"Does Martin read your books?" he asked.

She shook her head and laughed. "Not his genre. He's not a big reader to begin with."

"It's not really my genre, either," said Danny. "But the writing is so good, it really pulls you in."

When the plump waitress made her fourth visit, growing impatient, Danny and Lisetta finally ordered sandwiches. After she left, Lisetta leaned across the table toward Danny, made an impish grin and confided, "That's Harriet. She's been here forever. She's a real crab. I'm going to put her in one of my books."

"Ha, you should," said Danny. "You should put me in one too."

"Maybe I will."

"Can I be a white knight?"

"Sure. A white knight coming to the rescue of a damsel in distress. I'll put you on a horse."

"I've never ridden a horse."

"You'll like it. What should we name your horse?"

Danny mulled it over. "Sparky."

Lisetta broke up into loud laughter. "Sparky? That's a name for a dog."

That got Danny thinking about his own childhood dog. "Toby," he said. "Name him Toby."

"Toby? That could work." She started talking about the new novel she had in progress, a romance set during the French Revolution. "I love doing the research," she said. "But it takes so much time for something that will only sell like 10 copies and wind up in recycling bins."

"Don't say that," he said.

"It's the truth. If you only knew...." Her tone shifted, and for a moment her mood deflated.

"When I was young, I had this dream," she said. "I was going to be a bestselling novelist. I'd be in all the bookstores and libraries. I'd have millions of readers. Translated into dozens of languages, all over the world. I'd have long lines for book signings." She let out a sigh and pushed the thoughts away. "Youth is built on crazy dreams. You don't know better when you're 16. You think anything is possible."

"I had a really crazy dream when I was young," said Danny. "Do you know what I wanted to be? I was going to be an airline pilot."

"Really? A pilot?"

"Seriously. I didn't tell many people."

"That's so cool. That's a good dream."

"It still nags at me. I should've gone for it. But I never did. I couldn't pull the trigger."

"What's that John Lennon line? 'Life's what happens when you're busy making other plans.'"

"That's for sure." Danny paused. He wondered if he should release the next thought in his head. He decided to go for it. He had come all this way. There was no telling if he would ever have this chance again.

"Do you know what I really regret?" said Danny, and he looked into her eyes.

She asked, "What?"

"I wish I had more actively pursued you in high school."

Without hesitating, she replied, "I wish you had."

Danny was stunned. He wasn't sure if this made him feel better—or worse.

"Really?" he said.

"I liked you a lot, Danny. You couldn't tell?"

"I did—and didn't." He began to stammer. "I was an insecure kid. I didn't know what to believe...about anyone...or anything."

"You were good to me. Handsome. Fun. Smart." She was smiling. "I had feelings for you."

"I wanted so bad to make a move on you, but you had Martin."

"Yeah," she said, and her mouth formed a crooked line. "Martin. I stuck that one out. He has his good points and his not-so-good points." Hardly a ringing endorsement for a long-time relationship, thought Danny.

Their sandwiches sat cold on their plates. They had become so caught up in conversation that neither one had taken a bite since lunch arrived. Now Danny's stomach was in such knots that he couldn't imagine eating anything.

"Too bad we can't go back in time," said Lisetta.

"True." Danny stared down at the table, suddenly feeling very, very old.

"We made choices," said Lisetta. "Maybe not the right ones, but we have to live with them. You can't rewrite history."

Danny's mind searched for the right thing to say and he couldn't come up with it. He looked back at Lisetta. She was studying him. For the first time since they had met up at the front of the restaurant, there was a lengthy silence between them.

Then Lisetta spoke. Her dark eyes stayed on Danny. She spoke slowly and discreetly, almost a whisper. "I can't believe I'm saying this but...about a mile down the road...the main road here...out front, due west...there's a motel. It's called Countryside Inn. If you wanted to meet...."

"Like a...fling?" said Danny. "A one-night stand?"

She attempted to lighten the mood. "Not quite. More like a one-afternoon stand."

"And then what?"

"And then...? We get on with our lives, I suppose."

Danny straightened in his chair, heart pounding. "How about if we run away together?" he said.

Lisetta made a sudden exhale, like a small, scornful laugh. "Run away? To where?"

"I don't know."

"Danny, I have a daughter. I have a husband. I have a house and a job...I can't just run away."

"I—I don't want some cheap fling," said Danny, and his words quickly accelerated. "You're too special. You were the love of my life. I wanted to spend every day with you. This isn't about going for a romp in some motel room. I can't—"

She held up a hand to stop him. "I'm sorry. Forget it. Forget I ever made the suggestion. It was in the moment. It was crazy. I don't know what I was thinking. Let's just...stop."

Danny took a breath and said, "I'm sorry. I'll get the check."

She told him, "No, relax. It's okay. We're going to finish our lunch...like two old friends."

He swallowed, then nodded. "Okay."

"I didn't mean to freak you out," she said.

"You didn't."

"Let's just forget that part of the conversation ever happened. Erase it." There was a nervous jitter in her voice. "We don't need to live in the past. Those days are gone. Let's talk about the here and now. Tell me more about your job. Do you get to travel a lot?"

Danny didn't remember much about the rest of the meal. His mind was in a million places.

In the restaurant's white gravel parking lot, before splitting for their cars, they embraced once more.

Then Lisetta pulled back, looked at him squarely and said, "Oh, what the hell!"

She gave him a sturdy kiss on the lips.

The kiss was over before he could fully respond. Giving him a playful grin, she waved and skipped back to her car. Danny waved back but couldn't bring himself to say goodbye.

Chapter Twelve

Standing in his apartment, lights low, voice calm and even, Danny called Sandy.

"I wanted you to know I've started selling the assets of the business," he told her. "Reed kept excellent records of everything, so it's going very smoothly."

"That's good to hear. Thank you, Danny," she said. "I have total trust in you. I'm sure it will go well."

He added, "I'm not getting rid of everything. I'm keeping one of the fleet vehicles."

"I'm fine with that."

"Also, I'm not selling the warehouse. I'm going to put it under my ownership. I'll subtract its value from my share of the money."

She hesitated. "I guess that's fine. What are you going to do with all that carpet?"

"I don't want the carpet," he told her. "I have a deal to sell the inventory to Swanson. I just want the building."

She hesitated again, as if she hadn't heard him right. "Really? The building? That old thing? What on earth for?"

"For a physics project."

"Physics?"

"An experiment."

"Okay," she said in a tone that indicated she wasn't going to probe any further. "If that's what you want, Danny, go for it."

TRAVEL LOG:
REVERSAL 18Y 11M 22D

I'm soaring.

I'm elevated high in the sky in a Boeing 747, skimming the clouds like a surfboard. I am disconnected from the earth below, surrounded by eternal blue. My hands keep a firm and steady grip on the controls. The airplane glides powerfully and purposefully under my direction.

This is my life and I could not be happier.

My heart lifts at the sight of my wife Lisetta and our young son William shining at me from a color photograph I have posted in the cockpit. My family is everything to me. When I land, I know they will be excited to see me. I will experience the perfect finish to my perfect day: the homecoming.

I am 30 years old. I am achieving my life's goals. I am basking in the glory.

It's a spiritual feeling. The best way to describe it is pure bliss....

Part Two

Chapter Thirteen

Sticking out of the usual bulk of bills and junk mail in a mid-week postal delivery, Lisetta discovered a thick-textured, cream-colored square envelope with no return address and her name spelled out in elegant, formal script. The lettering had been carefully composed by hand with variances in line thickness, a departure from the cold, computer-generated mass mailings she typically pulled from the mailbox at the end of her driveway.

As she returned inside the house, delegating the boring mail to a sloppy stack on an entry hall table, she brought her personalized missive into the kitchen. Before pouring her customary after-work glass of red wine, she tore open the curious envelope, half-expecting a too-clever advertisement.

Instead, she slid out a cardstock invitation to a time machine.

You are cordially invited to
an exclusive trip to reinvent the past
at the request of Mr. Daniel DeCastro
who will unveil the miracle of his
TIME MACHINE
and the Open Horizon of Possibilities.

Lisetta broke out in a grin, charmed by the goofy creativity and titillating suspense. In smaller print, the terms were laid out:

Please note: this invitation is intended only for the addressed recipient and may not be transferred to or discussed with any other party.

At the bottom of the card, the instructions encouraged a prompt RSVP, providing a phone number to "secure your reservation for this once-in-a-lifetime opportunity."

"What...the...hell," said Lisetta, staring at the invite, still smiling. It was the most interesting piece of mail she had opened in forever and caused her heartbeat to pick up extra beats.

"You're crazy," she said to Danny's card, and she loved it.

She honestly had not expected to hear from him again. After their lunch meeting in Eldridge had ended with her awkward proposition and his uncomfortable sidestep, she feared their rejuvenated relationship had slipped off the rails. They shared a short email or two afterward, to reassure no bad feelings, but then there was a lapse of six months of silence.

Lisetta figured both of them had simply gone on with their lives—the ones that had been predestined and could not be interrupted.

And now this.

It was teasing and flirty and special and hinted at something that might pick up where they left off.

She studied the words on the invitation a couple dozen times. Then she hid it before her husband came home.

He picked through the bills and junk mail and groused. She had finished her second glass of wine and said very little to him, feeling warm under the flesh and coolly introspective.

The next morning, Lisetta called the RSVP number from her desk at the Eldridge Gazette. There was no one else around to eavesdrop. She was ready for the conversation to go wherever it was headed.

"Hello," she said, when Danny answered. She spoke in a jokey formal voice. "I'm calling about the time machine offer I received in the mail. Could you provide some more information?"

"I'm sorry, ma'am," said Danny, going along with it. "I'm

afraid we can't do it justice over the phone. We really need to sign you up for an appointment."

"I see," she said. "Can you tell me where this time machine is located?"

"No, ma'am. We cannot disclose that information."

"Really?"

"We meet at a prearranged destination and provide you with transportation to the site. Given the strict confidentiality of the project, you will be blindfolded and sworn to secrecy."

Lisetta felt strangely aroused at that moment in a way she hadn't been for many years. She almost had to put the phone down.

Finally, she broke character and became her true self expressing exactly what was on her mind.

"Danny," she said with a laugh, "what the hell is this?"

"I want you to come see my time machine!"

"That is the weirdest come-on line ever."

"I'm serious."

"Yeah, I bet." She glanced around the room to make sure her colleagues remained out on other business. "Listen—I would love to see you, time machine or not. But—"

She sighed. Reality and complications. Things like geographical distance. Oh, and being married.

"I don't know how..." she started. She was going to conclude with "...this is going to work." But then she stopped herself.

There was an opening.

"Okay, maybe I can visit," she said, remembering a notation on her calendar. "Just for a day or two. Next weekend—it's Martin's annual hunting trip. With his buddies. They go way out in the woods, no cell phone service. I'd have a window of maybe forty-eight hours. I could come see you. Then I have to come right back. Obviously—he can't know about this."

"You're the only person who knows about the time machine."

"I'm serious, Danny. He would kill me."

"The time machine will take care of everything."

She almost groaned at him. This wasn't something to be taken lightly. "Enough with the time machine. I want to see you. I—I think we can make this work."

"Good, good," he said. There was a tremble of excitement in his voice. "I'm looking forward to seeing you. How have you been?"

She answered honestly in a flat voice. "The same." Then she asked, "How have you been?"

"I'm doing great," said Danny. "I've never been better."

Lisetta pumped a playlist of 80s music in her car during the three-hour drive from Eldridge, Iowa to Chicago, Illinois, mentally preparing herself to journey back in time and erase the crummy memories of the 1990s and beyond. The playlist compiled her favorite tunes, beginning with "Under the Milky Way" by The Church, blasting "How Soon is Now?" by The Smiths at the halfway point, and finishing with the joyful thump of New Order's "True Faith." When the playlist concluded, she sent it back to start.

The journey was stubbornly non-scenic, flat and monotonous farm fields, allowing her to escape inside her head for a three-way battle between nostalgia, doubt, and fear.

She checked her phone frequently just in case Martin had a signal and wanted to reach her. Past experience reassured her both of these things were unlikely. She scared herself with "what if" scenarios involving engine trouble or being spotted by someone she knew at a gas station or from a passing car. This was the craziest, bravest thing she had done in ages, going against her slow, unfeeling descent into the unquestioned acceptance of life-as-it-is.

Danny had effectively taken hold of her heart and injected hope, or maybe just shaken her out of her doldrums with his offbeat, creative charm. She had packed more clothes than necessary for a quick weekend trip, solving the what-do-I-wear dilemma by stuffing her suitcase with options suitable for a variety of plotlines. This included sexy, slinky, silky red lingerie.

The only certainty was returning home by midday Sunday and scattering some books, magazines, and dirty dishes to accompany the illusion of a low-key weekend at home.

As Lisetta reached the city of Chicago, she quickly began looking for her exit. Danny had established a meeting place near the side of the highway, a dumpy bar called Perry's where they wouldn't be seen together by anyone in their respective social circles.

"It's a nothing place, a real hole in the wall," he told her on the phone.

"Great," she responded. "Sounds glamorous."

He promised to meet her at 2 pm, but her clumsy estimate of driving time brought her to the destination 45 minutes early.

She tucked herself in a back booth, head down, hoping to become invisible, but the place was nearly empty and a nice man kept coming back to refill her drink.

The first drink, vodka and tonic, disappeared in a flash in an attempt to settle her spiky nerves. She was the worst combination of nervous and tired. She hadn't slept well the night before, lying beside her husband in bed, feeling apprehensive about the knowledge she possessed that he didn't about the weekend to come. She became strangely paranoid that he could read her thoughts from such close proximity.

Then there was the fatigue from the long drive. Her brain wasn't at its best, groggy and undisciplined; at least that was her reasoning as she continued to nod for another drink.

On an empty stomach.

When Danny arrived at exactly 2 pm, she was comfortably inebriated and did not hesitate to jump up and give him a tight embrace. He quickly ordered drinks for the both of them, and she couldn't refuse. Her jagged edges continued to melt away.

They stayed for a couple of drinks and slipped into an easy, fun conversation. Danny wore an unassuming blue windbreaker, collared polo shirt, jeans, and neatly combed hair. His eyes sparkled as he spoke about the time machine, "my obsession of the past six months."

"How do you know it works?" she asked.

"I've tried it."

"Where did you go?"

"Back to my childhood."

She laughed. "You're blowing my mind."

"I have a chance to go back and fix everything that went wrong."

"But really—you visit the past?"

"I go through a passage in a higher dimension, it's like a hole in the fabric of Earth's physics."

"Can you go back, like, to the 1800s?"

Danny smiled. "No. It only works in your own personal timeline."

"So, I couldn't go back before I was born?"

"Right."

"Well, so much for a trip to see the dinosaurs."

"You're traveling the continuum of your own existence, and you can only go backward."

"I was never very good at science," she said simply. She finished her latest drink and had difficulty setting down the glass with her unsteady hand.

"Were you drinking before I got here?" said Danny, noticing.

She nodded with a shrug and screwed-up smile.

"You better not drive," said Danny. "We'll come back later for your car."

"Probably a good idea," she said.

She reached into her purse and handed over her car keys for safekeeping.

"There," she said. "The key to my heart." She spoke it spontaneously but felt no aftereffects. She decided it was no longer necessary to be under the pretense of subtlety.

He smiled at her and pocketed the key. "Are you ready?" he asked.

"I really want to go back in time," she said. The admission almost made her cry. Her head felt dizzy.

As they advanced outside, the sudden transition from dark bar to afternoon sunshine hurt her eyes. She stumbled and Danny caught her around the shoulders. He guided her into his car.

As they sat in the front seat together, Danny hesitated before starting the engine.

"For the time travel to work, its secrets cannot be revealed," he said.

"I won't tell anybody anything," she said, a touch slurred.

"Before we go, you must be blindfolded."

"What? Seriously?"

He reached into the backseat and, sure enough, pulled out a dark eye mask with an elastic band, the type used to help people sleep—or engage in S & M.

Fascinated, she accepted the mask and studied it in her hands. She placed it on her face without objection. It felt snug and cozy.

In the abrupt loss of sight, she became more lightheaded and off-balance. "Mmmm," she said, dropping her hands in her lap.

She heard Danny move in his seat and then his lips pressed lightly against hers. She accepted them and opened her mouth for a long, dark, mysterious kiss.

She felt a rush of feeling. After the kiss, she settled back in the passenger seat. Danny started the car and reversed out of the parking space.

As they slipped onto a street and picked up speed, Lisetta felt her body in motion, floating, then soaring, like a bird. Her imagination ran rich with abstract images. Then her senses morphed into a muddle of vague confusion, and she surrendered to alcohol, fatigue and overwhelm. She passed out without a fight, accepting the transition that awaited.

Chapter Fourteen

Lisetta resurfaced from sleep. Her head ached and her mouth felt dry. She felt the eye mask pressed against her face and reached up to peel it away.

A strange domestic environment slowly came into focus around her. She found herself on a bed, propped up against soft pillows. She stirred her limbs. Her brain emerged from a murky fog. Chipper, bouncy music greeted her with growing clarity. The Go Gos?

Lisetta sat up. Her hands clutched a thin bed cover beneath her. She bumped against some objects. Faintly familiar textbooks were laid out in front of her. One of them, split open, displayed geometry problems.

She stared down at a page of triangles labeled with numbers and letters. She lifted her head and scanned the details of her environment, certain she was dreaming.

She was sitting on somebody's bed—a made bed, not her own—in a youth's bedroom. Colorful hangings decorated the walls: an E.T. movie poster; a poster of the band Journey; and several large images of airplanes. Music played on an outdated, silvery stereo system nestled in a small wood cabinet. A black, vinyl record was spinning, and she watched it hypnotically for a moment before continuing to take in her surroundings.

Model airplanes crowded the top of a bedroom dresser. One remained a work in progress: tiny plastic parts organized alongside a sheet of instructions and tube of rubber cement.

Something about the wood-grained dresser—and the rest of the brown furniture—and the large-pattern wallpaper and multicolor shag carpeting—felt odd, a mixture of familiar and faraway.

She finally recognized the textbooks from high school. She realized she was dreaming about being a teenager again. Decades of adulthood had been stripped away to resurface old memories. Like all dreams, weird anomalies persisted: this was not *her* room.

Lisetta was afraid to move off the bed, uncertain of the turn this dream was destined to take. Her hands continued to move across the texture of the bed cover. It felt real, not imagined. The song on the stereo sounded rich and immediate. Lisetta felt a sudden urge to cry out and hear her own voice. Often in nightmares, she was mute, unable to scream for help.

"HELLO?" she shouted. Her own bellow startled her, bringing sharper reality to the scene.

She shouted again. "WHERE AM I?" Her voice shook with fear.

Abruptly the door to the bedroom opened. Someone entered the room holding a small wrapped present. He wore a yellow rugby shirt with green stripes and a white collar, acid wash jeans and striped Adidas. He appeared to be a teenage boy.

He stepped forward.

It was Danny DeCastro.

"Happy birthday," Danny said, holding up the gift. "I got something special for your sweet sixteen."

Lisetta swooned, confused, feeling swallowed up in a time warp. This was Danny's bedroom...from long ago...and they were back in high school? How was this possible?

Oh my God, she realized at that moment. *The time machine. It's for real.*

Her heart pounded with excitement. Her mind filled with wonder. She surrendered to the moment, letting her apprehension slip away, transporting herself mentally inside this physical environment.

I'm 16 again. Holy shit, I'm really—

Danny advanced closer, stepping out of the shadows and into the light.

The dreamlike fog lifted in an instant. Reality set in. Lisetta let out a small shriek.

This was old, adult Danny in a teenager's clothing: thin hair, face puffier and sagging, gray hair at the temples, potbellied.

She jumped off the bed. She stood before him on the carpet, frightened and confused, uncertain of what to do.

Danny frowned. "Don't ruin this."

"Where—where am I?"

"You're in my room."

"Your room?"

"Let me set up the scene."

"Scene?"

"We're doing homework together. It's your birthday. I got you a present."

"It's not my birthday."

"You just turned sixteen."

"This is the time machine?"

Danny nodded. He held out the wrapped gift in shiny, metallic paper. "Go ahead. Open it."

Adrenaline surging, Lisetta was now fully awake. The more she took in her surroundings, the more fake they started to look—fresh and staged, rather than lived in. The two windows had their shades drawn with no hint of outside light seeping in.

"Please, Danny, what's going on? I don't remember…how I got here. My head is a mess."

"It will all make sense if you open the gift."

Desperate for answers, she took the present from him. After a moment's hesitation, she peeled away the paper, letting it fall to the floor, uncovering a small jewelry box.

"Open it," said Danny, smiling.

She gingerly opened the jewelry box to reveal a beautiful, gold necklace.

She studied it, feeling even more confused. "I don't know what to say."

"Put it on."

"Not right now," she said. Her heart was pounding but no longer in a good way.

"That gift took a lot of courage for a 16-year-old. And a lot of lawn-mowing money."

"Thank you?" she said, and it came out more like a question. Everything had turned into a question.

"This is a course correction," he told her. "In an alternate version of this same scene, I gave you a stupid novelty card. That was foolish Danny, scared Danny, who had trouble expressing himself."

"I would be fine with a card."

"You weren't. I could tell it in your eyes. You were disappointed. Don't you remember?"

"I don't remember a card. Maybe a little bit. I don't know. That was so long ago." She held the jewelry box out to him. "Please take this back."

"But it's part of the process."

"What process? Where are we? What is this?"

The record player concluded playing the Go Gos album side. The needle entered the center groove, then lifted off the vinyl, bringing the scene's soundtrack to an end. Its absence plunged the room into starkness.

Danny refused to take back the jewelry box she extended toward him. Lisetta dropped her arm.

"This is what you wanted," said Danny. "This is what we both wanted. To go back and do it right."

"We're not 30 years younger, Danny. Look at us."

"Use your imagination. Go deep, like when you created those worlds in your books."

"My books?"

"Remember the time travel in *Whispers in Time*? You wrote about it. The science here is exactly the same. We're 'twisting the laws of physics.' That was your line."

"That was fiction."

"It came from your heart."

"What is going on, really?"

"This is the time machine," said Danny. "I set the controls for 32 years ago...5 months...18 days...for your 16th birthday."

"This is crazy."

"On this day, we were doing homework together in my bedroom."

"I'm done with my homework." She pushed the jewelry box against his chest, forcing him to catch it before it fell to the floor. "And you're taking this back."

"But that isn't in the script."

"Where have you taken me?"

"Back in time."

"This isn't funny."

"I'm not joking."

"I don't want to play this game. I want to leave."

"Leave?"

"Go home."

"What home?"

"Back to Eldridge."

"Your home in Eldridge doesn't exist. You're sixteen...."

"You're scaring me."

"Don't fight it. Go with it."

"This is ridiculous!"

"Calm down."

"I want out of here."

She gave him a forceful shove and he staggered back several steps. Lisetta swiftly headed for the bedroom door.

"Lisetta, please!"

She left the bedroom and plunged into a long, narrow corridor with a cement floor and high ceilings that vanished into darkness.

"What the hell?" she said, seeing no obvious exit in either direction—just a series of doors.

She ran to the first door and threw it open.

She faced an elaborate den with a large oak desk and crowded bookcase. The room was decorated with aviation images and small objects related to flying.

Lisetta dashed down the corridor to the next door and opened it to find an even stranger sight:

The room was empty and dark, except for the presence of an airplane cockpit.

Danny pounced on her, grabbing her wrists. "Stop opening these doors!" he shouted. "You're upsetting the space-time continuum!"

She wiggled loose and screamed in his face. *"What the hell is going on?"*

"I made our dreams come true."

"You're delusional!"

"You can't leave."

"You're kidnapping me?"

"No, I'm rescuing you. Like a white knight in one of your books. Like Ivan the Viking. I am the catalyst for the heroine to rediscover herself and take what she truly wants from life."

Lisetta's head was swimming. She hated herself for coming all this way on a whim, then drinking too much. This was not right. Danny was not stable.

"Where are my car keys? My cell phone?"

"Those things don't exist."

"Seriously? You can't keep me here. I'll tell the police you kidnapped me. My husband—Martin—he will kill you."

"You won't call the police."

"How do you know?"

"Because it's me."

She shook her head. "This is not normal."

"I'm not going to hurt you," he said. "You know that."

"That's not the point."

"We don't have to accept the reality we've been given. If we do, we surrender. We're stronger than that. Life is one big illusion anyway. Let's take control and go back to make it right. Everything we need is here."

"And where is here?"

"The time machine."

She sighed. "And exactly where is the time machine?"

He finally relented, offering some truth. "We're in a big space where no one will ever bother us. It's a building on the south side of Chicago. It used to be my father's warehouse."

"And all these rooms?"

"They're sets. Scenes. Moments. Parts of the life narrative that need a correction. I inherited some money. I've spent the last six months building this out…looking at details in old photographs to get it right…reading old diaries, doing research, finding things on eBay."

"And you did this all yourself?"

"Yes. I'll show you my lab."

"Your lab?"

"It's my secret lab, where the magic happens. No one else has ever been inside. You will be the first. Just like Professor Sotos in *Whispers in Time*."

"Professor Sotos didn't need eBay."

Danny laughed at her. "Come with me. Let me show you."

Cautiously, she followed.

He led Lisetta to the end of a long corridor. They passed through a black curtain and approached a secured door. He unlocked it and guided her inside, snapping on a light switch.

To Lisetta, the room resembled a theater troop's backstage storage, populated with racks of clothing and an odd assortment of furniture and props.

"Don't trip on Toby's water bowl," said Danny, and Lisetta just barely skipped past a dog's bowl at her feet. A yellow Labrador retriever scampered over to her, curious, tail wagging.

"Meet Toby," said Danny. "He's my dog from childhood. I use him in all the scenes from when I was growing up. I was just writing him into a new scene."

Danny walked over to a large, busy drafting table, covered with blueprints, handwritten notes and a scattering of old, faded photographs.

"This is where I design my sets," said Danny. "Right now, I have eight rooms, but I have plenty of space to expand." He grabbed a three-ring binder from a corner of the drafting table and opened it to show her a sampling of pages.

"These are my scripts," he said. "Are you familiar with role-playing therapy?"

Lisetta shook her head no.

"I rewrite scenes from my life and reenact them to go the way they should have gone. That's what gets performed on these sets."

She glanced at a page dense with dialogue between Danny, "Dad" and "Mom."

"Who plays these parts?"

"I hire local actors and actresses. Community theater people.

I tell them I'm a playwright trying out new scenes. I pay them well. They're starving artists. Everybody's happy."

"Why not just hire someone to be me?" she asked.

Danny shot her an incredulous look. "You? No way. We're going on this journey together. I can tell you want this as bad as I do. I saw it in your eyes. At the reunion. At the restaurant. At the bar...."

Next he showed her the handwritten pages of his time travel log. Each log entry represented a completed, reimagined episode of his past he had brought to life inside the warehouse, using props and hired performers.

"These are the parts of my life I've recreated so far," he said. "I redid them so they go the right way."

He showed her time travel entries reflecting the prevention of his mother's death and the thrill of his brother pitching a no-hitter.

"But it's not real," she said.

"The past is just a memory," he responded. "It only exists in our mind. We don't have to be a slave to something that no longer exists. We can correct it."

"By staging it?"

"All the world's a stage," said Danny.

She turned away, breaking from his stare and the time travel log book. She walked over to a box of baseball items: a jersey with the name DeCastro on it, a White Sox cap, and a baseball bat.

"So, you're a baseball player when you go back in time?" she asked.

"No. My brother is. He wanted more than anything to be a baseball player. That bat there, he signed it for me. It's from the American League playoffs."

"Okay," said Lisetta, unimpressed.

Danny turned toward the next batch of props, eager to continue the tour. He directed her attention to components of an airplane control panel. He kneeled down, picking through the pieces. "This is for the cockpit I've been building. You wouldn't believe how hard it is to get ahold of some of these parts. I've been to auctions, even scrap yards. The steering wheel is a beauty, it's an authentic—"

As Danny's back was turned, Lisetta slammed the baseball bat into the back of his skull.

Danny pitched forward into the tangle of cockpit parts, stunned and crumpled. His head began to bleed.

"You're fucking crazy!" she screamed at him, tossing the bat aside with a loud clatter.

He continued to sink to the ground, clutching the back of his head.

Lisetta left him semi-conscious on the floor and ran out of the room. She dashed into a long, narrow corridor of identical white doors. One by one, she threw open the doors, lost in a maze of madness, screaming for help, until she finally found the passage that led to freedom.

Chapter Fifteen

Danny sat on the floor of his time travel lab, petting Toby as the dog ate from his bowl. Toby's tail wagged happily as Danny stroked his fur for comfort.

Danny's head throbbed. The baseball bat lay nearby. He felt his senses return from a dazed state. His scalp was crusted with dried blood.

Danny did not notice Lisetta standing in the doorway until she spoke.

"I had to come back," she said. "I got worried that maybe I killed you."

"No," he responded slowly without looking up. "Just a really bad headache."

"I know you're hurting. On the inside. I can get you help."

"I don't need it. I've tried everything. I've popped every pill on the market. This is the only medicine I need."

"Okay. I can respect that."

"You don't have to be here. Go back to your life, Lisetta."

A long silence followed. Instead of leaving, Lisetta stepped into the room. Her voice quivered.

"I ran to the main road. I flagged down a cab. I was going to find someplace safe to call Martin. I was going to return to the life you took me away from. And then I realized, in that moment...I don't want to go back. I—I need time to think."

Danny looked up at her now. His hands slid from Toby's sides.

Lisetta said, "If I go back now...I'm giving in. I can't do that. I don't love him."

Lisetta cautiously stepped closer.

"You cracked my autographed bat," Danny said.

"I'm sorry. Maybe you can get your brother to sign another one."

"He's dead. It doesn't matter. I forged his signature on the first one."

"Reed died?"

"He had a heart attack six months ago."

"I'm sorry...."

"I'm fulfilling Reed's dreams here, too. He always wanted to be a baseball player. I'm fixing my whole family. I saved my mother from dying in that accident. I saved Toby from being sent away. It's all in the scripts." Then he added, "I wrote a script for you, too."

"For me?"

"Of course."

"Can I see it?" she asked, and her tone was sincere.

Danny stood up and walked over to the drafting table. He opened a three-ring binder and flipped the pages until he found the scenario.

"It's called 'Bestseller.' You're a best-selling novelist. You achieved your dreams. You're on *The New York Times* bestseller list. We're celebrating together."

He stepped back and let her read from the binder on the table. Her eyes became absorbed in his words.

"This is incredible," she said. "Total batshit crazy, but incredible." She continued looking through the pages.

"I'm creating new scenarios every day," he told her. "There's so much to be sorted out. At the reunion, I didn't tell you everything. I've had a rough go of it. My son, Adam—we haven't spoken in 10 years. He hates me. He moved to England. I was a terrible father. He grew up in a dysfunctional family. I had two terrible marriages. The first one, I was too young. The second one was too quick and desperate. I was filled with self-loathing. If I didn't like myself, why should anyone else? Throughout my life, I've been unable to hold down steady work. No job ever felt like the right fit. After my marriages, when I was on my own, it just got worse. I lied to you about the conference planning. I was fired from there almost a year ago. I only lasted about two months. I've been through a revolving door of jobs. I either get fired or I quit or a mixture of both. What I really wanted, ever since I was young, was to be a pilot."

"I remember you telling me."

She turned from the binder to face him. Her expression had softened. The edge was gone, replaced with pity.

"I'm on a journey to go back and fix everything that's wrong in my life," he told her. "I want you to be on this journey with me. We can rewrite both of our lives. There's a special energy between us. An imagination that's bigger than life. I know we can make each other young again."

"But what about our other lives?"

"We'll get rid of those lives." He smiled. "We're not those people anymore. You can write the obits. This is a new beginning."

She stared into his face and confused tears formed in her eyes.

"Give this a try," said Danny. "Please. Be crazy with me."

"Maybe I can stay…for a little while."

Lisetta reached out and hugged him. They held one another and, in that moment, grew stronger together.

TRAVEL LOG:
REVERSAL 18Y 6M 15D

We celebrated in our glorious penthouse apartment on Chicago's Gold Coast, an upper-floor corner of a high-rise overlooking the sparkling city skyline on one side and the wavy patterns of Lake Michigan on the other. Good wine flowed freely and gentle piano jazz tickled the air from our sleek, state-of-the-art stereo. We sat at the dining room table surrounded by a romantic array of candles.

My wife, Lisetta, had just topped *The New York Times* best-seller charts with her newest historical romantic fantasy, an epic of escapism called *Turn of the Century*.

As a special gift, I presented her with her book jacket in an elegant gold-leaf frame. The front cover displayed her name in big, bold letters—the way publishers do when an author becomes a brand. The back cover was dense with ecstatic blurbs from some of her favorite writers, as well as major media outlets.

Lisetta's publicist had just sent us a fresh set of reviews, and we read through them as we sipped our wine. The words of praise soared coast to coast, from the *Los Angeles Times* to *The New York Review of Books*. Trade publications like *Publishers Weekly* and *Library Journal* competed to come up with the most glowing superlatives. *Entertainment Weekly*, *People*, and *USA Today* made certain the book reached the attention of mass audiences with prominent coverage.

It was just the tip of the iceberg. A massive book tour was scheduled—bookstore signings and television appearances in the major markets—and Lisetta excitedly described the itinerary her publicist had compiled to meet an overwhelming demand.

"Oh, I almost forgot," I said, as we refilled our wine glasses, cozy and lightly intoxicated. "Your agent called. Another studio is in the running for the movie rights. They think they can attach some pretty big star power."

"Well," said Lisetta. "They know the terms. I want to write the screenplay."

"And you want a cameo?"

She laughed. "Of course. I think my fans would enjoy that."

"How's your wrist from the book signing this afternoon?"

"Still sore." She wiggled her right hand. "I can't believe they ran out of inventory. It's the biggest bookstore in the city."

"They'll have you back anytime you wish."

"I'm all over social media," she said excitedly. "My God, all the selfies. I'm glad I wore my blue blazer and my hair up—I think it was a good writer look. Not too pretentious, not too plain."

"You looked stunning," I said to her, admiring her beautiful features in the candlelight. "And you still do."

She smiled and I lightly touched her cheek.

As always, I was struck by the beauty in her eyes and the elegance of her face. I stood up from the table and circled closer to her. Her smile broadened. I leaned over and kissed her, gently sweeping away her long, lush hair. She touched me with her long, delicate fingers. The kiss was deep and heartfelt.

We advanced to our luxurious, Italian-designed sofa. We pushed aside the pillows and peeled away our clothes. In the soft illumination of flickering candles, we made love. Afterward, my wife fell asleep with her head on my shoulder. I remained awake, feeling her gentle breathing and the tickle of her long hair, warmed by the touch of our bare flesh, overwhelmed by the perfection of the moment.

Chapter Sixteen

In the days that followed, Danny and Lisetta set up simple living quarters in a section of the warehouse. The accommodations were strictly rudimentary as they spent most of their time in the lab, planning time travel episodes. Danny had steady income from the sale of business assets, providing a sizable budget for furniture and era-specific props to decorate the sets. Maintaining a purposefully stark environment outside the rich and vivid time travel rooms aided in transforming the latter into their new reality.

The early marriage scenes performed in the high-rise penthouse apartment were a smashing success featuring love, sex, and fulfilled ambitions. Lisetta assisted with the scripts, thrilled by the newfound freedom to reinvent herself. "This is more gratifying than the novels," she told Danny. "They were personal, but written to a formula for the romance audience. This writing now is the most liberating thing I've ever done. Anything is possible."

In the lab, alone with Toby, they brainstormed foundational scenarios. Danny described how some of his earlier time travel trips were designed to avert tragedy. Lisetta grew serious and pulled a troubling incident from her distant past.

"My cousin committed suicide," she said, seated in a simple office chair, stroking Toby's fur as he sat alongside her. "We were fairly close. She was 13. I was 14. She battled depression."

Danny listened carefully, notebook and pen in hand.

"She would go through these times of great sadness and point to things in her life but they were just your ordinary teenage problems like dating and grades and trying to fit in and find your identity. It was a chemical imbalance, I'm sure of it, and hereditary. But her family didn't believe in meds."

Lisetta's voice choked and tears formed in her eyes. "Danny, I want to go back and save her. If I had known then what I know now…I could have talked to her more, provided more support, convinced her to get help. I was young, I didn't know how to handle something like that. When she would get all melancholy on me, I wasn't a good listener. I wasn't very sympathetic. All of my life, since then, I have been rehearsing words in my head— the things I should have said to her. She looked up to me. I could have saved her life."

Lisetta shut her eyes and Danny watched as she painfully surfaced a memory that still clearly tortured her.

"I remember it was on a Saturday morning," said Lisetta. "I was planning to go to the high school football game. It was fall. The leaves were coming down, all over the yard. The skies were gray. I was figuring out what to wear. Then my mom came into the room. Her face was red and puffy. I had never seen her so distraught; she was good at holding everything in. She told me…."

Lisetta stopped for a moment to compose herself. "They found Gail in the basement. She had hung herself from the pipes." She looked up at Danny. "The last time we spoke, I hadn't been very nice. She was in a mood and I lost patience and said things like kids will say, you know, 'knock it off, you're such a downer, no wonder no one wants to hang out with you…' It was callous."

"You aren't to blame," said Danny.

"Maybe," said Lisetta, taking a deep breath. "But I could have done more to help."

Danny put aside the notebook and pen. He walked over and took her hand. He spoke gently.

"Here's what we're going to do," he said. "We're going to go back. We're going to go back to your bedroom when you were 14 years old. You will have a conversation with Gail. Those words you've been rehearsing in your head? They will become real. You will go back and save her."

Lisetta put her arms around Danny. "Yes. Yes, let's do that."

They spent the rest of the day designing the set for Lisetta's teenage bedroom. She recalled details while he took notes. They found much of what they needed online—often accompanied by the words "vintage" or "retro."

As they mapped out the elements, Lisetta grew excited. "I can't wait to go back to my old room," she said. "Sometimes I have dreams where I'm still in high school. I wake up feeling young again, so full of possibilities, then the feeling…it goes away."

"Life is one long narrowing of possibilities," said Danny. "That's why people love nostalgia. We want to go back to that time in our lives when our hopes and dreams might actually come true."

Lisetta began writing a list of items for the room. "I want to fill it with the happiest elements of my childhood," she said. As she described her childhood bedroom carpet—a late 1970s zigzag of red and black patterns—Danny laughed and nodded.

"That's an easy one," he said. "Let's go find it right now."

He led her to an area of the warehouse that contained a showroom with racks of carpet samples in 6 x 6 squares. Flipping through the voluminous options, she found the right one and exclaimed, "Oh my God. This is it!"

"It's so ugly that you're in luck," said Danny. "We probably still have it in stock." He led her to a main area of the warehouse that once housed aisles and aisles of carpet rolls. He followed the numbers and letters identifying each section. Many of the shelves were empty or close to it, but just enough carpet remained to instill hope.

"We sold most of the inventory to a competitor," said Danny, eyes searching the shelves. "But they didn't take everything. They left behind the really old, outdated fashions that would never sell in today's market. So, it's quite possible that…."

Then he said, "Aha," and pointed. A thick roll of Lisetta's bedroom carpet, matching the sample, sat on a barren shelf, lonely and left behind.

"That's it!" said Lisetta, and her voice cracked. "I never thought I'd get so emotional about an old carpet."

"The carpet is the first thing we need," said Danny. "Now we can start on the room."

Danny and Lisetta went to work, dedicating another parcel of warehouse space to time travel. They built an enclosed room matching Lisetta's remembered dimensions, positioning false walls to create the next set in the corridor of time passages. They found an online source for wallpaper matching Lisetta's memories and ordered several rolls, as well as other key items, including a dresser and bedframe.

Danny kneeled on the floor and got started cutting the carpet to fit the room. He used a retractable utility knife with an extra sharp blade to slice through the heavy material. Lisetta set up a small 1980s cassette boombox she had found in a second-hand thrift shop, along with a handful of cassettes of music from the era. "This will help set the mood," she said, and she punched "play," unleashing a string of tunes by Michael Jackson.

"Perfect," said Danny.

"I'm really looking forward to this," said Lisetta, picking up the unwanted carpet trims and collecting them in a cardboard box. "I want my room to feel warm and happy all the time."

"I hope you'll invite teenage Danny to come over," he said, looking up at her with a grin.

She returned the smile with a little shrug and sly voice. "Could happen…."

"We'll write a scene for it," he said.

"*I'll* write the scene. It'll be a surprise."

"I like that."

Their playful banter continued as they finished securing the bedroom carpet. The music transported them, the space was slowly coming to life, and Danny and Lisetta were happily consumed in the moment.

It took them nearly a minute to notice the tall figure standing in the doorway. Lisetta saw him first and gasped, causing Danny to look up and follow her gaze.

"What the fuck is going on here?" said Martin.

Chapter Seventeen

Martin Madison stepped into the room, examining the surroundings with anger and bewilderment.

"Did you think I would never find you? What is this? Some kind of weird hideout?"

Danny and Lisetta remained frozen, yanked from their fantasy world by an unexpected jolt of reality infiltrating their sacred space.

Martin stared at Lisetta with narrowed eyes. "I've been tracking your phone. I've been doing it for the past year. I always thought you were going to have an affair with that asshole Robie from the newspaper. But I see you've lowered your standards even further."

Martin stepped closer to where Danny was standing. Danny felt a rush of intimidation from the larger man. It took him back to the dizzying anxieties of high school. He said nothing as Martin looked into his face with a tight, simmering fury that looked ready to explode at any moment.

"Danny boy would not have been my first choice, but you left enough clues," said Martin. "That picture on the reunion website was pretty cozy. Then you had lunch together at Harvey's." He turned to face Lisetta. "Rather odd that you chose not to mention that to me, I had to hear it from one of the neighbors. Hey, it's a small town. You have lunch with a stranger, people talk. When I pressed you on it, you told me it was just Danny passing through on a business trip. Okay, weird, but I let it slide, because…it was Danny. Even then, I didn't feel like he could be a threat. I mean, look at the guy."

Softly, Lisetta said, "Martin, please stop."

Instead of stopping, Martin's voice grew louder. "I come home to an empty house. No note, no explanation, nothing. You think you can just disappear?"

Martin's hands had clenched into fists. He stood before Danny and Lisetta, blocking their only exit from the room. He looked back and forth between them, studying their faces as if trying to understand their relationship.

He said, "I waited...and waited. I waited up all night and you didn't come home. I tracked your phone. It told me you were in Chicago. I tried calling you. Many, many times. You didn't answer. So, I didn't know what the hell to think. When you refused to respond, I figured I had to come get you. I don't know what I was expecting, but I never imagined...this."

Lisetta had gone pale. Martin moved closer to his wife, filling her vision.

"Did you really think you could just get up and leave? Walk away from me? From Mindy?"

When she didn't answer, he turned and took a step closer toward Danny. Martin's nostrils flared and his chest heaved as his rage continued to boil.

"And you. Danny boy. We were friends once upon a time. When did this start? Were you fucking her back in high school? I knew you wanted to. A lot of people wanted to. I don't blame you for that. But we were buddies. You don't stab your buddies in the back. That's...just...not polite."

A long silence followed.

Then Danny spoke up. He said, crisply, "Please leave. You're not welcome here."

Martin smirked. "I see. I come for my wife...in this ratty shithole of a building...in this neighborhood of crackheads and gangbangers...to bring her home...and *I'm* not welcome?"

"That's right," spoke up Lisetta.

Martin abruptly whirled to face her.

"We're through," she continued. "We've been through for years and you know it. You're nothing to me."

"Nothing?" he said. He stepped closer and stood toe-to-toe.

Martin repeated, "Nothing? Zero? All those years together...

years of marriage…they all add up to zero? That's your math, am I correct?"

"Yes, Marty. *You* add up to zero."

Martin smacked her across the cheek with the back of his hand. The blow nearly knocked her to the ground.

"Don't touch her!" shouted Danny.

Martin turned toward him. "That was nothing," he said, "compared to what I'm going to do to you."

Martin delivered a solid punch to Danny's face that sent him backward into one of the movable walls, pushing it loose and out of alignment. Before Danny had even reached the ground, Martin was on him again, delivering more blows.

"Stop it!" screamed Lisetta, and she jumped on Martin from behind. They crashed into the small table that held the cassette boombox, bringing it down with a heavy landing that knocked out the batteries and silenced Michael Jackson's "Thriller."

Martin shook Lisetta loose and returned to beating Danny on the floor, reddening his lips and nose with blood. Lisetta jumped on Martin again, wrapping her arms around his neck, pulling back with all her weight, allowing Danny vital seconds to wriggle free from under the bigger man. From his back, Danny extended his leg and kicked Martin in the jaw, creating a loud crack. Martin reeled momentarily, then lunged forward, lifting Lisetta off her feet and throwing her into Danny. With both of them sprawled before him, Martin swung wildly with both arms, battering their bodies and faces with fast, hard punches as they scrambled to defend themselves against the blows. Martin threw his weight on both of them. Arms and legs entangled as the three bodies became a single mass, rolling like one monstrous being on the carpet.

Then, in the chaos, Martin let out a sudden howl.

Blood began to spurt through the air, accompanied by a series of hard, short chopping sounds. The fury of punching and kicking quickly lost its momentum.

Lisetta gasped.

The front of Martin's shirt had been slashed and blood streamed from multiple stab wounds. He wobbled on his knees, eyes wide in shock. His fingers trembled as he reached out into empty air. He choked, deep and hard. His upper body grew rigid and his expression dimmed.

Martin's life drained out before them in a flow of red from deep puncture wounds to his heart.

Martin collapsed to the floor. He shuddered a few times, then stopped moving, soaking in a pool of his own blood.

"Oh my God," choked Lisetta. "Oh my God."

Danny panted, catching his breath, dazed. His face and clothes were stained by Martin's blood.

Danny and Lisetta sat next to one another on the floor, staring in terror at the dead body before them.

Lisetta gripped the rug cutter. Fresh blood dripped from the blade, the handle, and her clenched hand.

"It happened so fast...." she said, staring down at the knife in her grasp.

Danny leaned closer to Martin, examining his lifeless form.

"I didn't mean to...." said Lisetta. Tears rolled down her cheeks. Her voice shook uncontrollably. "What are we going to do? Oh my God, Danny, what are we going to do?"

Danny fought to stay calm. The scene presented itself like a horrific crime drama. He kept his voice steady as the puddle of blood expanded.

He said, "It's okay. We're in control."

Chapter Eighteen

Under the cover of night, Danny and Lisetta drove deep into a network of gritty city streets to find a good location to ditch the body. "We're going to dump it in the worst part of town," said Danny. "Someplace so bad that not even the cops go there."

Martin's corpse had been rolled up in a carpet and stuck in the back of an old delivery van. His pockets had been emptied of anything that could identify him—wallet, phone, and keys. His stabbed body would become an anonymous "John Doe," unlinked to any local missing person, apparently killed and robbed by some ruthless crackhead.

"As far as we know, he didn't tell anyone he was coming out here," said Danny to Lisetta. "And no one knows you're out here, either. Chicago's not on the radar for either one of you, right?"

Lisetta nodded, occasionally lit up by a sporadic working streetlamp. She had said very little following Martin's death, slipping into shellshock. One of her few statements, spoken a while earlier, had been:

"I can't go to jail. I'm too old. Please, Danny, I would die there."

"You're not going to jail," Danny assured her. "All of this will go away. We will rewrite this story. It's going to be okay."

He found a dead-end alley, lit up only by the stab of his headlamps, dominated by crumbling pavement, outrageous potholes and an overflowing dumpster that appeared to have been taken off the route for sanitation pickup. Rats the size of raccoons scurried from the light.

Lisetta blinked back tears as she climbed out of the van

with Danny. They extracted the rolled-up carpet, each taking an end, struggling as it sagged badly in the blood-soaked middle. In small, staggering steps they reached the dumpster and unwound the body from its cocoon. Limbs flopping, Martin rolled partly under the dumpster, a fresh source of nibbles for the rodent community. Danny returned the carpet to the van and secured it in the back.

Danny looked around nervously, scanning the blank windows of nearby buildings for any observers, more worried about becoming a victim than being turned in for a crime.

"Hurry up," he said to Lisetta. She stood by her dead husband, staring at him with a face crumpled with many emotions. Finally, she reached down and gently touched his hand. Then she wordlessly returned to the van.

Danny, too, looked down at Martin's lifeless body one last time. The vision before him would soon be explained by alternate facts. He was in total control of the events along this timeline.

Danny also reached for Martin's hand. He tugged off the wedding ring from Martin's finger.

Minutes later, as Danny drove away, he rolled down his window as Lisetta softly wept. After a few blocks, he flung the wedding ring into the dark.

"What was that?" said Lisetta, catching a glimpse of him throwing a small object out of the car.

"Nothing," said Danny.

Back at the warehouse, Danny hid Martin's car in one of the garages and then worked with some heavy-duty carpet cleaner to remove the blood stains. He finally burned the stains out of the fibers with big black scorch marks and added the ruined carpet to a large heap of other scraps and discards, where it mingled anonymously.

Lisetta sat in his office, writing.

When Danny rejoined her, she had composed a script explaining Martin's death in a parallel universe, where the blame shifted parties and the demise took place much earlier—preventing her marriage to him from ever happening. He had been murdered by gangs during a drunken summer night bar hopping in the big city in his college years.

Danny read through the script, added a few small notes in the margins, then heaped it with praise. She smiled for the first time since the confrontation with Martin.

"We'll go into the time machine," Danny said, "and then it will become real."

"I'm scared," she said, eyes bloodshot and hair tangled and knotted by nervous fingers.

"We will leave the fear behind," he said. "There's no fear where we are going."

"We can never leave here," she said. "There's no going back, is there?"

"Not true," said Danny. "There's no going forward. We can always go back. Whenever we want. To any part of our lives. We will make everything right."

Chapter Nineteen

After traveling back in time to establish Martin had been killed in a tragic, random inner-city crime, Danny and Lisetta felt cleansed—no longer accountable for his death and freed to thrive in the new timeline of their lives. The path to Martin and Lisetta's marriage had been erased.

Lisetta authored an obituary for twenty-one-year-old Martin, drawing on her experiences writing obituaries for the Eldridge Gazette. She shared it with Danny as if it was an actual newspaper clipping from 1991, and they made it their reality.

Lisetta grieved Martin's passing and tried to move on. As the rewrite of history settled in, she still suffered from occasional crying jags. She found solace in the next trip backward to alter the future. A life had been lost, but now a life would be saved.

It was time to bring her cousin Gail back from the dead.

Lisetta relished in the writing—it was far more fulfilling than her forays into fantasy fiction. The romance novels were phony and cheesy, detached from any reality. This was true life. Her time travel scenarios were a direct reflection of her personal storyline. The characters were genuine. The control over their destinies was exhilarating.

This particular episode would be extra special because it was the first script she was authoring for a solo trip in the time machine. So far, the excursions had all been joint experiences with Danny. For this one, Danny would not be along for the ride.

This journey belonged all to Lisetta.

She shared the script with Danny, and he did not make any edits. "It's perfect," he told her, and she needed to hear it.

He said, "I think we're ready to advance to casting."

Together they scoured the web pages of local talent agencies, studying headshots for faces that resembled the young Gail. Several came close, even if wigs would be necessary to complete the illusion.

Danny scheduled auditions. He advertised that he was a playwright looking for an actress to participate in a dramatic reading of his new play-in-progress. He wanted to hear the dialogue spoken aloud to help him fine-tune it. He said he had co-authored the play with his wife, who would participate in the proceedings.

The initial readings took place in the audition room of Linehan Casting, an agency on the city's north side.

Danny and Lisetta identified themselves as Barb and Bob Kunkel. They sat at a table with stoic faces as a series of hopeful actresses read through a sampling of lines Lisetta had scripted.

Lisetta shared immediate reactions with Danny by scribbling quick notes that she slid across the table to him as the actresses delivered their dialogue.

No.

Maybe.

NO.

Too old.

Too skinny.

Too smiley.

Nope.

YES.

The all-caps "yes" led to a fresh-faced young actress receiving an invitation to a paying gig that Danny openly admitted was unusual.

Her name was Selene Browning. She was 18 but could pass for 14, blessed with lovely soft features and lively eyes.

"Wait, so this isn't for an actual production?" she asked, as Danny tried to explain the situation.

"The play is still being written," said Danny. "We hire actors and actresses to perform certain scenes so we can hear the dialogue and make adjustments. We find it helpful to the editing process."

"Okay." She shrugged. "So, you want to schedule a time to come back?"

"We don't do it here," said Danny. "We have our own rehearsal space. With sets. It's all very elaborate."

"Wait," said Selene, trying to make sense of the arrangement. "You've built sets for a play that you're still writing?"

"It enhances the creative process," said Lisetta.

Danny quickly got to the point. He knew that most of these local actresses made very little money. "It pays extremely well. We pay a premium price. We would provide you with the script in advance to give you time to memorize your lines, and then you would do a single, clean run-through on our set."

"Sure," she said. "Whatever works." Then she asked, "When this play hits the stage, can I audition for it?"

Danny and Lisetta glanced at one another for a quick moment before both nodded in agreement, a simple lie to continue the pretense that this was for a theater production, with no mention of the time machine.

"The time machine only exists for us," Danny had told Lisetta at the beginning of her immersion into an alternate truth. "We don't discuss it with the outside world. They wouldn't understand. They would destroy everything we are trying to achieve. Don't worry, this will work."

Danny had experienced previous success in hiring theater performers for supporting roles in his time travel episodes, including scenes with his mom and dad. The one hire who wasn't a professional actor or actress was the young woman portraying college-era Cheryl who was, in actuality, a whore. She was paid not to have sex but aggressively attempt it in a critical dorm room scene. Having a prostitute represent Cheryl worked well in Danny's mind and he considered it effective typecasting.

A few days after Selene's audition, Danny greeted her at the front of the shuttered carpet warehouse and immediately sensed fear in her eyes as she took in the stark, isolated surroundings.

"We're renting space for our sets," he told her. "You can

imagine how expensive that gets downtown, so we've converted this old warehouse building. I know, it's not the greatest neighborhood, but we have everything we need here. You're going to be really impressed."

"My boyfriend knows where I am," she said. "This better be legit. I'm not some naïve kid."

Danny responded with hurt in his eyes. "Of course, it's legit. I swear to you."

Danny brought her inside. They advanced past the main warehouse area to the back offices. Danny guided her past a black curtain and through a winding corridor of closed doors until they reached one with light seeping out from underneath.

"Ready to see your set?" he asked.

She nodded, lips pursed, apprehensive.

He opened the door to the bright, cheerful bedroom of teenage Lisetta. Lisetta, dressed in colorful 1980s teenager's clothing, stood in the middle of the set, wearing a big smile.

"Gail, it is so good to see you," she said.

Selene advanced slowly, looking around. The bedroom had a full set of furniture, and posters of long-ago teen heartthrobs decorated the walls. "You really go all out. This is really detailed. Like a movie."

"We spare no expense to get it right," said Danny. "There's nothing phony about it."

"Do you like my room, Gail?" said Lisetta in a playful, bouncy voice.

Selene smirked and went along with it, responding with youthful enthusiasm. "Oh yes. It's totally awesome."

Lisetta beamed.

"Barb here will play the character of Lisetta," said Danny.

"I see she's dressed for the part," said Selene.

"And you will be, too," said Danny.

"Seriously?"

"We have a wardrobe for your character."

"No way."

"It helps us with the writing. We want every detail to be perfect. It fires up the imagination."

"I've never seen anything like this before."

"We take our work very seriously."

"Obviously."

"Do you have your lines memorized?" said Danny.

"Yes, just like you told me to."

"Excellent. Then we'll get you changed, and you and Lisetta will perform your scene."

"Do I have to change?" asked Selene, with an expression of discomfort.

"We have a private dressing room," said Danny. "Please. That's why we're paying a premium."

"You do know, this is kind of weird," said Selene.

"Not to us," said Danny.

"See you soon, Gail!" said Lisetta with a cheerful wave.

Danny guided Selene to a private room and presented her with a teenage outfit from the late 1980s: white painter's pants and an orange turtleneck sweater.

"I'm serious," said Selene. "I have my boyfriend on speed dial. Any funny business and he is going to be here in a heartbeat with the cops."

"This is real," said Danny. "I promise you. We are very real here."

Selene changed into her character's costume. She stepped out of the changing room, wearing a tense face that said "I just want to get this over with."

As Danny walked her back to the set, he told her, "I will not be in the room. It's just you and Lisetta."

"But how will you know…?"

"I trust Lisetta…Barb…to assess how it goes. She's the primary writer of this scene. I'm not in it—I mean, not as involved."

Selene shrugged, still getting used to the eccentricity of the whole affair.

"When you enter that room," instructed Danny, "you will immediately become Gail. Begin the scene right away. Whatever you do, do not break character. If you forget a line, improvise, keep going. Think of this as one take, no interruptions, and when you are done, you will come back out into this hall, right here."

"And then I can leave?"

"Yes."

"And when do I get paid?"

"I will pay you here, in cash, after the performance."

"One thousand dollars?"

"That is correct."

Her mood lightened. For a gig this brief, the money was very, very good; even better than the dumb roles she occasionally scored in corporate training videos.

Danny said, "Now become Gail. Show me Gail. The sadness, the confusion, the despair. You are struggling with your suicidal impulses. Yet you retain a spark of hope, deep inside, that maybe not all is lost. Got that?"

Selene nodded, taking it all in. "I'm ready," she said, and she advanced to the bright light of the set.

Afterwards, Selene stepped into the hallway outside the 1980s bedroom set and said, "That's it?"

"That's it," said Danny.

"A twenty-minute scene, and you just want one run-through?"

"You're done."

She sighed with a puzzled smile. "All right, then."

Selene returned to the wardrobe room and changed back into her street clothes. Danny paid her one thousand dollars in crisp hundred-dollar bills.

"Thanks," she said. Then she added, "You know, you two are pretty out there."

Danny smiled. "Perhaps."

"But, hey, if you have any more of these twenty-minute gigs for a thousand dollars, give me a call."

Danny just continued to smile.

After Selene left the building and returned to her car, Danny rejoined Lisetta, who had stepped out of the time machine.

"How did it go?" he asked.

"Perfect," said Lisetta, and she started to cry. "I did it. I did it, Danny. I saved her life."

TRAVEL LOG:
REVERSAL 34Y 6M 15D

Lisetta here. I am writing today's entry in the travel log. This was my first *solo* excursion in the time machine. I am still shaking from the aftershocks. This trip was very important to me. I needed to correct an error from my past that has haunted me for a very long time.

I hugged Danny goodbye and entered the sightless, soundless tunnel that twisted time and place to transport me to my childhood. I stepped out of the darkness and into the light and colors of long ago.

I entered the bedroom of my teenage years. It was an overwhelming sensation. I welcomed a rush of good feelings. I felt safe here and comfortable. The world was a less scary place back then. The future held no threats of despair and disappointment, just sweet, naïve joy.

To be young again!

I hugged my ratty old teddy bear, Mr. Jeepers. I shook off my shoes and enjoyed the familiar soft carpet under my bare feet. I revisited my room's cheerful décor and adolescent clutter. It fit me snugly like a favorite old coat.

After basking in the warm glow of nostalgia, I turned serious and focused. This was not a pleasure trip. I had a critical mission. I was here on this particular day in my timeline because I had invited my cousin Gail over to my room—something I had neglected to do in the past, even though we attended the same high school and she lived nearby. Sadly, I had been dismissive toward her. Not cold—just indifferent.

Gail was different than me—bottled up, melancholy, and

slow to make friends. I had been on her case about her downer attitude. Her moody personality got on my nerves and took me out of my selfish, happy zone. I had resisted her overtures to be more than just relatives and enter a genuine friendship.

My treatment of her wasn't much different than everyone else in her life. Other girls didn't want to hang out with her. And the boys—they could be downright cruel.

One of the earliest taunts was "Gail, Gail, the garbage pail." Even the bullied kids picked on her, establishing Gail at the lowest end of the pecking order.

I had never really thought of the cumulative effect of all this on a delicate teenager with super low self-esteem.

But now, armed with better insights, heightened empathy, and a more mature perspective, I was prepared to handle the situation.

I couldn't relate to her pain back then, but now I could. In my adulthood I had developed a better understanding of a wounded psyche and the entrapment of depression.

I could feel Gail's pain.

There was a hesitant knock at my bedroom door. I quickly welcomed Gail inside.

She stepped forward with uncertainty. She had never been in my room before. I had never invited her, until now.

She almost seemed suspicious of my overtures of friendship.

But we soon enjoyed a good, flowing conversation. I played my new REO Speedwagon record. We talked about school and boys. We complained about our parents. She opened up to me about some of her struggles, exposing her insecurities. She told me how useless and undesirable she felt. She started crying.

I reassured her that her feelings were not unusual. She was not alone. I told her I could relate. I said we all go through dark clouds.

I convinced her she was going to emerge out of her depression and find true happiness.

"It sucks being a teenager," I said. "Sometimes I hate my life too."

"Really?" she said. "You do?"

"You're not alone. Everyone I know—they act happy on

the outside. But they have the same fears and bad feelings. Sometimes I cry for no reason, it can be anything. My mom says it's because our body chemistry is changing. School is full of pressures. And the other kids, they can be so mean."

It felt so good to look into her eyes, speak the right words, and watch her lift out of her personal darkness. We had a therapeutic conversation. We promised to have more like it.

"You need anything, anytime, someone to talk to, promise you'll call," I said to her.

"I promise," said Gail. "Thank you for hearing me out. You made me feel better. I feel less alone. I guess these feelings are just something you grow out of."

"You are going to become a happy and beautiful young woman," I told her. "I know these things. I've seen the future. There are good things in store for you. Just hang in there."

If Gail had entertained thoughts of ending her life, they were gone now. I was sure of it. I knew my discussion had done some good.

It was a little moment in the grand scheme of things, perhaps, but with implications that renewed a life.

Chapter Twenty

Energized by her scene with Gail, Lisetta brought a rush of enthusiasm and imagination to the continued reinvention of reality. She worked alongside Danny as he covered a long wall of the office with sheets of paper posted in a linear sequence to form a timeline of key moments in their interwoven histories. The first, unsatisfactory pass-through of the story of their lives was represented on yellow sheets. Proposed concepts for "take two" turning points to replace the original experiences were written out on green sheets. The current timeline mostly contained yellow sheets with an occasional presence of green for the completed time travel trips so far—such as Martin's altered death scene. Underneath the main timeline, bunches of green sheets waited for their moment to leave the sidelines and enter the field of play. Danny and Lisetta had written summaries of nearly two dozen scenes that required a passage through the time machine to fix the nagging errors of their past.

"We will rebuild the timeline until there are no regrets," said Danny. "We will turn the entire timeline from yellow to green. We will do it one episode at a time. We don't have to be chronological about it. This is like filming a movie or writing a book—the construction can come in pieces, as long as all the pieces work together in the end."

Lisetta planned more new scenes to represent milestones in her writing career—selling her first novel, her first number-one bestseller, her first movie deal.

Danny's life choices mostly revolved around relationships—especially family—and his childhood dream to be an airplane pilot. He created placeholders for the day he graduated flying school and the day he obtained his pilot's license. He looked forward to pulling down his two failed marriages and replacing them with his marriage to Lisetta. He looked forward to erasing all of his bad jobs.

Toby kept them company during the long hours in the office, tail wagging, generally pleased about everything around him.

For ideas and details, Danny consulted a small stack of childhood diaries and personal journals, which ended in adulthood. "I stopped writing because nothing interesting was happening," he explained. He also dug into old emails and online research to establish the right dates for time travel trips. He reviewed a shoebox of childhood photos and filled in the blanks from memory.

Props, furniture, and fashions were very important to creating the right vibe. Danny and Lisetta searched eBay and other online sites for the key items they needed to rebuild their realities. They also visited Chicago-area resale shops for secondhand items from prior decades, which required rare trips out of the warehouse and into an uncomfortable present tense. The harsh mental adjustment required to switch environments convinced Danny and Lisetta to keep such excursions to a minimum and stick to online shopping.

The warehouse became a growing collection of elaborate sets, divided by false walls. Danny and Lisetta each had teenage bedrooms that needed to be just right to trigger the right mindset.

It was fun.

Even more enjoyable, they got to imagine all-new sets that never existed for an exciting new branch in their life story: their marriage.

They dreamed up the ideal "first apartment" for themselves.

They designed rooms for their perfect "first house" in the Chicago suburbs, after Danny's career as a pilot and Lisetta's success as an author took off. The house featured a handsome dining room, a fancy kitchen, Lisetta's office, Danny's den and, of course, the master bedroom.

One of the most critical time-travel props required a great

deal of online searching and a big outlay of cash. Danny found someone in Muskegon, Michigan selling the exact make and model of the Chevy he drove during his teenage years. The Chevy was necessary for a crucial scene in the turning point for his relationship with Lisetta: the kiss that didn't happen. He would rewrite the night they sat in her driveway after an emotional high school party. Now, clearly defined on a green sheet of paper, the kiss was really going to happen. The yellow sheet in the current timeline that described the blown opportunity would be replaced with a correction.

"I'm nervous," he told Lisetta. "It's going to be our first kiss."

"Nervous is good," said Lisetta. "Nervous is cute."

Rolling open a huge aluminum door intended for carpet delivery trucks, Danny drove the Chevy inside the warehouse. He parked it and then went to work building a set around it: black walls, stars in the ceiling, and dim lighting representing moonlight.

Soon after establishing the set, Danny and Lisetta traveled back in time to alter the course of their relationship at that fateful moment in their innocent youth.

The scene turned out perfect.

Afterward, Danny couldn't wait to swap out the yellow sheet of past regret with a green sheet of course correction.

The timeline of their lives continued to turn colors.

Still exhilarated by the "first kiss," Danny proposed they skip ahead a few years in the timeline for a sex scene.

"I can't help it, I'm aroused," he said. "We had to keep that first kiss as a first kiss."

"You want to experience our first time making love?" she asked.

"No," he said. "Not yet. That will be too awkward. Let's go farther up the scale. Like our fifteenth or twentieth time. When we're better at it. We can go back and do the first time later."

"Let's write the scene out," said Lisetta with a smile on her lips. "I've drafted a few sex scenes in my day."

"I can't wait," said Danny.

Danny brought Lisetta with him on his next visit to see his father at the residential care facility in Kenosha.

George DeCastro sat in his favorite chair, wide-eyed and unshaven, still in his pajamas and bathrobe at noontime.

Danny and Lisetta sat on the small couch across from him. "Dad, you remember Lisetta?" said Danny.

George DeCastro nodded slowly with some uncertainty, acknowledging his son's words.

"We're going to be celebrating our twentieth wedding anniversary," said Danny, taking her hand. She smiled.

"Hello," said George in a fragile and gentle voice.

"We have good news to share about our son," said Danny. "He's going to medical school. You know, William, the Eagle Scout?"

"That's good," said George, appearing a little surprised, but it was his natural look these days.

Danny continued to describe his new reality to his father, who accepted it as fact over any remaining pockets of memory of Danny's other life. The dementia had mostly erased Danny's original history. Now, to establish a better reality for his father's final years, Danny had created the ideal storyline. He would reinforce it during every visit until his other path of existence disappeared for good.

Danny told his father about Reed's amazing success as a Major League Baseball player.

Danny's father smiled, and he perked up in his chair. "Can we watch him on TV?"

"Of course," said Danny. "We will do that together one day." Danny considered his options—could he turn on a random game and identify a random player as Reed? Did his father even remember what Reed looked like? Whatever his father believed became his father's new reality.

"We all live in our heads anyway," he told Lisetta during the drive back to the warehouse.

He felt good about the narrative he had shared with his father, who did not question any of it. His father would go to his grave with a different outcome for his two sons. When Danny described his recent travels as an airline pilot, his father's eyes twinkled with wonder, awoken from their frequent deadened state.

"You fly…in the sky?" he said.

"Yes, dad," said Danny. "I can do anything."

Danny and Lisetta set up a small table in dim light with two, tall-backed chairs. They added a linen tablecloth, linen napkins, shining silverware, elegant salt-and-pepper shakers, an ivory votive candle, a bottle of red wine, two crystal wine glasses, and a menu stolen from one of the fanciest restaurants in Chicago.

Having established the set, they filled the table with delicious food and started the scene: their twentieth wedding anniversary dinner.

Danny was adamant that they go back in time and cement this scene early in their agenda of trips to the past. "If we have this scene in place, then we have confirmed the success of all the scenes that come before it. We just backfill. It's good to know our destination."

They toasted to the next 20 years. They spoke with smug pride over the endurance of their marriage. "We stayed together, while so many others have failed," said Danny. "Out of everybody we know, we have the best, most long-lasting marriage."

Their conversation included references to other couples whose marriages had crumbled, whose children had become losers and criminals, whose families had dissolved into chaos through drugs, alcohol, mental disorders, hideous illness, and unforeseen tragedy. In particular, they altered the fate of couples they had previously envied who seemed to have "perfect lives." They reserved the perfect life for themselves, made all the more sweet by the downfall of the people they used to admire.

This included Mark Benedict and Pamela Whittaker, a flawless couple who met in high school (Prom King, Prom Queen), never separated, found spectacular jobs and wealth, produced immaculate children, and lived happily ever after. In just a few swift exchanges of dialogue, Danny and Lisetta knocked them off their pedestal and took over their roles as the high school couple everyone wanted to emulate.

They talked about their upcoming high school reunion, certain they would turn heads—Danny and Lisetta, a perfect pair living an ideal life.

It would be nothing like the high school reunion they attended in their previous reality, which became an uncomfortable spotlight on two miserable souls filled with regret.

That yellow sheet would be replaced with green, and soon.

Dear Friends,

Season's Greetings from the DeCastro family!

We hope this letter finds you well as we come to the end of another wonderful year and reflect on our blessings. Danny and Lisetta (the authors of this letter!) recently enjoyed their 20th wedding anniversary and our love has never been stronger.

Life is good at Casa DeCastro. Danny always has his head in the clouds—that's life as a pilot! He is a senior captain with four stripes. You could say his career has really taken off (ha ha). Lisetta continues to hit the bestseller charts and her most recent novel debuted at number one! She has made several trips to Hollywood to meet with stars interested in the movie rights to her books. Two major films are already in production based on her works.

This year's vacation trips circled the globe—including Barcelona, Athens, and Paris. We also enjoyed quiet time in our summer home by the lake in Door County, Wisconsin, simply enjoying the natural surroundings and each other. We are fortunate to be fit and healthy, keeping the weight off, staying busy with our many volunteer and charity efforts. You never know what the day might bring. Yesterday, Danny rescued a stray kitten!

Our son William continues to amaze us with his good looks, high ambitions, and intelligence. He wants to go to medical school and pursue a career as a pediatrician.

One of the highlights of the year was going to Cooperstown to see Danny's brother Reed inducted into the Baseball Hall of Fame to commemorate his stellar career. His acceptance speech was a true Grand Slam!

Danny's parents are doing well, healthy, and happy as Danny's dad enters retirement. He recently sold his booming carpet distribution business for $3.6 million and looks forward to relaxing, traveling the world, and playing lots of golf.

The Christmas holiday is always precious to us and we look forward to hosting a big Christmas dinner for the entire family. There will be Christmas caroling, good food and wine, and brightly colored packages under a giant, twinkling Christmas tree.

As we head into the new year, we know that more fun and excitement await. It is a great time to be alive. We wish all of our friends and family the very best in the times ahead.

Merry Christmas and happy new year from the DeCastro family!

Danny, Lisetta, & William

Greetings and happy holidays.

I apologize for the lateness of this traditional Christmas letter. Life got in the way.

As you will see at the bottom of this letter, there is only one name. Pamela and I split up this year after a long, painful decline in our relationship. I find it ironic now that so many people considered us "the ideal couple." Anything but! I'm glad she's out of my life and I know she feels likewise.

It has been a sad, miserable year in so many ways. Our son, as many of you have undoubtedly suspected, is a junkie. He is prone to getting wasted and committing foolish acts, like petty theft and public indecency. Our daughter continues her battles with anorexia and has been in and out of hospitals.

In other news, our garage caught fire and burned down our house, and I have six months to live. The disease I have is so rare they have no name for it, so they will be naming it after me. That will be my legacy. Look for me in medical journals soon. The early symptoms have caused part of my face to swell and deform, so no Christmas photo this year.

I hope you are having a better year. Do not feel bad for me. Deep inside, I probably deserve it.

Best,
Mark Benedict

Chapter
Twenty-One

Danny and Lisetta needed to pick out the ideal son, a fully-grown young man who would embody the outcome of an exemplary childhood and perfect upbringing. Their son would make his time travel debut at a family Christmas dinner the year of Danny and Lisetta's 20th wedding anniversary. Danny didn't discuss Adam, his original son, much at all with Lisetta. That experience had turned out poorly for the parent and child. This would be a major "do over" to set things right, and it would further cement his relationship with Lisetta.

Danny and Lisetta landed on a name for their son: William.

They agreed he would be handsome, athletic, intellectual, warm, witty, and a doctor who made a lot of money and saved a lot of lives. Someone they could brag about profusely.

Standards set high, they gathered in the office and began reviewing head shots on talent agency websites.

They rejected most of them.

Their mutual agreement was that the chosen son had to be someone they could both live with; if one of them liked a boy's appearance and the other didn't, it was a no go.

"Crooked smile."

"Nose too big."

"Shifty eyes."

"Looks nothing like me. People will talk."

They finally picked out two young men for auditions. Both failed their auditions. One had a voice that annoyed Danny. The other felt too slick and mechanical for Lisetta.

Next they reviewed websites dedicated to Chicago's theater

scene and scrutinized photos of young actors in plays. The frustration was building as no one seemed to fit the mold.

"I have this image in my head," said Danny. "And no one is nailing it."

Then they came across Harold Beyer.

Harold was the star of a military courtroom drama that had just been extended for a few weeks at a small but well-respected theater in Lincoln Park. The play, *Perfect Order*, featured a young sailor fighting corruption in the Naval ranks after discovering a high-ranking officer taking part in a drug smuggling scheme aboard an aircraft carrier. A large photo of clean-cut Harold bravely testifying in his crisp blue uniform grabbed the attention of Danny and Lisetta immediately. He had a square jaw, piercing blue eyes, and an aura of honesty and integrity.

Danny and Lisetta bought two second-row tickets to see the play—more specifically, to observe Harold.

They immediately fell in love with him.

"He's perfect," whispered Lisetta.

"That's my boy," said Danny.

At the end of the play, as the performers took their curtain calls, Harold received thunderous applause.

Danny felt proud.

They finagled their way backstage to meet Harold. He stood in his own space, away from the other performers, wiping off makeup.

"We just wanted to tell you, we were blown away," said Lisetta. She held Danny's hand tightly, nervously. "You were brilliant."

Harold responded with sweet modesty, not a hint of arrogance or aloofness. He was half out of his costume, in white t-shirt and slacks.

"My wife and I, we're playwrights," said Danny. "We're working on a new play—a domestic drama about a family. To help us with the writing, we employ actors and actresses to do these very elaborate staged readings of certain scenes—almost like small performances, without an audience. We have sets, props, wardrobe…."

Harold's eyes narrowed as he held onto his smile, retaining politeness while uncertain of how to receive this eager couple.

"We would like to hire you to perform in a few of our scenes," said Lisetta sweetly. "You would be perfect—absolutely perfect—for one of the roles. I know you must be very busy and in demand...."

"This show runs a couple more weeks," he said.

"It wouldn't take long," said Danny. "We would send you the script in advance. How about three thousand dollars...for a couple hours of your time?"

Harold stared at them, retaining his unflustered composure, even as his response wavered with uncertainty.

"Well, I don't know," he said. "You could contact my agency...."

"We'd rather deal directly with you," said Danny. "Why give some agency a cut? Tell you what, we'll make it thirty-five hundred dollars."

Harold considered this, then responded. "Four thousand."

Lisetta broke out in a smile. "I like how you think."

"He's nobody's fool," said Danny, equally impressed by the young man's smooth bargaining skills. "Four thousand it is."

"Hurray," said Lisetta.

"We have ourselves a deal," said Danny, and he shook Harold's hand. "From now on, your name is William."

"Okay...." said Harold with a small shrug.

During the drive back to the warehouse, Danny outlined the new norm. "My son will love and respect me. We will be close. I will not make any mistakes this time. I've learned from my past. The past was just a rehearsal. This, now, is the real thing."

Lisetta placed her hand on Danny's shoulder and smiled at him from the shadows of the passenger seat.

"I need to write us a new scene," she said, "for when William is conceived."

Danny purred with arousal. "How quickly can you get that drafted?"

As he drove through the stop-and-go city traffic, she kissed his neck.

They ran a red light and escaped laughing, unharmed.

In that moment, Danny felt neither young nor old. He felt ageless and invincible.

Chapter Twenty-Two

L isetta woke up in the middle of the night screaming. She flung herself from her cot, and collapsed into the pitch black of the Neutrality Room.

The Neutrality Room served as living quarters for Danny and Lisetta when they weren't planning or embarking on time travel. It was carefully designed to represent a timeless state—a plain, minimalist environment where any items identifying a specific era, such as cell phones, were not allowed. There were no mirrors to capture their age and just a few bare necessities, such as a shower and toilet.

It helped to further block out the outside world. But it could do nothing to prevent remnants of the past from invading their dreams.

Lisetta had just experienced a vivid dream that took her back to Eldridge, reunited with Martin and Mindy.

When she awoke, and they vanished, she exploded into a panic.

Danny quickly climbed out of his cot and snapped on a dim light. The room remained dark with the walls painted black.

"I have to go home!" exclaimed Lisetta, seated on the floor, shaking, as Danny quickly joined her and put his arms around her.

"This is your home."

"No, no," she said, crying. "My house. In Iowa. Where I live with my family."

"Martin doesn't exist anymore."

"But my daughter Mindy—"

"She's away at college."

"I can't just disappear on her. She needs me." Lisetta struggled to stand up, but Danny's embrace was firm.

"She's strong, she's independent. You told me so yourself. She's left the nest."

"Danny, I can't breathe." Lisetta gasped, nearly hyperventilating. "I feel so much guilt...."

"There's nothing to feel guilty about. You're a different person now."

She tried to shake off Danny. He wasn't letting her leave.

"I want my car keys!" she shouted.

"Lisetta, listen to me!" Danny's voice turned loud and his eyes stared into her face with a sudden fierceness. "You must cut your ties for this to work. That world out there with Martin and Mindy, it no longer exists. You can't do this halfway. It's all or nothing. Don't you like your new reality?"

"It's selfish," she said, and tears striped her face. "I've abandoned my daughter."

"You're gaining a son. You're living your dream career. You have me...."

She stopped struggling and held on tight to Danny.

"You don't want to go back," said Danny in a calmed voice, nestling his face into her hair, speaking close to her ear. "In that world, in that time capsule, you are a killer. If you go back, you will be arrested for murder. You will be sentenced to life in prison. No matter which path you choose, this one or that one, you will be separated from your daughter."

She erupted into sobs. "I didn't mean to kill him...."

"That is why it is being erased."

Danny gently pulled away from her. He took her hand. "Come with me."

He led her out of the Neutrality Room and they walked the short corridor to the office. He flipped on the light, waking Toby, curled up on his rug.

Danny and Lisetta stood before the wall that displayed the changing timeline of their lives.

"It's a mix of green and yellow," he said. "I know it must feel like you have one foot in two stories. We're making progress every day. Your world is shifting. We will turn all of these yellow sheets to green. You will have just one lifetime again, the right one, the one you deserve."

"Yes," she said quietly, studying the colored sheets, feeling a comforting detachment, as if truth and fantasy held equal weight. The dueling narratives existed outside of her conscience, posted objectively on a wall in plain handwriting.

"You can't go back," said Danny. "Neither one of us can. We are committed to this."

"The dream with Mindy…." said Lisetta. "It was so real."

"That's all it was," said Danny. "A dream. Let it evaporate, like all dreams do."

Lisetta nodded. She said yes with a heavy punch of exhalation. She slowly gathered her composure and said, "I can do it. I think it's already fading away."

Chapter Twenty-Three

A small crowd gathered at 9 am on a Tuesday—actors and actresses, quickly developing an animated camaraderie, chatting curiously about the odd location and strange solicitation that brought them here.

Punctual to the minute, Lisetta opened the old metal door with a loud, uneven scrape, and the performers glanced at one another before going inside, hesitating only briefly, figuring, *Well, safety in numbers.*

Plus, they were being very well paid for this gig.

Lisetta led them into a big, open space where, she explained, carpet used to be stored. She brought the group to the rear of the warehouse where there was a long, plain table surrounded by folding chairs.

At each setting at the table, there was a script and bottled water.

"This is where we will have the table reading," she said. "And here is my husband...."

Danny stepped out of the darkness, smiling, clutching his own copy of the script. Toby followed him, tail wagging.

"Thank you for entering our domain," said Danny. "We call it The Idea Factory. It may look unorthodox, but we find the isolation and emptiness conducive to creativity."

Several of the performers nodded; they felt right at home with a couple of quirky artists.

"Please find the script with your character's name written on top," said Danny. "That will be your seating."

The actors and actresses moved around the sides of the

table, filling slots as they found their parts.

Once everyone was seated, Danny took his chair at one end of the table and Lisetta sat at the other end.

"A quick roll call and then we'll dig in," said Danny.

He ran through the cast of characters and each one had a representative: his parents, George and Karen; his brother, Reed, with his wife, Sandy, and two daughters; and his son, William.

His own script was for "Danny" and Lisetta's script was marked "Lisetta." They would be playing themselves, of course.

While he didn't have his own script, Toby had a part, too. He was "Toby Jr.," portraying his own descendant, since it was mathematically impossible to extend the original Toby's life so many years into the future.

Details mattered.

"Everyone's accounted for," said Danny, pleased. "With that, I think we can get started. Again, this is just a table read. We will schedule an actual live performance in the future. But first, we want to make sure everyone is comfortable with their parts and the script is in tiptop shape."

Both Danny and Lisetta had pens alongside their scripts, at the ready, to make notes or edits in the margins.

The DeCastro Christmas dinner got underway.

Reed: "What a fantastic meal."

Karen: "Yes, everything is so lovely."

Lisetta: "Thank you."

Karen: "It is so wonderful to get everyone together."

Danny: "We're delighted everyone could be here. Dad, can I pass you the mashed potatoes? Or have you reached your limit?"

George: "Well, I've already had one big helping...."

Karen: "Go ahead. It's the holidays. Besides—you just had your annual checkup. The doctor said you are in excellent health."

Reed: "That's great, dad."

George: "So, William, tell us about medical school."

William: "It's my dream, Grandpa. I love making sick people well. Especially children."

Lisetta: "He's going to be a pediatrician."

Karen: "I am so proud."

William: "Thank you, Grandma."

Karen: "So many of my lady friends, they have grandchildren who are lazy, or dopers, or disrespectful to their elders. How did you turn out so fine?"

William: "Blame it on Mom and Dad, I guess. They're the perfect parents. Obviously, they knew what they were doing."

Danny: "Your mother has been stellar. Give credit where credit is due. I'm not always home, with all my flights and traveling. Your mother has always been there for you."

Lisetta: "I've been very fortunate to have a career where I can work out of the house. I have my home office; the hours are very flexible. Being a best-selling author—it's a good life. I can play hooky whenever I want. The money never stops flowing—movie rights, foreign rights, audiobooks, I can't keep track of it all. Fortunately, my accountant does, ha ha!"

Reed: "I heard one of your books is becoming a miniseries."

Lisetta: "Yes. I've been invited to visit the set and make a cameo!"

Sandy: "Reed, tell them your news. You're about to go in front of the cameras, too!"

Danny: "What's this, bro? Getting into the baseball Hall of Fame wasn't enough?"

Reed: "I've been recruited for a second career. Sports broadcaster for one of the major networks."

George: "That's terrific!"

Reed: "I think it will be a lot of fun. It's a way to continue my passion for sports. Obviously, I don't need the fame or money, I'm all set there, ha ha!"

Karen: "I am so proud of my boys."

George: "I am grateful you didn't join the family business. Sure, I was disappointed in the beginning. But you have really emerged from under my shadow to become very successful in your own right."

Danny: "Who knows, Dad. Maybe your business would've been less successful if Reed and I helped run it."

George: "I've been very fortunate. The carpet business has been very, very good to me. I never dreamed I could one day sell it for so much money and retire with a gigantic nest egg."

Karen: "Now we're going to travel the world."

George: "I'm just glad we can afford your addiction to shopping!"

Karen: "I can't wait to go shopping in other countries."

George: "We're going on a couple of cruises next year. I hope the cruise ships have plenty of storage for everything you'll be bringing home!"

Karen: "Oh, George, you make me sound like such a consumer! You know I give a lot of money and goods to charity, too."

George: "It's true. She's very active in the community. She gives to the poor and gives to the church. She's a very generous woman."

Karen: "And I am very fortunate to be married to a brilliant, wonderful man!"

Lisetta: "Here, here. Me too."

Sandy: "Me three."

Danny: "This is the best Christmas ever! I propose a toast. Everyone lift your glasses...to the DeCastro family!"

Overall, Danny was pleased with the table reading. In a few instances, he reminded the performers to smile, to exhibit an extra boost of warmth and happiness. The line readings were strong and precise, with the banter bouncing between the players in a steady, peppy rhythm.

Danny outlined the next steps: "Lisetta will pay you in cash for today's services. I will work with your schedules to find a time in the next week or two for a full-on performance. It will be here. We will have a set, props, and wardrobe. We will expect you to have your lines fully memorized. We will send you any script updates. I know I have a few edits based on today's reading, and Lisetta, I saw your pen moving as well. We will make sure the dialogue is perfect."

As the group of performers broke up to begin exiting the warehouse, Danny fielded a few concerns.

Harold approached him and spoke in a low, respectful tone. However, his words were not filled with praise.

"I'm not sure I get this," he said.

"Get what?" said Danny.

"This play."

"You're only seeing one small part."

"Yes, granted. But this scene today…it's just one long, happy conversation."

"And there's something wrong with that?"

"Well, sort of. Where's the conflict, where's the drama?"

Danny looked at him, confused. "Why do we need any of that?"

"Your script needs some spice. This stuff is—I'm sorry—it's really bland."

"I did not feel blandness at that table," said Danny, quickly getting defensive. "Do you know what I felt? I felt joy. What's wrong with that?"

"Nothing," said Harold, wrinkling his brow, searching for a better way to get his point across. "Maybe I just don't understand my character. What's his motivation?"

"Motivation?"

"Yeah. Like, my backstory. What drives me?"

Danny responded, "You're a high achiever. You love your family. You're very successful."

"And—?"

"And what? That's it."

"But I need to have some flaws. That's what makes us human. Some kind of fear or anger beneath the surface. Maybe I'm harboring a dark secret. Like a problem with my sexual identity. Or a rare blood disease. Or a gambling problem. Or—or—"

"*No*, absolutely not!" said Danny. Then he stated clearly and firmly, "You are not the writer here. You are being paid—very well-paid—to speak these lines and become this person. Nothing more, nothing less. Do we have an understanding?"

Harold hesitated, thrown off by the sudden aggressiveness, and finally shrugged with a half-chuckle. "Sure. Right. Whatever."

Next up, Danny was confronted by the two teenage actresses who were playing the parts of Reed's daughters.

"How come we don't have any lines?" said the older one. "So, we just sit there?"

Danny had not come up with any compelling dialogue—or any desire to reshape their identities—and left them as a silent presence at the dinner table, playing on their iPhones, which was more or less realistic, too.

"Children should be seen and not heard," said Danny.

"Can't you like, just stick a mannequin in my chair then?" said the girl with a sour pout.

"What's the matter, you don't like money?" said Danny. "I'm sure I could pay some other kid five-hundred dollars to sit there and be quiet."

"You're weird," said the girl, and she left with her fictional sister, who looked equally annoyed but had successfully held back any rude comments.

After the warehouse cleared out, Danny hugged Lisetta.

"All things considered, I think that went very well," he said. "I started to really see them in their roles."

"It's a good ensemble," said Lisetta. "William was good."

"He's getting there," said Danny. "He asks too many questions. But he'll settle in. He'll become the part."

"I like him," said Lisetta wistfully. "I'm proud he's our son."

Chapter
Twenty-Four

Even as Danny's fantasy life blossomed, he remained loyal to one painful reality outside the warehouse walls: his weekly trip to visit his father at the Kenosha residential care facility.

Occasionally there were small lifts of optimism where Danny could convince himself his father was improving a little bit, but mostly he was a helpless witness to slow-motion deterioration.

Following on the heels of crafting an exciting new storyline for his father, the return to illness and despair struck Danny hard. The transition between dueling universes made his head spin.

On this Tuesday afternoon, Lisetta stayed back at the time machine office, working on scripts and ordering period-specific props and costumes. Danny arrived at his father's room alone, knocked on the door and waited patiently to introduce himself, hoping for a glimmer of recognition.

George DeCastro opened the door and smiled. "Reed?"

"It's Danny."

The visit did not get any better. His father's shirt was stained with a big spill and Danny traced it to a half-full glass of juice on the kitchenette counter. Danny helped his father change into a clean shirt and then noticed the bruises on his arm.

"What happened here, Dad?"

"I don't know."

"When was the last time they were here to check on you?"

He offered a guess. "This morning?"

The rest of the conversation predictably veered between

blank stares, irritability, and confusion. At one point, his father asked, "Where's Karen?"

"Shopping," said Danny, choosing something pleasant and dishonest over the real answer: "Dead for thirty-eight years."

His father seemed more restless than usual and paced around Danny for several minutes in his bare feet before opening the door to a closet.

"What are you looking for?" asked Danny.

"The bathroom."

"It's over here." Danny led him to another door. "Do you want me to go in with you?"

"Why?"

Danny watched his father enter and said, "Be careful."

Before George DeCastro shut the door, he mumbled, "What a stupid thing to say."

The forty-minute visit was more emotionally grueling than normal. Before leaving, Danny hugged his father, and it felt like embracing a limp, distracted child.

As Danny exited the senior memory care facility, his eyes grew wet with tears. He felt the cold slap of a stinging wind from a lingering spring chill. He stepped toward the parking lot.

"Heyyyy," said a voice.

Danny turned and saw the last two people he wanted to see right now.

Cheryl and Barry walked over from where their car, a red Honda Civic, sat parked near the front of the building. They had been waiting for him.

Danny acknowledged Barry's smarmy greeting with a glare. He stopped for a moment and shoved his hands into his pockets.

"What are you doing here?" he asked.

"We've been waiting for you," said Barry in a friendly tone that was obviously false.

Cheryl spoke next, offering no attempt to sound pleasant. "You haven't responded to my calls or emails. We had to come here. The woman at the desk said you're here every week at this time."

"This is time reserved for my father," said Danny. "It's not for you."

"Listen," said Barry. "You can't avoid this. This is important."

"What is it? I have places to go."

"We heard about the business," said Cheryl.

"What business?" said Danny.

"Your father's business. You sold it."

"Why is that your concern?"

"Because you owe me money," said Cheryl.

"That's bullshit," said Danny.

"Heyyyy," said Barry. "Hear us out. Don't be acting rude."

"Acting rude?" said Danny. "You ambush me here, where my father is very sick...."

"You know what this is about, Danny," said Cheryl sharply. "You owe back alimony. I brought up Adam under financial and mental hardship. You pitched in nothing. Now that you've sold the business, we expect you to pay what you should have been paying all those years. It's only fair."

"You made a lot of money off the sale of that business," said Barry. "Meanwhile, Cheryl here went into debt bringing up your child."

"My child? You wouldn't even let me near him!"

"You were in no condition to be a father."

"Says who?"

"Let's not argue here," said Barry, acting like the voice of reason. Danny considered him a colossal asshole, oozing with bogus charm. "Where can we discuss this reasonably, like adults?"

"There's nothing to discuss," said Danny.

"We don't even know where to reach you," said Cheryl. "Where do you live? What's your phone number?"

"It's none of your business," said Danny.

"Danny," said Barry. "Let's face it. Maybe you didn't have money before. But now you're loaded. I know how much that business sold for."

"That money is reserved," said Danny.

"For what?" said Cheryl.

"A physics experiment."

Barry held back a chuckle. "A what?"

Danny could take no more. "I'm leaving," he said. "Don't ever bother me here again." He walked between Barry and Cheryl and headed into the parking lot.

"We will send a lawyer after you!" said Cheryl, loud and shrill. "We have a lawyer and he is *ruthless*."

"He will annuitize the sale of that business to apply to back alimony," said Barry, his voice also rising. "You're going to court, and this money will be allocated appropriately. You will not shut us out, Daniel."

Danny said nothing. He climbed into the carpet delivery van he used for transportation. He locked his door and sat in silence, watching them from his window.

He did not want them advancing into the building and, God forbid, pestering his father in his current state. What if they got him to agree to some arrangement for the money from the business sale, taking advantage of his addled mind?

Danny watched Barry and Cheryl talk to one another for a moment, probably discussing their next slimy plot. They nodded to each other in agreement and returned to the red Honda Civic.

Danny hated them both with a passion. His entire body shook.

After they left the parking lot in their car, Danny followed in his van.

He trailed them on a long stretch of road that cut through the scenic Wisconsin countryside on the way back to the main highway that sent people north to Milwaukee or south to Chicago. The terrain consisted of woods and farmland, laid out under gray, emotionless skies. Only an occasional car or pickup truck zipped by in the opposite direction. Danny got close enough to read the smug bumper sticker on the Honda Civic: "I'd Rather Be Golfing."

He could see their outlines in the front seat, heads turned close, undoubtedly talking about him and scheming....

Belittling him...plotting to sic their "ruthless" lawyer on him...eager to seize his bank account and steal his money.

Danny's blood boiled with anger. They were going to take

away the warehouse. He would lose the time machine and, with it, all hopes of a better life. He would lose Lisetta.

"*No*," said Danny out loud. He wasn't about to let that happen.

This cruel thievery had to stop, and it had to stop now.

The red Honda reached a short, wooden bridge stretched over a rocky, fast-flowing river. Danny gunned the engine of the delivery van. He let out an angry yell.

Danny slammed hard into the back of the Honda, hammering the bumper and crushing the car's left brake light. He pushed the vehicle to the far right and off the road. Swerving wildly out of control with squealing tires, the Honda slid across the slim shoulder and broke through a brittle wooden guardrail.

In a surreal moment of silence, the car plummeted forty feet in a freefall. Then it splashed into the shallow river, quickly striking bottom and flipping upside down.

Danny stopped the van. He could see the tires and undercarriage of the car just barely breaking through the water's surface. All else was submerged—including Cheryl and Barry, trapped and mangled in their car seats, taking in the rush of cold water that would displace all of their oxygen in a matter of minutes.

Danny checked his mirrors and windows for any witnesses and found none. Just some birds and a squirrel. He didn't hear any screams coming from below—perhaps they were unconscious or dead or busy drowning.

He felt nothing about their fate. They weren't even real anymore. Just a couple of pencil sketches about to face the eraser.

Danny stepped on the gas. He left the scene.

Danny returned to the time travel offices, fighting to stay calm. His clothes stuck to his body with sweat. He scratched Toby's head and told Lisetta, "During the drive home, I—I had an idea for a new scene in my timeline."

Lisetta looked up from the script she was writing, a bidding war for one of her books between two Hollywood studios.

"I need closure with my first wife," he said. "I've already prevented us from getting married. But she's still a presence in my new life, she's out there, you know. She married that asshole

Barry Cody, and the two of them are still running around, being jerks to everyone they meet. If this new life is to be perfect—then they don't exist."

Lisetta said, "You're going to repopulate the world to remove people you don't like? That's going to be a lot of work."

Danny thought about it. "No. Not everyone. Not like the people who cut in front of you in line at the grocery store. That list would go on forever. But Cheryl and Barry…I already have it written in my head. I know what I want to do. For my own peace of mind, I'd like them to have an accident."

Lisetta smiled, intrigued by the drama. "An accident."

"I'll need your help. Your skills as a journalist. Your expertise with HTML coding and design. I'm very excited about this."

"You do seem a little breathless."

Danny declared, "Let's prepare the time machine."

TRAVEL LOG:
REVERSAL 14Y 9M 21D

Today, I discovered tragic news.

I was home at the apartment with Lisetta, during one of the mandated breaks in my busy flight schedule. We were enjoying a day of good food and lovemaking.

During a casual glance at the local news headlines on my laptop, I chanced upon a story about the deaths of two people I knew.

Cheryl and Barry Cody.

I had dated Cheryl a few times in college and then initiated a breakup once I realized she was not a good fit for me. She was loud, aggressive, and scheming. She was preoccupied with money in a bad way. Years later, I heard through the grapevine that she had married a lunkhead named Barry Cody. From a friend of a friend, I was told he was a very snide, artificial man. He was condescending as a survival tactic, because he was really quite lowly.

So, it was with mixed emotions that I read the shocking online article. Cheryl and Barry were dead! As much as I disliked them, I would never wish them any harm. Surely this was an act of God.

During a drive in the Kenosha countryside, they experienced a blown tire. Unfortunately, it occurred on a bridge. The car veered off the road, broke through a fence and crashed into a river.

Barry died instantly from a broken neck.

Cheryl died slowly, trapped upside-down in the smashed car, smothered in the freezing water, unable to escape. Battered and bloody, she drowned as the Earth continued to turn on its axis indifferently, shedding a useless life.

"Hey, honey, check this out," I called to Lisetta.

My wife came over and read the news headline and first few paragraphs of the story.

"I used to date that girl in college. We broke up. She wasn't right for me."

"What a terrible way to die," said Lisetta.

"I'm glad I never stayed with her," I said. "I can't imagine being married to her. I'm glad you're the one I married."

"Thank you, Danny."

"You're the only one, now and forever."

Lisetta shook her head sadly at the story on the laptop monitor. "Terrible, terrible tragedy...." Then she brightened. "Hey, you want to make love?"

Chapter Twenty-Five

Adam DeCastro awoke to the sound of a buzzing cell phone vibrating on the dresser.

His wife, Janis, was a light sleeper and hopped out of bed to answer it as Adam continued to stir free from his murky dreams.

Janis spoke a few words in a hushed tone—"Yes, yes, just a moment"—and then said to Adam: "It's from the States. It's for you."

Adam slowly sat up.

Janis came over and handed the phone to him. She stayed close.

Adam had been living in the Marylebone neighborhood of London for ten years, working for an architecture firm while his girlfriend taught at the University of Westminster. His ties with the United States had slowly dissolved over the years, so an overseas caller was rare. London was his longtime home now. His few American contacts knew how to maneuver time zones, so the middle-of-the-night call immediately spiked him with alarm.

"Hello," he said. "This is Adam."

He listened, absorbed the message, and then shut his eyes. He slumped with despair, unable to find many words, just monosyllabic responses to acknowledge he was taking it all in as the caller continued to dispense information.

Janis stood in their bedroom in her long nightshirt, studying him with wide eyes, anxious. She started biting a fingernail. Her husband's expression and body language were not good.

When the call ended, she asked, "What is it?"

Adam stared in disbelief at the phone in his hand. In a foggy voice, still trying to absorb the news, he uttered a short, crumbling statement. "My mother and stepfather...they're dead."

Part Three

Chapter
Twenty-Six

On the plane from Heathrow to Chicago's O'Hare International Airport, Adam tried reading, sleeping, listening to music on his earbuds and could do none of the above. His mind swam. The reality of what had happened was still sinking in, making the grueling transition from a disorienting shock to cold reality.

The limited details he had of the accident were enough to create ugly pictures in his mind. He envisioned his mother and stepfather screaming inside their car as it lost control and skidded off a bridge into the river. It was a short bridge and shallow river, but the hard impact of the fall injured and trapped them beneath the water's surface. Being a low-traffic roadway in the Wisconsin countryside, there were no immediate passersby to jump to the rescue or contact police and paramedics.

The two of them died at the scene. If it wasn't instant and simultaneous, one of them probably experienced the death of the other.

Adam felt overwhelmed with guilt and regret. He had not been in regular contact with his mother and Barry for many years. A phone call here and there, Christmas cards, and the occasional email when there was something noteworthy, like a new job. But he had not visited the US in nearly a decade, and they had not come to the UK to see his new life.

Adam knew he was to blame for creating the distance between them, a geographical separation that led to an emotional detachment. His younger years were not good ones. His parents split when he was just a few years old. His mother was small but exhaustively overbearing, and Adam failed to connect with her new husband. His true father lived nearby throughout much of Adam's childhood, but their attempts to connect were clumsy and ultimately combative.

Adam's teenage years became his "Who gives a shit" phase, ditching classes, smoking pot, engaging in marathon sessions of playing video games and hanging out with the "wrong crowd."

At age 18, Adam left home to "backpack through Europe" with a loose itinerary and few belongings. He quickly ate through meager savings cobbled from birthday and Christmas cash and a brief stint as a second-rate pot dealer, mainly selling to his friends. He stayed in youth hostels and worked odd jobs in Italy, France, and Spain. He made love to women drawn to the novelty of a free-spirited, unsophisticated American tourist who did not speak their language.

After a year and a half of aimless adventures and avoiding adult responsibilities, he settled down in London. He met a group of gregarious young Brits in a pub on a Friday night and wound up working with one of them as an office assistant in an architecture firm. It was a real job, and he worked hard to step up to the occasion.

Adam gradually learned enough about the business to take on expanded duties as the firm took off with a growing client list. His boss saw potential and subsidized evening classes, and Adam embarked on a gradual climb to assistant landscape designer for public spaces.

Then one day, through a friend of a friend, he met Janis.

Janis taught literature at Westminster, two years older than Adam, lovely and wise. Adam pursued her for several months, and she gradually warmed to his advances. Her demeanor was stoic but sly, with a wicked, unsmiling sense of humor. She was a hard-fought conquest, and once he won her over, he did not let go.

She warned him she was "not the marrying type" and didn't want children, and he readily agreed to both. As a product of—and contributor to—a dysfunctional family, he had no interest in creating one of his own. Adam and Janis were happy to be two friends and lovers living together, and that would be the extent of their relationship, with no further ambitions.

It worked really, really well.

Adam sent photos of Janis to his mother and Barry, as well as pictures of his handsome office space, evidence that he was settling down and not the reckless, directionless delinquent of his past.

"She's very pretty," wrote his mother.

"When will we meet her?" wrote his stepfather.

"One day," he responded, and now, in the blink of an eye, "one day" had become never.

Adam's birth father didn't even know Janis existed. Adam had cut off all ties with him many years ago, following an incendiary senior year at high school. It was one of the worst periods of Adam's life.

As much as his mother annoyed him, and his stepfather was a glib jackass who ignored him, Adam's dad was the biggest pain point. The two had stopped talking long ago. In fact, he wasn't sure his dad even knew he was living in England.

During Adam's childhood, "Real Dad" was a mopey, mumbling man who lived across town and did not offer him anything in the way of interest or encouragement. As an adolescent, Adam spent many dull weekends staying at Real Dad's apartment, hoping they would do something fun together and then usually stuck watching TV with him—the shows his dad wanted to watch—or accompanying him on boring errands for groceries or mundane items at the local hardware store.

In those early years, he simply felt bad for his father. After the divorce, his dad moved too quickly into another marriage, hooking up with an equally gloomy woman named Marci. Someone had fixed them up because they were both newly divorced and miserable, mistaking it for a common interest. Adam didn't like Marci—she was a heavy drape of melancholy with odd phobias, like a fear of fish. She despised sports and would not enter a room where any type of sporting event was on television or part of a discussion. She only smiled with effort.

Adam's dad and Marci divorced within a few years, leaving Adam's dad more bitter and lost than before. Adam tried to connect with him, but always found it very difficult.

Adam knew he was the reason his parents got married—not love. Perhaps his father resented him as a symbol of that horrible, forced marriage to a woman who constantly berated him. She seemed to recognize and feed his self-loathing.

On the other hand, Adam's "new dad" was hardly a winner, either. Adam felt that Barry resented him just as much for other reasons—Adam was a symbol of his wife's previous marriage, a product outside his own creation and therefore unworthy of more than simple, manufactured flattery and feigned affection.

Barry Cody was a salesman, and he could convincingly sell the concept that he cared for Adam, but over time it was easy to spot the calculated mechanisms of his self-marketing, the same approach he employed as a successful insurance salesman.

Barry was so good at selling insurance that he worked his way up the ranks to manage other salespeople. As part of his career path, he was assigned to a regional sales director job in Connecticut for one year and promised a big promotion when he returned to the home office in Chicago.

He leapt at it.

He rented an apartment in Hartford and Cheryl moved in with him under the guise of not wanting to be separated from her loving husband, but more likely due to the fact that she did not trust him alone and feared the apartment would become a bachelor's pad for flings and hijinks.

The one-year assignment in Connecticut took place during Adam's senior year in high school, and Adam was encouraged by Cheryl and Barry to stay behind and not break continuity by finishing school someplace else. That was fine by Adam; he didn't want to move to Connecticut for a year and squeeze into an apartment with the two of them.

He expected to live alone in the house for a year, taking care of himself without any bothersome parents. He privately grew excited about the prospect of no supervision, consumed with visions of the parties he would host, the weed he would smoke, and the young women he would entice into the bedrooms.

His teenage fantasy immediately dissolved when his mother and Barry informed him he would not be trusted alone at the house—he would be staying with his father at his dad's apartment.

"You will spend your senior year with your father," said Adam's mom. "You are not old enough or mature enough to be living by yourself. It's already arranged. It will be a good thing for the two of you to spend time together. After all, he is your father. He's shirked enough responsibility over the years. He will take care of you, and make sure you are eating properly, going to school, and staying out of trouble."

"I know it's not ideal," said Barry with a salesman's smile. "I know your father is not the best when it comes to being a father. But you need adult supervision, you're just not old enough to go it alone. We'll be back in 12 months. You'll have lots of opportunity to visit, I promise. I know you'll miss us a great deal. After we come back and I get the promotion, we'll go on a fabulous vacation together—the three of us. You can choose where we go!"

Adam simply said, "I don't want to live with him."

His mother answered, with equal conciseness. "You don't have a choice."

Thus began a year of hell.

Adam's father was ill-prepared to suddenly deal with his son, and Adam wanted nothing to do with his dad. They bickered endlessly about everything. Adam's father offered no pleasantries, only criticisms over Adam's study habits, hygiene, diet, length of hair, disregard for curfew, addiction to videogames, curious bloodshot eyes, "bad influence" friends, "easy" girls, and general sloppiness disrupting the tidy order of the apartment—perhaps the only thing Adam's father had successfully been able to control in his sad-sack life of a perpetual victim.

His dad was constantly irritable, transitioning between jobs and without a girlfriend—or many friends at all, for that matter. His hours were sometimes unpredictable, which made ditching school a gamble unless Adam hung out at the mall or local public library.

For eleven months, they argued and fought until they were exhausted and fell into an easier pattern of just ignoring one another. Adam didn't complete his senior year and when his mother and Barry came home for the graduation ceremony, and Adam was absent from it, there was monumental hell to pay.

Adam's father received the brunt of it; after all, he was "the adult in charge."

"I tried, I tried everything!" insisted Adam's father.

"I question your methods and sincerity," said Barry, and that's when a fistfight almost broke out.

After that awful year, Adam managed to pass his GED exam to finally receive his diploma, which he threw at his mother.

Following moving out of his father's apartment, Adam never spoke to him again. He didn't plan it as an act of hostility, it just fell into place naturally.

Adam felt his father was a big loser. He also began to realize he was a big loser, too. The only route out of his predicament was to leave the whole hot mess behind and start a new life somewhere else that included none of them.

Adam packed up, wrote a note for the kitchen table, and left for Europe.

And now—nine years later—he was returning to the States. It was one of the few things that could truly beckon him back: a funeral.

He had convinced Janis to stay behind. She had essays and midterms to grade. She had never met his family, and he wanted to keep it that way. He expected to see his father at the funeral, and he knew it would be a very awkward reunion to add to the drama.

"I'd rather go it alone," he told Janis. And she kissed him and granted him his wish with minimal argument, sensing the truth and pain behind his eyes.

He deeply appreciated that.

She understood him.

He felt closer to her than anybody else, ever, in his life. It gave him the strength he needed to journey back to his past and confront old demons.

He was a very different person than the eighteen-year-old hothead who ran away from home, scrawling an angry note that finished with: "I just want to be left alone."

Life was different now.

He no longer wanted to be alone. He had Janis.

He no longer wanted to run away from home. He had found home, in another country.

Perhaps these two tragic deaths were just another step toward completely severing the ties to a past that seemed more distant and faded all the time.

Adam knew he would cry at the funeral. He would crumble and it would hurt. Adam would grieve for his mother, for his stepfather, and a whole lot more.

Chapter Twenty-Seven

Adam felt like a stranger at his mother and stepfather's funeral at St. Anne's Church in Barrington. It was crowded, an unusual joint service with two coffins. He sat up front, stiff, stoic, and blurry eyed, wearing a dark suit and accepting the embraces and cheek kisses of a steady progression of people he did not know. Occasionally, he encountered a faintly recognizable face—a cousin, a former neighbor—but for the most part his life had been wholly detached from this world. It moved around him in a haze of vague familiarity, like a soft dream.

After the service, the mourners moved about to engage in small conversations around the pews. Adam repeated his storyline at least twenty times: living in London, happy in a relationship with a school teacher named Janis, sad that he had not been back to the US in a long time. In return, he heard numerous compliments about how the little boy they remembered had grown up to become a handsome young man.

Adam talked with Aunt Mia, his mother's sister, from California. He had met her a few times when he was young, just enough to feel a slight connection now. She looked like a sagging, crouched alter ego of his memory of her. She wore a lopsided wig and quickly explained it—chemotherapy. Adam felt awful. On top of cancer, she had to deal with the sudden, tragic death of her only sister.

And she was the one feeling sorry for *him*.

He hugged her, entering the ring of aroma of her "old lady" perfume, squeezing out tears for her and everybody else, but somehow not himself.

Adam felt more stunned, confused, and overwhelmed than sad. He knew an outburst of sorrow would come later, in a big way.

"What were they even doing out there?" asked Aunt Mia.

"Excuse me?" said Adam.

"Your parents. Driving out in Kenosha, the countryside. There's nothing out there, where they were. I don't know. It's strange, don't you think?"

Adam didn't know what to say. To him, the location of their car accident was irrelevant. It happened, they died. It could have happened on the Chicago expressway.

"Maybe they were visiting a friend out that way," said Adam.

"No one knows," said Aunt Mia. "It's weird. No one knows where they were going or coming from."

Then she asked the question that he had been asking himself for hours.

"Where's your father?"

"I don't know," said Adam.

"Have you heard from him?"

"Not at all."

"How strange."

"We don't really talk."

"Still...." said Aunt Mia. "I get it, it's his ex-wife, they divorced a long time ago. But at least go to the funeral. Show some respect."

"My dad's kind of a recluse," said Adam. "He doesn't do well in social situations." Then he realized he could be describing himself.

As the church started to empty out and their conversation winded down, Mia said warmly, "She was proud of you, Adam. Your mother would talk about you, and yes, you were apart, but you were in her heart. She was so happy that you were happy, and you had gotten your life back together."

Adam smiled, said nothing, and tears surfaced in his eyes.

A little while later, during the drive to the cemetery, Adam spoke aloud in the rental car, rehearsing what he would say if he came across his father. He could fully imagine his dad staying clear of the church service but making an appearance at the burial, standing back, staying away from conversation, but witnessing the lowering of the coffins into the ground.

Maybe he would be sad, maybe not, but he would be drawn to the closure....

However, Adam did not see his father at the cemetery.

He began to feel angry. It was rude and self-centered. And wholly consistent with the father he remembered, who upset him so much as a teenager.

A chubby older woman with thick glasses and a long coat stood near him and kept looking at him, sad-faced with a gentle expression of sympathy. He smiled back politely as the priest delivered his graveside remarks.

The burial service concluded with both coffins descending into the earth, adjacent plots, as designated in Barry and Cheryl's joint will. They had always wanted to be buried together. *I'm sure they never dreamed it would be on the same day*, thought Adam.

The chubby older woman in the long coat stepped over to him. She started to say, "You probably don't remember me...."

But he did, in that moment.

"Marci," he said.

It was his dad's brief second wife. He hadn't met her too many times—the marriage crumbled fast—but the encounters were always amicable.

"That's right," she said, surprised to be recognized. "You remember me."

"Of course," he said.

"I know you must find it strange to see me here.... But I got to know Cheryl a little bit. We have something in common, you know.... Your father."

"I'm sorry it didn't work out," said Adam. "For both of you. My dad has a hard time in relationships. We had our ups and downs, too."

Marci dismissed his comment with a wave of her hand. "That was so long ago. We move on."

"Yes," said Adam, with full understanding. "We move on."

"I find the cemetery peaceful," she said. "I come here a lot. I have family in this cemetery."

Adam nodded as she shared some more musings in her soft, melancholy voice. She asked about his life and he gave her the UK update. Then he found an opening and asked her the question everyone had been asking him: "Have you seen my father?"

She shook her head. "Not for years. I ran into him at a Walmart store, maybe five years ago, in Arlington Heights. He wasn't much into talking. You know how he is."

"But isn't it weird that he's not here? I mean, they were married. Maybe just a few years, but still." He wanted to add, but held back: "Wouldn't he want to at least see *me*?"

"Your father's had a tough time, from what I've heard," said Marci. "He might not want to be around other people. His brother Reed died, just in the last year."

"Uncle Reed?" Adam was stunned. He had heard nothing about it. He grew angry at his father for not telling him, and then realized his father probably had no contact information for him. "What happened to Uncle Reed?"

"Heart attack."

"Oh my God. He wasn't that old."

"Hey, we're all getting into that age group, me included," said Marci with her typical tone of glum futility. "Who knows, they could be burying me next. I've already reserved my lot."

"Uncle Reed died...." said Adam, still letting it sink in.

"I missed that one. I heard about it later, otherwise I would have gone," said Marci, with a drag of disappointment in her voice. She kept talking, but Adam became lost in a swirl of his own thoughts.

Finally, he blurted, "I need to find my dad. Do you know where I can reach him? I don't have a current address or phone number."

"I don't know," said Marci. "I think he moved from this area, but I'm not sure. He moves around a lot, you know."

"Right," said Adam, suddenly determined to find him.

Then Marci said, "Why don't you call Reed's wife? She'll know. She's in the area still, I'm pretty sure. What's her name? Sandy. That's it, right? Sandy."

"Yes," said Adam. "Aunt Sandy. I'll start there. I'm going to find my dad. I just think...I should."

"Tell him hi for me," said Marci. "I still want him to do well, you know. Just because we didn't work out, I don't hold that against him. Tell him Marci says hello and to hang in there."

Adam nodded. The mourners were beginning to move back to their cars, heads hung low, solemn and quiet. His mother and stepfather were in the ground, lives finished.

"Yes," he said to something or nothing, his mind buried in a cloud of thoughts.

Back at his hotel room near the Chicago-Skokie border, Adam set up his laptop and searched for a phone number for Sandy DeCastro. He eventually tracked it down and successfully reached her, prepared for an awkward, uncomfortable call.

"Hello, Aunt Sandy? This is a name from the past," he said. "It's Adam DeCastro… the son of Danny DeCastro."

"Yes, of course," she responded warmly but with a tinge of alarm, unsure of his reason for calling.

"First, I'm—I'm sorry to hear about Uncle Reed. I didn't know. I only recently found out. I've been living in London."

"Thank you, Adam," she said. "Yes, I heard you were in London. You've been there for some time?"

"Almost ten years," he said. "I'm back in the states for the first time in a long time. There was a tragedy…I don't know if you heard…. My mom and stepdad died in a car accident."

She gasped, unaware, and immediately offered her condolences.

After he hurried past the news of the crash and assured her he was okay, devastated but managing through it, he moved the dialogue to his real reason for calling.

"My dad wasn't at my mom's funeral," he said. "I don't know where he is. I would really like to contact him and see him, while I'm in the states. I'm worried about him. I have an old phone number and address, but they're outdated."

"Yes," she said. "I can help you. I have a phone number. As for an address—I think he moved recently, but I'm not sure where. I do have a post office box. I've been sending him various documents—you know, they sold the family business."

"Yes, I heard," said Adam.

"I can understand him not going to the funeral," said Sandy. "He—he really keeps to himself, as you know."

"I know."

"He's had a very rough couple of years. He's been bouncing from job to job. His brother died. His father is in terrible shape...."

"Grandpa DeCastro?" said Adam.

"Yes, he's got Alzheimer's," said Sandy, continuing a tone of sadness. "His health is really declining badly. He's in a residential care facility up in Kenosha. Reed used to go there with Danny to visit, and he'd come home in tears...."

Adam froze for a moment, gripping the phone. "Grandpa DeCastro is in Kenosha?"

"They found a good place—not as expensive as the ones closer to Chicago. I've been there, it's nice."

"Kenosha," said Adam again, softly.

After he concluded the call with his Aunt Sandy, Adam immediately tried reaching his father at the phone number she had provided.

He called repeatedly, into the night, without success. Each time, after eight rings, he was dumped into a generic voicemail inbox. Twice, he left a message, short in length but encouraging contact.

He sat in his hotel room, television murmuring on low volume, barely watching it, eating room service food, waiting to hear from his dad.

His father did not call back.

The next day, still determined to connect with his elusive father, Adam used the mailing address Aunt Sandy had given him. He drove to the post office facility where his dad had a P.O. box. He parked across the street in the rental car, sat and waited.

Sooner or later, he figured, his father would appear to get his mail.

Adam listened to music through a pair of earbuds, observing every patron who entered the building.

After four hours, he grew restless and hungry. He made a

brisk visit to a Subway restaurant next to the post office for a sandwich, bag of chips, and soft drink. He returned to Subway an hour later for a bathroom break.

After seven hours, he questioned his plans. What if his dad only picked up his mail once a week?

After eight hours, Adam was ready to return to the hotel. It was getting dark. The post office service windows were closed, but residents could still come in and access their post office boxes in the front lobby area.

Adam didn't even know if he could identify his father—all these years later—in the dying light.

Then, as the sunset completed and night fully took over, Adam saw his father appear, as if lured out of hiding by the shroud of darkness.

Adam seized up with anxiety and ripped the earbuds from his head. He pushed closer to the window glass and studied the slow, thick man who approached the front doors of the post office, pulled one open, and stepped inside.

Heavier, yes; thinning hair, yes. Still recognizable as his father, yes.

Adam wanted to jump out and confront him but quickly recognized a nighttime ambush was the wrong way to start the reconciliation. He felt like a stalker. He knew this reunion would be fragile as hell. He wanted it to work.

Adam chose to follow his father to his home. That would give Adam a street address and then he could pay a visit in the more reasonable daylight hours with a casual opener. "I was in the neighborhood…."

Adam watched his father emerge from the post office with a handful of mail. He climbed into a branded delivery van that belonged to the family business, DeCastro Carpet Distributors. The van drove off. Adam waited ten seconds, then started up his engine and followed.

Adam stayed close, not wanting his father to suspect someone was tailing him. His father drove deeper into the city, cutting through a low-income residential community that soon gave way to a rundown-looking commercial district. As the traffic around them dropped off, Adam felt more noticeable, and he increased the distance between them.

Adam shuddered. They were entering a really rough-looking neighborhood. Then the delivery van took a turn, traveled through what looked like an industrial park, and Adam realized where he was.

Grandpa DeCastro's carpet warehouse.

Adam had worked there a couple of summers as a young kid, between his final years of high school, helping out with a variety of odd jobs such as cutting and organizing carpet sample squares and sweeping the showroom.

The van turned onto a driveway. Adam stopped following his father. He pulled over to the side of the road and dimmed his lights, watching the van drive up to the warehouse and then slip behind it, disappearing into a back area with garages and a loading dock.

Adam's heart filled with sadness. Was his father living in the old warehouse? Was he broke? Was he unwell? The whole thing didn't sit well: his absence at the funeral, the unreturned calls, the unlisted address.

Adam stayed for forty-five minutes, hoping his father was just making a delivery of some sort and didn't actually live here. But his dad did not drive back out. The few lights inside the building soon went dark.

"Oh, Dad…." said Adam in a sad whisper.

Adam began to notice a couple of scruffy individuals inching closer to his car—homeless? drug addicts?—and decided it was time to leave.

Adam drove back to the hotel, emotionally exhausted.

As soon as he got back to his room, he called Janis. He told her everything.

"I don't know what to do," he said. "I can't just leave him like this."

"You have to go back there," she said. "Tomorrow, during the day, go back and talk to him."

"I don't think he wants to talk to me. It's no different than ten years ago."

"You must do it," said Janis, always the voice of cool reason in her British accent. "You're in Chicago. This is your big chance.

Who knows when you'll get another? Adam, you'll regret it if you don't go."

"I know," he said. "You're right. Jesus, what a week."

"Be strong, babe. I love you."

"I love you, too." The separation across the ocean was killing him.

After the call ended, Adam stared out the hotel window for a very long time, watching the street traffic slowly reduce in volume and hoping he could settle down his jumping heart.

Chapter
Twenty-Eight

Adam returned to the warehouse in the daylight, after a quick breakfast and extra coffee. He was surprised to find a cluster of cars parked outside. He pulled up his rental car alongside them. His curiosity deepened: *What kind of operation is going on in there?*

The front entrance to the building did not respond to his tug: locked. He circled the structure to try other doors and found them equally secured. He peered in several windows and observed nothing of interest. The place was dark and appeared largely empty, except for some leftover carpet rolls in batches on the floor and slotted in shelving units.

Adam knew the warehouse fairly well, having worked there a few short stints as a summer job. Adam's Uncle Reed helped manage the business, but Adam's father had no interest, even when better employment opportunities proved elusive. Grandpa DeCastro ran the company with hard-nosed focus and passion, with little patience for Adam's teenage slacker attitude. It was not one of Adam's fonder memories, and he could now fault his own abrasive immaturity as a bigger factor in the unpleasantness than the environment itself.

Looking for an entry, the best option appeared to be a cracked-open, tilt window in an alleyway, well above his height.

He found several old, wooden pallets he could stack, but they promptly came apart as he moved them, rotted with age and pulling loose from rusty nails. As he looked around for something else to elevate his height, his eyes stopped on his rental car. He strolled over, hopped in, and drove the vehicle into the alley, as close as he could get to the building without scraping against it, positioning under the window.

Fortunately, the grounds were desolate and abandoned, so there was no one watching his obvious break-in. He climbed onto the roof of the car, reached the window, and widened the opening by tilting the framed glass up. He stuffed himself forward, held onto the window rim the best he could and swung his legs through. He hung for a moment inside the warehouse, felt hopeful about the cushion of carpets below, and let himself drop.

He landed with a bruising thud, kicking up a nasty cloud of dust. He remained still for a long moment to see if anyone heard his arrival, but the large, open-area warehouse stayed silent. He stood up, brushed himself off, and walked down an aisle of tall shelves. He felt awkward about his sneaky entry but knew he couldn't return to England without seeing his father and checking on his well-being.

What the hell is he doing in here? thought Adam. *Running a meth lab?*

The notion made him laugh and increased his discomfort. Whatever was going on, it didn't feel right. His father didn't seem like the type to set up an illegal enterprise, but he was a remote and unpredictable man, spending more time in the privacy of his own thoughts than engaging with the world around him.

Adam advanced across the warehouse, stepping around debris, until he reached the back wall. He passed through the entryway that led to a long hall of offices, employee facilities, and smaller stock rooms.

The area was lit up. A moment's pause confirmed the presence of people. Adam could hear a distant, lively conversation.

And music.

By the upbeat tone of the voices and melodies, the gathering sounded like a party.

Adam smiled. He continued to stand still for a moment, listening, and then his smile faded as he grew perplexed.

The music...sounded like Christmas songs.

In the summertime?

Not moving, Adam continued listening. It was definitely a Christmas tune.

Santa Claus is Coming to Town.

He couldn't quite hear the content of the conversations, but it certainly sounded happy with frequent eruptions of laughter.

"This is so fucked up," said Adam, and he advanced further into the back offices. The space had changed from what he remembered. There was an area blocked off by a large black curtain. He pushed through the curtain and entered a dark corridor. He walked through a strange, narrow maze of plain walls and closed doors. It smelled like fresh construction. As he continued toward the party, he heard the clinking of silverware, plates, and glasses; there was definitely some kind of festive meal going on. He caught a whiff of food. Adam swore he could smell ham... and gingerbread?

And the pine needles of a Christmas tree.

The sounds of celebration brought him to a closed door outlined in a thin frame of light.

Winter Wonderland played loudly now. Someone was singing along.

Adam could hear the assorted voices of men and women. Was something kinky going on? The party sounds continued to erupt in periodic laughter, like a big, private joke.

The mystery was too much. Adam couldn't stand it anymore. He grabbed the handle and threw open the door.

Adam's vision filled with bright light and color, and it took a moment for his eyes to adjust. He stood before a big dining room filled with people and decorated for Christmas. The participants, old and young, were neatly dressed for the holidays, seated around a festive dinner table, enjoying a feast of food and wine. Against the wall, a Christmas tree sparkled with lights and tinsel, surrounded by a cluster of brightly wrapped packages. A stereo system played music from a compact disc player. A dog in a Christmas sweater circled the table, sniffing for dropped food.

Adam recognized no one in the room—except for his father, who sat with his arm around an unfamiliar woman. He wore a red and green sweater. He looked straight at Adam and his big smile collapsed.

"Dad?" said Adam.

Everyone around the table immediately stopped talking and stared at the intruder, halting their conversations in midsentence.

The room turned silent, except for the continued jingle of Christmas music.

Danny stared at Adam.

Adam stared back. He waited for his father's reply.

Danny appeared stunned, flustered. He looked around the table of holiday dinner companions. Then he returned his gaze to Adam...and slowly broke out into an uneasy grin.

He stood up from the table and offered his hand.

"Why, hello! Look who's come to join us," said Danny. "It's Cousin Bert!"

Adam absorbed the comment, wrinkled his brow and said, "Uh, no, Dad. I'm your son."

Adam's remark was met with a hard chuckle from his father. "Son? That's not true." He turned to a handsome young man in a matching sweater who sat next to him at the table. "William is my son."

"Excuse me?" said Adam.

"This is William. My son. Bertie, what has gotten into you? Have you stopped taking your meds?"

"I'm not...Cousin Bertie," said Adam in a perplexed voice. The whole scene appeared like a hallucination or twisted dream.

"Of course you are," said Danny. "Would you like to join us for dinner?"

Adam looked at the silenced faces around the table.

Danny gestured to them, one by one. "Bertie, you know my parents...George and Karen. And this is my brother Reed, his wife Sandy, and two daughters...."

Adam grew speechless. None of them looked like the real thing—perhaps some vague similarities, but it wasn't helped by the fact that two of the individuals around the table were, in fact, dead in real life.

"Reed has been sharing exciting news," said Danny proudly. "He's getting into his second career, sports broadcasting."

"Reed" smiled and nodded, then took a long sip of wine.

"This is my son, William," said Danny, gesturing to the young man in the matching sweater and placing a hand on his shoulder. William wore an expression frozen with uncertainty. "He's going to med school. He's going to be very successful, and he *loves* his mother and father."

Adam could feel an intentional sting in his father's tone.

"And this, Bertie, as you will remember, is my wife, Lisetta." Danny leaned over an attractive, heavily made-up older woman in a festive dress. He gave her a gentle kiss on the cheek.

She smiled at Adam and said, "So good to see you, Bertie."

"Lisetta is celebrating her new bestseller," said Danny. "It just topped The New York Times bestseller list."

Adam said nothing. He looked around the room. Was this one big practical joke? A bizarre prank? What was the point of such an elaborate room full of make-believe?

"Last, but not least," said Danny, reaching down to scratch the head of the wandering dog, "this is Toby Junior. Do you like his sweater?"

"Dad," said Adam, "are you out of your fucking mind?"

Danny's face immediately switched from jovial to stern. "Bertie, I would like to have a word with you in the other room." He turned to Lisetta. "Honey, take care of our guests. Make sure everyone has enough wine. I'm going to step out for a moment."

"Of course, darling," said Lisetta.

The next holiday song kicked in: *It's the Most Wonderful Time of the Year.*

Adam followed his father out of the Christmas scene.

They stepped into the dull light of the plain corridor.

"What the hell are you doing here? How did you get in?" snapped Danny, immediately dropping the holiday cheer.

"Why does it matter how I got in? I'm in, I'm here. I was worried about you. You weren't at the funeral."

"I didn't need to go."

"She was your wife."

"No. She was never my wife."

"What are you talking about?"

"Lisetta is my wife."

"I went to that funeral alone. Everyone was asking about you. Even Marci was there."

"Marci? I don't know who that is."

Adam let out an exhale of exasperation. *"Your second wife."*

"I've only had one wife. Lisetta."

"Dad, you know that's not true."

"Don't tell me what's true," said Danny. "What you're talking about—none of it matters."

"Why are you acting this way?" Adam felt a rush of emotion. "My mother is dead. She died in a car crash."

"Big deal," said Danny. "So did mine."

Adam stared hard at his father, speechless. His head was spinning.

"I did something about it," said Danny. "I went back and changed my life. I rebuilt this family. You know how you wrote me out of your life? Well, I've written you out of mine."

"Dad, I...." Adam didn't know what to say. Was this the final result of their long separation? A refusal to even acknowledge him anymore?

"Dad, I'm sorry," said Adam. "I know we've been apart. But it's not too late...to fix things between us."

"It *is* too late," said his father, matter of fact, unmoved. "I've gone back in time. I have rewritten history. You don't even exist anymore. You never happened."

Adam felt an ache of sorrow. "Dad, you're not well. I don't understand what's going on here, or who those people are, but it's not right. I think you need help. I'm being as honest and open as I can be."

"I want you to leave," his father said firmly. "I need to get back to my Christmas party. I have family to get back to."

"Yeah," said Adam. His throat tightened, and he could no longer speak without choking back more tears. He turned and left his father. He moved back through the strange maze of walls and doors. He pushed past the black curtain, seeking only one thing—the exit.

Chapter
Twenty-Nine

Danny fought past the confusion in his head, agitated by the disruption to his time travel, as he moved the Christmas props into the storage room. Lisetta worked silently at his side, handling wardrobe and wigs, putting everything in their proper place.

"We can't have any more interruptions like that," said Danny. "The time travel is sacred—you can't have elements from the old narrative interfering with the new."

"Do you think he's coming back?" asked Lisetta.

"He doesn't even live in this country anymore," said Danny, angry. "He moved across the ocean to get away from me. He should stay away."

"You recovered the scene nicely," said Lisetta. "Cousin Bertie. He's just a bit player in our larger universe."

"There will be no more scenes with Cousin Bertie," said Danny. "That was a brief cameo, nothing more."

Lisetta placed the box of Christmas tree ornaments on a high shelf. After a few minutes, she stepped aside and covered her eyes.

Danny watched her. "Are you okay?"

"Yes. Never mind. I'm just—"

"What is it?"

"I started thinking about Mindy."

"Don't do that."

"I can't help it. I know we have William. But you have another son, I have a daughter...."

"Not in this new life," said Danny firmly. "We have to

erase them from our mind. Otherwise all of this...the time machine...it all breaks down. You have to believe. You can't doubt."

He embraced her, and she hugged back, tight. She sniffed back a few tears, then regained her composure.

"I had never met him before," said Lisetta. "I guess it just got to me...actually seeing him for real."

"I haven't seen him in years," said Danny. "And that's the way he wanted it."

Danny tried to downplay it to Lisetta, but he couldn't get Adam out of his head. His son's image stayed in his thoughts, no matter how hard he tried to push him out. One thing in particular made a haunting impression—how much Adam resembled Danny at that age. In a twist of time, it was almost like encountering his younger self. The height, build, hair color and facial features were all there.

Danny let go and stepped back from Lisetta. He stared into her soft, pretty face and the small smudges of mascara around her big, dark eyes. This was the face he needed to replace all other thoughts and images. The woman he loved more than any other person on the planet.

"No more disruptions," he said to her. "We will be strong together. We will make this work. There's no going back."

Unable to sleep, Danny gently climbed out of bed, careful not to wake Lisetta. He maneuvered through the cramped Neutrality Room that served as living quarters. He had a craving. He needed a time travel trip to settle his nerves. It was still a few hours before dawn, but he couldn't wait. His dreams and thoughts were stubbornly focused on the wrong narrative, the one he was working so hard to replace.

Danny passed through the black curtain. He chose not to turn on any lights. He wanted a warm entry into his refurbished past. He knew the skinny corridors of the back warehouse quite well, grazing the walls softly with his hands and following each turn. He mentally prepared himself for the transition to his sacred aviator den.

He stepped through the passageway toward his destination.

He reached across darkness for a door handle—and grasped air.

The door was already open.

Danny froze and his senses jolted fully alert. He caught a whiff of an awful smell. The room reeked of piss and body odor. He heard the rise and fall of a raspy, gurgling snore.

Danny moved quickly for the light switch and his foot hit something unexpected on the floor. He yelled out, heard another voice yell, and almost tumbled to the ground. He slammed against the wall and smacked on the lights.

There was a filthy, bearded man in tattered clothing on the ground. His eyes bulged large with fright. He threw up his arms to defend himself, as if expecting to be kicked again.

"Who the hell are you?" demanded Danny.

"Nobody!" said the man in a rough, hoarse voice, followed by a deep cough.

"How did you get in here?"

"I'm sorry!" The man started to rise, struggling for balance on shaky legs. "I din't know anyone was in here."

Danny's mood turned from startled to angry. It was a bum, a homeless derelict, probably accustomed to finding shelter in abandoned buildings. He appeared scared and confused.

"You have to leave here now!" said Danny forcefully.

The intruder nodded vigorously. "Yes. Yes."

"Danny, what's wrong?" Lisetta shouted from the outside corridor, awakened by the noise.

"Just a...." Danny struggled for a politer word than bum or hobo. "Transient."

"A what?"

He walked the man out of the aviator den and led him back through the black curtain. They entered the main hall, which was now fully lit.

Lisetta, in nightgown and robe, gasped. Toby Junior, at her side, started to bark at the stranger.

"He's leaving," said Danny.

"I'm leaving," muttered the homeless man.

Danny took him through the warehouse to one of the exits. They passed a broken window, revealing the visitor's entry point. Before shutting him outdoors in the black of night, Danny warned, "I have a gun. If I see you again, I will shoot. This is my home, do you understand?"

The man nodded, staring at Danny for a long moment before he left, as if Danny was the crazy one.

Rejoining Lisetta, Danny was jacked up, wired with tension. "I found a broken window near the front. It was that easy. He just broke a window with a rock and climbed inside."

"It's an old, decrepit building," said Lisetta. "He probably thought it was empty."

"God dammit, you can still smell him," said Danny. "He better not have touched anything. It's bad enough we're getting mice in here. This is *our* story, and none of this other shit is allowed."

"Honey, it's okay," said Lisetta, stroking his arm, trying to calm him. "Let's go back to sleep. We'll board up the window in the morning."

Danny felt derailed, pushed off his rightful narrative by an invisible force. "For this to work, it has to be a controlled environment," he said. "We have a plan. We have scripts. We write the stories. We decide the cast."

"I know," said Lisetta. Toby Junior remained close to their side, tail wagging with blissful obliviousness. Danny reached down to scratch the dog's fur.

"You, me, Toby, this is *our* life," said Danny. "Everyone else—it's invitation only."

"Life isn't that predictable," said Lisetta.

"Yeah? Well, we'll make it go our way."

Two days later, Danny and Lisetta awoke to the sound of Toby Junior barking. Danny sat up, jolted awake. Lisetta froze still, eyes opened wide.

"Listen," she said.

They heard voices, laughter.

Toby Junior anxiously paced at the door, wanting to be released from the room.

"Intruders," said Danny.

"Now what?" groaned Lisetta.

"You stay here," said Danny. "I'm getting the gun."

"Danny!" she exclaimed. "Please be careful."

Danny pulled on pants over his boxer shorts and quickly laced on a pair of gym shoes. "Toby, you stay here," he instructed, but the dog very much wanted to follow him. Danny had to partially open the door and squeeze out, keeping Toby inside the room with Lisetta. "Stay. Good boy."

Danny hurried to his office, feeling through the dark corridors. Inside his office, he turned on a small lamp and reached into the back of a bottom desk drawer. He pulled out the handgun, checked to make sure it remained loaded, and paused to listen for voices.

It sounded like they were in the main warehouse, creating a trail of excited chatter that bounced and echoed in the large, open space. He wasn't sure how many of them had invaded the building.

Danny moved quickly, determined to protect his home at all costs from unwanted elements.

Entering the main warehouse, his eyes caught the movement of a long flashlight beam several aisles away, and now the voices were clear enough to hear words.

"Just a bunch of carpet, man!"

"Maybe they got computers and shit."

The voices sounded like teenagers.

Danny hurried across the aisles in a crouch, getting closer but staying out of the path of their flashlight. He got close enough to see their outlines—two animated shadows, tall and gangly, energized and giddy. He was unable to identify any ethnicity—white, black, Hispanic—and it didn't matter. They were one thing: intruders.

"Freeze!" shouted Danny, and his voice boomed and echoed. "I have a gun!"

Startled, the boy handling the flashlight dropped it to the concrete, where it smacked apart, releasing the batteries and plunging the warehouse into near-total darkness.

"Shit, man, there's somebody in here."

Danny remained very still. After a long pause, the boys bantered in a harsh whisper.

"Which way?"

"I don't know!"

"This is fucked, man!"

"How was I supposed to know there's a security guard?"

"Ssh, don't move."

Danny could sense their location in the dark. He cleanly maneuvered the warehouse space from memory. He reached a long aisle of shelving units that separated him from the boys on the other side. There was a narrow, steel rolling ladder a few steps away to give him easy access to the top of the shelves.

Still gripping the gun in one hand, he took hold of the ladder rail with the other. He ascended to the top, occasionally making metal creaks that caused the boys to reengage in chatter.

"What's that?"

"I don't know."

"Is he close?"

"Shut up, he'll hear us."

Reaching the top shelf, elevated fifty feet from the ground, Danny slowly began walking the length of the aisle. He stepped carefully around leftover rolls of carpet. He kept as quiet as possible.

Nearing the end of the aisle, he moved toward the edge… directly above the two would-be thieves below.

He was perfectly positioned to aim the gun downward, at the tops of their heads, and shoot them dead.

He thought about it briefly and disregarded it.

He had a better idea: the twelve-foot, tightly wound carpet roll at his side. He leaned down and dragged one end of the carpet ninety degrees to position it lengthwise at the edge of the shelf.

"Do you hear something?" said one of the voices below.

Danny didn't allow the other boy time to reply. He shoved hard, and the carpet fell from the shelf, plunging to the ground.

With a thud, it landed on the two intruders, knocking them flat.

They shouted in surprise—then in pain. One of them, in particular, howled about his arm, probably broken by the sudden body slam to the concrete floor.

"Get out of here!" Danny shouted down at them. *"Now!"*

"Fuck you!" one of them hollered back up at him.

Danny didn't like the response. They were slow to move from their spot—too stunned or too stubborn? He quickly stepped across the shelving platform, returning to the ladder. A part of him surged with the adrenaline of adventure, recalling the times he played in the warehouse as a young boy with his brother Reed, turning the surroundings into his own personal playground. His father always yelled at them for climbing the shelves like a jungle gym—but the thrill outweighed the threats and warnings of danger.

Danny knew what he wanted to do next. In the slight lighting, he maintained a sense of direction and stepped quickly across the warehouse floor. He advanced to another aisle where he remembered seeing one of the forklifts. It had been idle for a long time, sitting in the same spot since he moved in, but he knew the thing was reliable and old-world sturdy, ageless in a way.

Danny charged the two intruders with the forklift, blinding them with the headlamps and pounding on its horn.

The two teenagers quickly scampered from where they had been regaining their senses. One of them limped, the other held his arm.

Danny herded them like cattle, chasing them back to where they originally broke in—at the loading dock. Somehow, they had partially rolled up the door and slipped underneath.

He trapped them against the door and they scrambled through the narrow opening at the bottom in a frantic crawl on their stomachs. Perhaps they had some broken bones, but they were well enough and motivated enough to make a swift getaway.

Danny climbed off the forklift and held the gun steady for any retaliation.

He could hear the boys running away, screaming "motherfucker" at him, kicking up gravel, no longer giddy and laughing, now justly injured and terrified.

And never coming back.

After a few minutes, Danny unlocked a side door and

stepped outside the warehouse. The moon illuminated the weedy, broken asphalt. He closely surveyed the dock bay. A broken padlock rested on the ground. The intruders had cut it with bolt cutters. He found the bolt cutters several yards away.

"Thank God you're safe," said Lisetta, when he returned to her. "You didn't take your phone. I had no way to reach you. I was going to come find you, but I didn't know—"

"I took care of it," said Danny. He placed the gun on the dresser in their makeshift bedroom. She stared at it. Toby Junior wagged his tail, nosing his way between them.

"You didn't...." said Lisetta.

"No," said Danny. "I didn't fire a shot. I didn't need to."

"I don't feel safe here."

Danny hardened. "We're safe. We're safer here than anywhere out there. It was just a couple of stupid gangbangers. Forget them. They won't be back."

TRAVEL LOG: INCIDENT REPORT

There are people who don't want this experiment to succeed. They threatened to deny me this road to a better life.

Last night my laboratory was invaded by government spies. They broke in with the goal of stealing the secrets of time travel. I could not allow this to happen. Lisetta and I have committed everything to erasing the past with a new storyline. I will protect this undertaking with everything in me. I have created a controlled universe. The outside world is not welcome.

I defeated the attempts of the government spies to raid my time travel machine. They broke in through the loading dock. I have my father's gun. I chased them out with warnings to never return.

Nevertheless, I am weighed down by a blanket of insecurities. Will there be more attempts to stop me? Is another raid coming? Perhaps I will be arrested on false charges and taken away. Maybe our living quarters will be bugged, placed under surveillance or worse—firebombed by the FBI or CIA.

I am not naïve. I knew that meddling with the laws of science and physics would draw misunderstanding, opposition, and danger. I will be waiting. I will not back down.

Chapter Thirty

Detective Chico thrust out his hand. "Thank you for agreeing to meet with me."

Adam shook it firmly and said, "Absolutely."

"You want some coffee?"

"No thanks. I'm good."

"We'll go into my office."

Adam followed the tan-skinned, broad-shouldered cop out of the reception lobby, through a set of thick double doors and into the main area of the Kenosha Police Department. They passed an open section of desks humming with monotone phone conversations and keyboard pecking. Chico led Adam into his cramped office behind a glass wall and sat behind a desktop filled with tidy paper stacks and manila folders. Adam dropped into one of the plastic visitor's chairs. The detective reached for a pad of lined paper, flipped it to a new page, and clicked a ballpoint pen into action. He scribbled something, perhaps a header for the notes to come, then placed the pad back down.

He spoke in a calm tone. "As I mentioned on the phone, there's an active investigation into the death of your mother and stepfather."

"Yes," said Adam. "I'm interested in hearing more. In the beginning, they were saying it was maybe a blown tire."

"Well, in the beginning, it wasn't conclusive one way or the other. But we've been working with the Wisconsin Highway Patrol on an analysis of the crash: reviewing the car damage, the condition of the road, the tire marks, the angle of the impact, the pattern of debris. We have reason to believe your parents' car was struck by another vehicle just prior to going off the bridge."

"Another vehicle?" said Adam, surprised. "What, like a hit-and-run?"

"Yes."

Adam let it sink in. "So, someone hit them and just left the scene of the accident?"

"If it was an accident."

Adam settled back in his chair. He struggled for words. "You think—you think someone did this intentionally?"

"If another vehicle rear-ended them like that and left the scene, it's a criminal offense, whether the impact was intentional or unintentional."

"Who—why would someone do that and just leave?"

"I don't know. That's what I want to talk about. We have no witnesses, just the truck driver who discovered them when it was too late."

"I don't know of anybody that would want to do that. I don't know my stepfather that well, if he had any enemies. I—I don't know why anybody would go to that length. Maybe it was some kind of road rage with a stranger."

"Tell me about your father's relationship with your mother," said Detective Chico.

Adam took a moment and responded. "Well…they don't have one."

"Was there animosity?"

"Well, some," said Adam. "But it was so long ago. They both moved on. Why would my dad factor into any of this?"

"We have a lot of unanswered questions," said Chico. "Quite frankly, we don't even know why they were in Kenosha, forty-five miles from home. Did they have friends or family out this way?"

"No—" said Adam, and then a thought hit him, and he almost blurted it out before stopping himself. *My grandpa is in a nursing home in Kenosha.*

Chico studied him, catching a flash of alarm.

"Is something wrong?"

"No," said Adam, quickly settling into a more relaxed

expression. "I'm just—this whole thing—it's been very difficult."

"I've spoken with your aunt," said Chico. "Mia Peller. Your mother's sister. She expressed some surprise that your father wasn't at the funeral."

Adam nodded. "That's right. Yes. Not that big a surprise. Like I said, they've been apart a long time. They didn't stay in touch. Like I said…they moved on."

"But that's pretty insensitive. Not to go. She *was* married to him. They had you."

"Yes. They had me."

Chico sat back in his chair. He said, "We want to speak to your father, but we've been having a hard time reaching him. No one seems to know where he lives these days. No one has a working phone number. I would imagine you have some kind of contact with him?"

"Well," said Adam carefully. "We had a falling out. It was bad. We don't—I don't—I live in England. I don't even live in the United States anymore. I haven't been close to my mother or father in a long time."

"I see," said Chico. His eyes seemed to be studying Adam. Adam felt extremely self-conscious about everything in that moment—his expression, his tone of voice, his choice of words.

"Adam, do you know where I can find your father?"

Adam slowly shook his head. He shrugged, maintaining a blank look. "No…I'm sorry."

Chapter
Thirty-One

United flight 613 received clearance for landing.

The flight instruments glowed green on the control panel. The steady roar of the engines filled the cockpit. Captain DeCastro checked the altitude and speed indicators. He spoke to the tower on his radio.

Danny loved talking the pilot lingo. He loved the snug fit of the cushioned headset. He loved the feel of his fuzzy sheepskin upholstered chair. He felt proud in his crisp white aviation shirt, black tie and the four stripes on his shoulder that indicated he was in command.

As he reached for the throttle, he spoke to his copilot and best friend, first officer Christopher Ridley. The two shared a special bond over the magic of flying. They were an inseparable team, sharing stories and owning the skies together as they regularly crisscrossed the globe.

When Ridley didn't respond, Danny repeated his line.

The expected response remained stillborn, and then Danny turned from the instrument panel to look at his partner.

Then Danny exploded.

"What the hell is wrong with you? Put that fucking thing away!"

Ridley was on his iPhone.

"It's 1997, that doesn't exist. You are ruining this!"

Ridley remained focused on the phone. "Hold it, man. I told you, my girlfriend's sick. This could be important."

Danny threw off his headset. "You've ruined the whole fucking scene!" He released himself from his seatbelt and stormed out of the cockpit. He passed through an opening that led to the rest of the room, revealing the absence of a passenger cabin, just open space and the tools of illusion to create a cockpit set.

Danny shut off the noise machine that replicated the heavy whine of jet engines. He could no longer fool himself into feeling immersed in blue sky and clouds: now he only saw crudely painted walls. The pilot console was powerless, an assembly of make-believe. The voices from the radio tower didn't exist except in his head.

And his "best friend," the best friend he never had, was not playing the part.

Ridley stepped out of the flight deck, headset hung around his neck, quickly stuffing the iPhone back into his pocket. "Relax. I just had to check on her, it's a bad flu. We can pick up where we left off. It's not like there's an audience or something. Let's get going."

"No," said Danny firmly. "I can't. I was in the zone. I can't just go back. You ruined the continuity. The scene is tainted. You were told to leave your phone outside. This doesn't work when you bring a piece of the present into the past."

"You have weird rules," said Ridley. "This whole set is fake. You know, your airplane doesn't actually fly."

"We're using our imagination," said Danny. "You're an actor. Act."

Ridley shook his head. "I'm trying, but this is bullshit. I'm just not feeling it."

Danny flew into a rage. He fired his actor on the spot. He demanded for him to leave. "And don't take the uniform!" he added.

Ridley shrugged wordlessly, expressing no dismay over losing the role. He left the cramped airplane set and entered a skinny corridor. He began pulling off the shirt as he walked away. "Careful with the buttons!" Danny shouted after him.

Ridley retreated through the black curtain and returned to the changing room.

Lisetta caught up with Danny in the outer hallway.

"What's all this yelling?"

"In the middle of the scene, he's texting with his girlfriend!

He brought his cell phone. The scene clearly says March 12, 1997. Does it not?"

"He knows the rules. We briefed him."

"I can't believe I cast that idiot as my best friend."

"He was good in rehearsals."

"No. He was okay."

Before leaving, Ridley returned in his street clothes to address them a final time. "You two are nuts," he said. "I hope you seek help. You're a couple of lunatics with some kind of weird fetish. I don't know what your scene is, but something's not right."

"Go back to your amateur theater," shot back Danny. "We only want real actors here."

Ridley chuckled, more amused than offended, and left.

Danny began pacing the floor, worked up. Lisetta suggested something to settle him down: an impromptu time travel to their teenage years. "Let's just hang out, me and you, watch some TV or something, without a care in the world."

Danny stopped pacing. He thought about it. "Yeah. Okay."

They changed into colorful, youthful Eighties teen fashions. They fit into wigs that helped transform their look into shaggy kids. They picked a specific date and transitioned through the dark time warp tunnel to Danny's boyhood bedroom. Once there, they lounged on his bed and watched period-specific television shows to feel snug in the warm blanket of nostalgia. They watched episodes of *Family Ties, Mr. Belvidere,* and *The A Team* from a hidden DVD player as if they were viewing live TV. Later they played Top 40 hits from 1988, pretending they were tuned in to an AM radio station on a clock radio, keeping the real source—an MP3 player—hidden out of view. One of Lisetta's favorite songs came on: "Never Gonna Give You Up" by Rick Astley. She got giddy, and soon Danny and Lisetta were making out like teenagers on the mattress. He felt himself get hard, but she wouldn't let him go all the way. "Your parents are home," she said.

"No, they're not," he said. "They—they went out to a movie. They went to see—what came out in 1988?"

"I don't lose my virginity yet," she told him. "Not now." She stroked his wig for a moment, which he could barely feel, and it made him self-conscious and irritated about the balding head beneath.

Later in the day, after traveling back to the present, Danny and Lisetta huddled in the office to determine the next episode in their timeline.

"I know what it is," said Danny. "I think we're ready for the big one. I want to go back in time and marry you. I think we're ready for the proposal scene."

Lisetta let out a happy gasp. "Really?"

Danny looked across the lengthy timeline taped to the wall. He pointed to a gap waiting to be filled. "We've had so many scenes come before and after, but not the big moment itself. I want to write the script where I ask your hand in marriage."

"Make sure I say yes," said Lisetta.

"Of course you will," said Danny. "It's already destiny."

"I can't wait to see what you write."

TRAVEL LOG:
REVERSAL 24Y 10M 21D

Today I went back in time and created the very best day of my life.

I told Lisetta I would pick her up at five in the morning for a special surprise. She wanted details and I playfully refused. I took her to Waukegan Memorial Airport, thirty-five miles north of Chicago, where I had rented a Cessna 172 Skyhawk, a cozy, single-engine, propeller aircraft.

"Aha," she said. "We are going to celebrate your pilot's license."

I just smiled, because we were going to celebrate something much more.

My timing was precise and exquisite. We lifted from the runway and took off into the skies just as dawn began to break. We flew along the shoreline of Lake Michigan, watching the sunrise on the horizon as it spread a golden shimmer across the water.

We ascended to ten thousand feet above ground level, cruising at a hundred fifty miles per hour. The engine hummed around us like a warm hug.

"It's like heaven," said Lisetta.

The moment was so perfect and magical, I didn't want it to ever end.

As we soared above the earth, illuminated by the embrace of a new day, I proposed.

I presented her with a diamond ring and asked her to marry me and unite our lives forever.

"Yes," she said, not once, but exactly five times. "Yes, Danny. Yes. *Yes*. Yes!"

We kissed delicately, straining against the safety belts of our leather seats, lips connecting in the middle of the tiny cabin.

The rest of everything else disappeared and it was only us, in this glorious moment in time, above the earth, rewriting history.

Chapter Thirty-Two

A dam sat on the bed in his hotel room, looking down at his shoes, immobilized by the steady push of disturbing thoughts.

Dad is sick. It's his mental health, he's unhinged.

Is he connected with that car crash? Why would he do something like that? What's the point?

Do I let the police talk to him? What will they think of his condition? Does he need a doctor? Is he dangerous?

Why is he living that bizarre life in the warehouse? Who is that woman with him? Is she crazy too?

Janis had been calling Adam daily for updates. He had been telling her everything...up until now. He couldn't bring himself to articulate suspicions that perhaps his father had something to do with the fatal car crash.

She wanted him home. She didn't understand why he still hadn't booked a flight back to England.

It was complicated. He wanted to go home...but this was also home, for better or worse, and he needed answers before he could leave his family a second time.

Adam let out a sigh—more like a painful shudder. He knew he had to return to his father and talk with him, better assess the situation and make a firm decision on what to do next. He wasn't nineteen anymore. He couldn't just run away and avoid his family's pathetic problems. In a strange twist of fate, he had possibly become the family's only remaining responsible adult.

In the bright sunshine of a new day, Adam returned to the warehouse. He parked the rental car and stepped up to the main entrance, a thick and scarred door, securely locked.

Adam pounded on it. He yelled out his father's name. He made the only noise on this stark block of forgotten commercial buildings, shattering the stillness.

Adam knew his presence was not welcome but felt determined to persist until someone came to the door to stop him.

Finally, he heard a dog bark.

The barking continued, getting nearer, and then the door opened following the chunky sounds of disengaged bolts and chains.

An older, haggard-looking woman stood at the entrance with a yellow Labrador retriever.

"What you want?" she said, leering with suspicion. It was the woman Adam's father had identified as his wife at the bizarre Christmas dinner scene. Only now she wore no makeup or flattering wig, covered in frumpy clothing. Her tone was unpleasant.

"I want to speak with my father."

"He's not here. He's on an errand."

"Then let me come in and wait for him," Adam said. "It's important."

"No," she said, without hesitation.

Adam shook his head in amazement. Who did this woman think she was?

"You can't just say no," said Adam. "I'm his son."

"No," she responded, with a firm tone and hard stare.

"He's my father," said Adam. "We are family. I don't know who you are, but you are not part of this family. You are bullshit."

The woman reacted with a stung expression. The wrinkles tightened across her face.

Adam didn't know who this person was, but he knew he hated her and held her accountable for contributing to his father's messed up state of mind.

"What have you done to my dad?" Adam demanded.

"He's not your father," the woman responded. "You're not his son. You don't even exist."

"What the—?" Adam lost his temper, giving in to rage. "You crazy bitch, I'm his real family. Who the hell are you? Where did you come from? Who do you think you are trying to prevent me from seeing my father?"

"*William* is our son!" she shouted at him in a coarse voice. "William, William! Our child is William, not you, not Mindy, it's William!"

Adam stared at her for a moment. "Who the hell is Mindy?"

The strange woman's expression turned from anger to shock. The name apparently triggered alarm. After appearing frozen for a long moment, tears began to fill her eyes.

"Who is Mindy?" said Adam.

She slammed the door on him.

Chapter Thirty-Three

Lisetta staggered back into the main nest of the warehouse, heart pounding in a sickening electrical crackle through her veins, head spinning. She despised herself for opening the door, allowing the outside world to creep into the sanctuary she and Danny had worked so hard to build physically, mentally, and emotionally.

Danny's son had punched a hole through the wall of her new world, representing an alternate version of the truth, a symbol of everything that still lived outside the warehouse, including her daughter Mindy.

Lisetta cursed. She had done so well training her mind to erase Mindy and allow her to slip away in a fog like some distant dream. But now the harder Lisetta fought to push away her memory, the stronger it seemed to push back.

Knees weakened, Lisetta nearly collapsed in the time travel office, as if gravity wanted to beat her down to the ground. She desperately needed Danny to return, her anchor in this other narrative, but he was out buying supplies—props, toiletries, food—basic necessities. Without his presence to assure her of the victory of time travel, she felt like she was sliding into a pit of terrible truths that clawed upward to reclaim her.

Lisetta sobbed, hyperventilating. *"I've abandoned my baby."* She desperately needed to see Mindy. The floodgates had opened, and every repressed flashback flickered bright like a movie. She tore into a closet and dug deep to retrieve forbidden things—her Iowa purse and pocketbook, filled with identification and collateral belonging to a different woman than the one fabricated through time travel. This other woman had married another man, moved to Eldridge, and lived a long and boring life made bearable by the presence of a wonderful, beautiful daughter.…

Lisetta pulled out a small photo of Mindy from her pocket-book, tucked between old coupons and credit cards. If Danny had been present, he would have stopped her and blocked the reentry, but he was gone, absent at the worst possible time, unable to prevent this horrible and stomach-churning relapse.

Lisetta stared at the sweet face of her daughter and confronted the unthinkable: a child with a dead father and missing mother, life shattered, lost and alone.

A war broke out in her head, voices fighting back and forth, as if two personas battled for dominance.

Mindy is not real. You have replaced that life and now it never existed.

Mindy is waiting for you. You are still her mother. You cannot change your life story. You cannot alter who you really are.

In the office, inserted between a desk and the wall, Danny had stashed a bathroom mirror he had taken down when they settled in together. One of the very first rules of time travel had been no mirrors, no reflections of any kind, to betray their altered storyline. She had not seen herself—stared into her own eyes—since freshening up in the bathroom of the Chicago bar where Danny met her after she left Iowa.

When she applied makeup now, it was from memory or with Danny's assistance. In particular, he loved to apply the mascara. He was generous with it. He said it made her eyes more "alive".…

Face your reality.

Don't do it. Everything will be undone!

Do it for Mindy. You need this. You can't hide from the truth any longer.

Lisetta slid the mirror out of the narrow space. She turned it around and settled the four-by-three-foot frame against the wall, propped to face her, filling her eyes with an abrupt, close-up reflection.

Lisetta entered the forbidden world.

She was old and puffy. Her bloodshot eyes were ringed with dark folds. Wrinkles invaded her features and created sagging jowls below her pale cheeks. Her hair was not luscious and full, but thin and dry and surrendered to streaks of gray. Her neck was thick and graceless, wired with ugly, prominent veins and discolored with age spots. It was everything she didn't want to be.

She also glimpsed the beginning of her torso and unconsciously placed her hands on her body, feeling the awkward bulges of body fat, the inevitable casing of someone whose trim youth had all but disappeared.

Lisetta screamed in hatred at the woman revealed before her. She spun away from the mirror and grabbed the back of a wooden desk chair. She slammed the chair into the mirror, shattering the glass to pieces. She pounded away repeatedly, solid blows, pulverizing the despised woman to oblivion, until the chair broke apart and there was nothing left to smash with or against.

But the image continued to exist. It lived inside her head now. She punched at her skull and tore at her hair, but it refused to go away.

Chapter
Thirty-Four

Danny discovered Lisetta sitting on the floor of the office, shaking and wide-eyed amid shards of mirror and chunks of broken chair. She was breathing heavily. When he asked what was wrong, she exhaled two words. "Panic attack."

Her purse sat on the ground nearby. Then Danny noticed the small photograph in her trembling hand...a high school graduation portrait of her daughter, Mindy.

"You're going to be okay," said Danny, crouching alongside her. "Everything's fine. You just had a...moment." Slowly he reached over and slid the photograph out of her grasp, carefully watching her response, prepared for a jump.

She did not resist.

Danny inserted the photo into the breast pocket of his shirt. He asked, "Would you like a drink? Something to settle your nerves?"

She shook her head, not looking at him. She stared forward at the wall, where the mirror had been.

"I feel claustrophobic," she said. "Like the walls are closing in."

Danny lowered his crouch to sit on the floor alongside her, careful of the pieces of broken mirror. He put his arm around her, gently.

"It's just a little cabin fever," he said in a soothing voice.

"I need natural light. I haven't been out in the real world for days. Or is it weeks?"

"Honey, this is our reality."

"I don't know what's real or not anymore." Then she hung

her head, as if in shame. "My daughter needs me."

Danny tightened the arm around her shoulders. "I need you. William needs you. Toby needs you."

When that didn't generate a response, he said, "You're finally getting the life you always wanted. That you deserved."

"I'm old," she said. "I'm fat."

"No. You're not. I don't see it, so it's not true."

Her body seemed to relax, slowly, and her breathing became softer, settling down.

Danny stroked her hair, continuing to speak in a steady, reassuring voice. "I have an idea to make you feel better. Let's go on a special trip to the past. You need to feel young again. There's too much angst about aging. Let's turn back the clock. Let's be twenty-one again. In fact, let's celebrate your twenty-first birthday. How does that sound? You want to be twenty-one?"

She nodded.

He smiled.

"I'll get to work on the script right away," he said. "Here's the concept—we're in a bar, a nightclub, on your twenty-first birthday, celebrating your first legal drink. Doesn't that sound fun? Just me and you. We'll dress up. The club will play all your favorite music. We'll be madly in love. What do you want for your first drink? A mixed drink? Some Jell-O shots? Whiskey sour? Gin and tonic? Rum and Coke?"

Her lips formed a thin, wavering smile. "Rum and Coke... sounds nice."

"Rum and coke it is! And we'll create a special driver's license for when you get carded, and you prove to the world that you have just turned twenty-one."

Her smile grew. "Can the ID have a photo? Of me at twenty-one?"

"Of course," said Danny. "That's easy. A little magic, a little Photoshop, and you are twenty-one again."

As Danny prepared for the time travel trip, his cell phone buzzed several times with an annoying poke from his faded, but not totally absent, prior life. Adam was trying to reach him again. Danny finally tossed the phone in a drawer and shut it with the ringtone muted. He refused to acknowledge Adam. Eventually Adam would get the hint and go away, returning to his own alternate life in England. There was no reason either one of them needed to revisit the mistakes of a storyline both had abandoned.

Danny sat at his desk and quickly wrote a script for the twenty-first birthday. It flowed out of him as if unfolding in real time. He captured the dialogue overheard in his head and described the setting he could practically observe in front of him.

The set was easy: the club was dark. All he needed was a table, a couple of chairs, two tall drinks and an "off-screen" music source populated with the right playlist.

Getting them into the proper appearance took longer. Danny and Lisetta spent over an hour in the wardrobe room. Sample photos filled the walls, cut out of old magazines and posted with adhesive tape, to inform period-specific clothing and hairstyles, including Danny's personal favorites. Lisetta squeezed into a corset and wore a large wig of big hair that was stylishly feathered in layers. She wore a hot pink blouse with a low neckline and pumped-up shoulder pads. Her black leather skirt hugged tight, like a second skin. Danny helped her apply light-colored lipstick, thick eyelashes, and pink rouge. In turn, she adjusted his hair. Danny wore a shaggy brown toupee to cover his bald spot. He slipped into loose parachute pants and a striped rugby shirt. He pulled on tube socks and a pair of striped Adidas gym shoes.

Danny felt jittery with excitement but could sense Lisetta was still not fully in the mood, complying but quiet.

Danny and Lisetta entered the ritual of time travel, setting the controls for the desired year, month, and date, mentally blocking out everything that existed outside of the chosen moment. They slipped through the split in the black curtain, entering a dark and twisty passage, advancing toward the faint glow of a doorknob. Once the door was opened, and light returned to their eyes, the void was replaced with a warm immersion into a precise setting at an exact moment. In a crashing wave of letting go, nothing else existed.

They took their seats to the playful dance music of Madonna. They exchanged banter with an unseen, unheard woman named Mary, who was tending to the tables and accepted their drink orders—after requiring Lisetta to show her driver's license, which she did with prompt confidence.

The drinks appeared on the tabletop and Danny cheered on Lisetta to take her first legal sip of adulthood.

She did, modestly, and made an awkward attempt to smile.

Danny could sense something was still not right.

Nevertheless, he moved forward into the prepared conversation with gusto.

She responded gamely, but soon drifted off script and appeared distracted. Instead of expressing happiness, she was speaking of discontent.

"Those aren't your lines," hissed Danny under his breath.

But she continued to improvise, inappropriately for the scene, speaking in a manner that did not fit the mood and setting.

He began to get mad, prodding her to get back on track.

"The foot scene," he said.

"What?"

"God dammit, you know, you saw the script—there's the foot scene, remember?"

Danny had crafted a kinky moment where Lisetta, giddy with birthday alcohol, kicked off her heels and planted a black-stocking foot in his crotch, massaging it under the table, teasing him into arousal in the private shadows of the public setting.

"I don't want to," she said.

"It's in the script."

"This is a public place."

"Well, yes and not really. You know what I mean. Nobody will see. It's fun. It's something a couple of horny kids would do."

"But I'm not in the mood."

"It's the perfect time and place. It fits into the narrative arc."

"Narrative arc, Jesus Christ, you are so rigid about this shit."

"That's not true." Danny leaned back in his chair. He threw his hands up in frustration. An upbeat love song played in the room, now an inappropriate soundtrack to the scene.

"Lisetta, you are breaking the number one rule—and now you have me doing it. We don't talk about the process, the scripting, when we are in the middle of a trip in time. We just dive into the moment and enjoy it. You're killing the magic."

"I have a lot on my mind. I can't remember my lines right now, okay?"

"You want me to feed them to you?"

"What am I, a fucking parrot?"

"No," said Danny sharply. "You're a fucking pain in the ass."

Tears began to fill Lisetta's eyes, leaking mascara.

"Don't cry," said Danny. "I'm sorry. Please don't cry. It's not good. I'm sorry I got mad. I won't be mad, and you don't cry. We're supposed to make this perfect."

Lisetta got up and left the set.

Danny followed, head spinning from a juxtaposition of now and then, plunging back into the dark corridor to follow her. He found her slumped in a narrow passageway between two sets, crying.

Danny felt his heart sink. "We'll...we'll do another take, another time. We'll wipe that scene from the logbook. Never happened. We'll go back and make it right. We won't argue. We'll be perfect."

"There's too much pressure in being perfect," said Lisetta. "Just stop. I'm flawed. You're flawed. That's life."

"We can still make it better," said Danny.

"I need to lie down," said Lisetta. And she immediately added: "*Alone.* I just need some space. I feel like I'm trapped in here. I'm suffocating. Why are we doing this? It's like some kind of self-imposed exile."

"It's better than what's out there," said Danny, aiming a finger beyond the warehouse walls. "Believe me. We'll make this work. So, the time machine had a breakdown, a malfunction. We'll manage through. The next trip will be better. It will be—"

"Don't say 'perfect,'" she stopped him.

"Okay." He tried to smile. He restarted his statement. "It will be *wonderful.*"

Danny plunged all of his focus into a climactic scene in the new timeline: their wedding night in an extravagant hotel suite overlooking the sparkling city skyline of downtown Chicago. This pivotal moment would cement their bond with fresh affection and tender lovemaking. He believed it was exactly what they needed right now. They had populated the timeline with new memories before and after their wedding. But the wedding itself had been saved, something to look forward to with a heightened anticipation, an event deserving of rich details, total immersion, and the performance of a lifetime.

Danny immediately got to work building the set: a bridal suite brimming with passion and intimacy. He installed a luxurious bed with a sheer white canopy, lace pillow covers, and soft, fresh linen. On the bedspread, he arranged red rose petals in the shape of a heart. He set up a small table with a bottle of champagne in a stainless steel bucket, two thin-stemmed champagne glasses and a small bowl of chocolate-covered strawberries. He arranged candles to illuminate the room in a soft, flickering glow. He selected romantic music to play in the room and drafted a poem to recite, expressing his eternal love. As a final touch he installed window frames over large poster prints of a spectacular view of nighttime Chicago.

When the set was ready, he couldn't resist showing it to Lisetta for a sneak preview.

She smiled at first. She said a few kind words. But Danny sensed a lingering tension. He spoke delicately, not wanting to veer back into squabbling. As they quietly admired the ideal bridal suite, the mood was broken by the abrupt appearance of a black rat scampering across the carpet and disappearing under the bed.

Lisetta screamed.

"God damn it!" screamed Danny.

Lisetta left the set and Danny chased the rat away, sending it under a gap between the wall and the floor. He vowed to buy rat poison.

He tried to cool his temper. He felt cracks in the foundation of his fantasy. It hurt his bones. "Mind control," he told himself in a harsh whisper. "I must wipe that vermin out of my head. It's not part of this world."

He found Lisetta in the corridor, hugging herself with a sad face, leaned against a wall between doorways to the 1980s and 1990s.

"Let's go to the office," said Danny. He had the perfect distraction for her. "Let's pick out your wedding dress."

They sat together in front of the computer and spent an hour and a half looking at options before finally settling on a classic ivory ball gown, strapless and sultry. Lisetta became fully engaged, leaning forward to get closer to the images on the monitor. Danny moved quickly to place an order with the fastest shipping possible.

He kept her focused on the Big Day, skipping past any distraction or hint of conversation that would drag them back into their former lives. The dress arrived within twenty-four hours. He tore open the box and quickly ushered her into the wardrobe room to try it on.

She squeezed into it and made an uncomfortable face.

"You look like a princess," said Danny.

The top fit tight, showing extra bulges. The billowing skirt flowed to the ground, bunched up with extended length.

"You'll need heels," he said.

"I want to see what it looks like."

"It looks beautiful."

"I want a mirror, Danny."

He stared at her and slowly shook his head. "You know we can't do that."

"I don't care. I want a mirror. It feels like it doesn't fit right."

"We don't have any mirrors here."

"Then go out and get one. You got the dress. You got the bed. Now get a mirror!" The tension rose in her voice with every word.

"Please," said Danny softly, refusing to engage in bickering. "Calm down."

Lisetta looked like she might start crying. "I'm not feeling it anymore," she said in a trembling voice.

"Just try. It will come back."

"I've been trying. I think I'm done."

"We will make this the best scene of our lives. It will be incredible."

She hung her head for a moment, examining the fabric on the dress, pinching it between her fingers, and then running her hands across the shape of the body underneath.

"I promise you. The dress looks fantastic," said Danny. "I am your mirror."

Lisetta looked up at him and said, "I want my photo back."

He tilted his head and wrinkled his brow. "Photo?"

"You know what I'm talking about. The picture of my daughter. You took it."

"You don't have—"

"*Give it to me now!*" she screamed.

He took a step back. Her face was flushed red with anger, eyes hardened with fury. It looked all wrong against the soft and delicate contours of the white wedding dress.

"I—I don't have it anymore."

"You're lying."

"No, I'm not."

"Give it to me."

"No."

"You're a pig." She spat it out with such piercing contempt that he couldn't help but give in to a burst of anger. He spoke words he knew he would regret.

"*I burned it.*"

In a sudden flurry, Lisetta began tearing the wedding dress from her body. As the room filled with her stomping and the sound of ripping fabric, several cockroaches shot across the floor in fast, jerky movements. Lisetta screamed at them, she screamed at the dress, and she screamed at Danny.

Danny reached out to grab her, wanting to calm her down, and she slapped him away, half naked as she tore free from the wedding gown.

"What does this mean?" he shouted. "You're not doing the scene? We have to do it, it's pivotal to everything we've built around it!"

"No," she said. "I'm not doing the scene." He watched her disrobe, stunned into silence. After she changed back into frumpy, timeless street clothes, including tattered gym shoes on her feet, Lisetta dropped the bomb:

"I'm leaving."

He felt knocked backward by the statement. "What? No. Of course not. That can't—"

"I want out. This is a prison."

"You're being ridiculous."

"There's a world outside this bunker, Danny. We can't go on believing it doesn't exist. I have a daughter. And you have a son. He came here looking for you. I closed the door on him."

Danny took this in, then narrowed his eyes and immediately tried to purge the thought.

"He cares for you. I can tell," she said.

"You don't know anything about my family."

"I know what's real."

"There isn't a single reality," he told her. "Reality is the product of our minds. It's perception. We create our own worlds, whether it's in here or out there."

"Well then, this reality is no better than that one. It's just as broken."

"What do you mean? Here, you're a best-selling author. Out there, you're nothing. I built your website. I created your wiki page!"

"It's all a lie. Take it down."

"It's not a lie. It's the new truth."

"I'm going home."

"*This* is your home."

Her face sagged with sorrow. "We made choices. Maybe not the right ones, but we have to live with them. We can't just run away. Life is sloppy, okay? That's the way it is. You can't just go back and make it all neat and organized and perfect like you see it in your head."

"But we are! We are making it better!"

She shook her head. "No. I'm still not happy. I thought this would make me happy. Maybe it's me."

"How can you say that? This is our paradise."

"*Paradise?*" she said. "Come on. Look at us. We're getting on each other's nerves. This life is just as fucked up as my other one.

I'm still not satisfied, Danny. Don't you see? It's not about chang-ing the sets or the scenery or the players around us. It's still us. We can't escape ourselves. We can't change it. We are what we are."

"And what does that mean?"

"You're still selfish and self-absorbed. And I'm still a horrible neurotic."

"You can't leave." His tone turned desperate, pleading. "We're getting married."

She made a small, sad laugh.

He continued. "You can't call off the wedding. It's impos-sible. We had our twentieth wedding anniversary! It's already in the timeline. We were married in all those scenes together, our apartment on the Gold Coast, you're a novelist, I'm a pilot, we have a son going to medical school. It's already destiny!"

"You can't make all those things happen. That's not how it works."

"Yes, it is."

"You're a control freak, Danny."

He produced a grim smile. "Yeah, right. That's a laugh. I've never had any control over my life. I let it all slip away. I became a passenger in my own life story. That's my problem. This is a chance to start over."

"It's too late," she said.

"What you mean 'too late'?"

"You can't undo what's already done. None of this—what we're doing—is rational. I can't believe I got so caught up in this play-acting. I believed because I wanted to believe."

"What's wrong with that?"

"Oh, Danny, everything."

He shook his head. His body felt clenched in one big ache. "Why are you doing this to me?"

"I'm not doing anything. You're doing it to yourself. Go take a good look in the mirror, if you can find one."

His shoulders slumped. He struggled for words. "So, you're turning against me?"

"I'm sorry, Danny. I can't do this any longer. I just think we should part ways."

"Incredible," he said. "You're just like everyone else. My ex-wives. My son. My bosses. You're no better than them. You're all in this together."

She said, "Did you ever stop to think that maybe it's you?"

The statement stung. Danny could not respond. He paced a small circle in the wardrobe room, mind racing. Finally, he stopped and faced her with the worst truth he could throw at her.

"You killed Martin. If you go back, you will be arrested and thrown in jail, and you will never see your daughter again. I will tell the police the truth. That you stabbed him to death in this warehouse. You're nothing but an old hag *murderer*."

She stiffened, waited for the impact of his words to wash over, and then made a simple, final statement.

"I wanted to love you, Danny, but I don't. I can't. Maybe no one can."

Lisetta left the wardrobe room and Danny remained frozen, staring down at the tattered remnants of the wedding dress pooled on the floor.

His heart pounded so fiercely that it hurt.

The rest of him couldn't move.

He knew she was really leaving him. She was retrieving her purse and personal identification and car keys. She was escaping from the second life he had worked so hard to create for them. She no longer wanted any part of it.

His passionate love for her churned and soured and became a fiery and bitter dismissal.

Fuck it, he told himself.

Perhaps she wasn't satisfied, but neither was he. She never lived up to his dream image of her, no matter how hard he tried to script it. She was more alluring when she was unattainable. And she dared to criticize him? Life with her was no bowl of cherries, either. She was a nut, a basket case, emotionally unstable and physically deteriorated decades past her prime.

In the ideal state created by his hopeful mind, she had lost her flaws, but now, if they were going to shine the spotlight of reality on one another, she was genuinely broken and probably impossible. That's why she never got the life she wanted. The world didn't want to give it to her. She was a human mess.

"Good riddance," he uttered to no one and everyone.

Danny returned to the office and, indeed, her purse and car keys were gone. The room was gripped in stillness.

He stood at his desk, where he had scripted so many scenes, alone and cowritten with Lisetta, but could not muster the energy for a new entry in his time travel escapades. He simply felt empty inside.

He remained standing, dwelling on the situation, starting to feel nauseous. Toby Junior wandered into the room and Danny met him on the floor and hugged him, finding comfort in his furry warmth.

"She left," he said to Toby Junior. The dog simply wagged his tail in response.

Eventually, Danny returned to the desk and pulled out a pen and opened his notebook to a fresh page.

He felt compelled to create...what?

The silence in the warehouse was deafening. His paradise was rotting. He felt like a pathetic derelict isolated in a big, dirty building crawling with vermin. It was as if a curtain had fallen away to expose the grungy mechanics of an amateur stage play. He couldn't continue alone. This needed to be a shared universe.

He needed Lisetta to come back.

This wouldn't work without her.

Together they could rekindle the magic and imagination necessary to spark the time machine back to life.

Approximately one hour after Lisetta had left the premises, Danny pursued her. He jumped in his car, floored it, and headed for the highway with a handgun under a blanket in the passenger seat.

Chapter Thirty-Five

Adam moved through Monroe Hardware filling a small basket. He grabbed a crowbar, pliers, screwdriver, hammer, and flashlight. As an afterthought, he added a sturdy axe. It was time to take drastic action. He was going to break into the warehouse any way he could and confront his father.

The strange woman who answered the door wasn't going to let him inside. That was a given. His father wasn't answering Adam's repeated calls and text messages. That was equally futile.

At the same time, Adam had not responded to follow-up calls from Detective Chico. He felt sick not sharing his father's whereabouts as the police investigation continued. He couldn't just send the cops his father's way, without advance warning. He had to talk to him and hear from him firsthand. Adam felt partly guilty about his dad's deteriorated mental condition—had he not moved out of the country and cut ties with his father, could he have helped to prevent this pitiful current state?

On top of everything else, Janis, the woman he loved, had grown impatient and upset with his extended stay in the states, insisting that he return to her, unaware of the latest twist in the drama around his parents. How could he even articulate that the auto accident appeared to be a homicide and his father was wanted for questioning?

Adam bought the supplies from a cramped, inner-city hardware store, paying the elderly clerk in cash. The clerk bagged the tools wordlessly and Adam returned to his rental car. He climbed behind the wheel, let out a big sigh, and headed for the carpet warehouse.

He parked in a hidden spot tucked behind an abandoned building next to DeCastro Carpet Distributors. He observed no other vehicles in the area. He took hold of his bag of tools and approached the warehouse at a casual pace, keeping watch for any signs of people. He found none. He could hear distant traffic and feel the urban bustle that stirred one block away, but his immediate surroundings felt encased in a bubble of lifelessness.

The old warehouse appeared more secured than the time of his first break-in. The upper window he had climbed through was firmly closed shut. That was fine; he was prepared to create an opening any way possible. His adrenaline raced with determination. He would not leave without talking to his father.

As he circled the structure, he came across the discarded Christmas tree from the holiday dinner. Some tinsel still clung to its branches. He kept walking and reached the adjacent garage that once housed the company's fleet vehicles. He attempted to look inside the garage through a window, but the interior was too dark. The flashlight beam could barely penetrate the glass, which was clouded by years of spiderwebs. There was a nearby side door with a padlock. He loosened some screws, wedged the crowbar between a metal plate and the deteriorated wood, and popped the door open without having to disturb the padlock itself.

He found a single delivery van inside with the familiar company logo gracing the side. He approached the vehicle's rear doors. He studied the handles and then tugged on one, gaining entry with a sharp *creak*. The van's cabin appeared empty. His flashlight beam touched inside and began to bounce around, stopping when he realized he had glimpsed something curious. He illuminated the floor of the van and stared at a dark, dried puddle of something....

Could it be blood?

Adam nearly dropped the flashlight. He probed some more and found additional smears and splotches of the same brownish red color.

What the hell?

Adam pulled away from the rear of the van. He took a deep breath. Maybe it was blood, maybe not. Whatever it was, it was not fresh. He slowly circled the side of the vehicle and pointed his flashlight through every window. When he reached the front of the van, he looked down and saw something that made him gasp out loud. Then he wanted to cry.

The front bumper was damaged and hanging loose. The grate and hood were dented inward, as if the van had struck something with force.

Adam leaned forward and brought the beam of light closer to the damage. "No," he murmured. "Oh God. No, no, no."

His mother and stepfather had died in a red Honda Civic.

There was evidence of red paint etched into the point of impact at the front of the van.

Chapter Thirty-Six

Danny's rage mounted until it seemed to tint his entire vision blood red. In the hours it took to drive from Chicago to Eldridge, Iowa, his obsession deepened and his fury for Lisetta's betrayal exploded. *After all we created together.... After everything I've done for her... How can she do this to me?*

His entire universe shriveled to one tenacious commitment: bringing Lisetta back to their rightful existence in the new narrative made possible by time travel. Nothing else mattered—not hunger pains, not the ache of his hands as they clutched the steering wheel so tight his knuckles turned white.

The faster he accelerated, the more he reduced Lisetta's head start, guaranteeing that she wouldn't be home long without him.

Danny flew off the highway and sped through the sleepy Iowa town, guided by GPS, cutting through a residential neighborhood, watching the distance diminish between him and Lisetta on his iPhone. His senses burned in overdrive with flames that intensified as he drew closer.

When he reached the house, he recognized her blue sedan in the driveway. He parked behind it, slamming the brakes, and barely avoiding a collision. He flew out of the front seat and stumbled into the yard.

Danny ran to the front door, crashing it open. He immediately encountered Lisetta in her living room.

Lisetta sat on a sofa with an older woman who looked like an aged version of herself. It had to be Lisetta's mother, he immediately determined.

The two of them held one another. They had been crying. No doubt, Lisetta was telling her mother everything, puncturing the special fantasy world they created together with the ugly reveal of a magician's secrets.

They screamed at him in shrill voices and he screamed back. Everything became a crazy blur of frenetic action. Danny produced the handgun to keep the mother at bay. He grabbed Lisetta by the collar of her shirt and pulled her with him, gun in her ribs, back outside. He promised to shoot if she resisted, and the raw passion in his voice cemented his credibility.

He shoved her in the back seat, jammed the gun in his waistband, and quickly pounced to tie her wrists together with twine. His experience using this same twine to tie up thick rolls of carpet came in handy. His knots were perfect on the first try. She screamed horrible things at him, and he told her to stop, this was for her own good, she would thank him for it later.

Did she really want to return to this dreary life? thought Danny. How could she possibly explain her husband's disappearance? Did she want to go to jail? What had she told her mother? How long had they been talking? It couldn't have been long, not with his amped-up highway speed.

With Lisetta securely bound in the back seat, he silenced her squealing by pointing the gun into her face. He hated to do it, but the screaming was horrible and unnecessary.

Danny climbed into the front seat, started the engine, and reversed out of the driveway just as the mother came running out of the house.

Face wet with tears, she dashed at Danny's car, begging him to stop. He cursed at her, backed into the street, and then quickly shifted gears to shove the car into drive.

What happened next unfolded in a matter of seconds.

Danny slammed his foot on the accelerator to propel forward, just as Lisetta's mother came running in front of the car to stop him. There was no time to yell out, to brake, to do anything but witness the ugly sight of the car striking the mother hard, smacking her down to the concrete, and then two awful thumps as the wheels ran her over, crunching her bones. The car continued forward with unrepentant force.

Danny glanced in the rearview mirror and caught the grim image of Lisetta's mother crumpled, broken, and lifeless. Her hair was askew, covering her crushed face.

Dumb bitch ran in front of the car. What was I supposed to do?

"What have you done?" screamed Lisetta from the backseat.

He turned to look at her and waved the gun as a reminder. "Stay down. Stay quiet. The next noise you make...you will regret."

She lowered her voice to a whimper. "Why are you doing this? Where are you taking me?"

Danny responded, "Our story's not over."

Chapter Thirty-Seven

D anny sped back to Chicago, the gun in his lap, music blaring on the car radio to drown out and finally silence the unwanted, improvised dialogue in the backseat. Lisetta's outbursts did not fit the narrative. He needed her back in the time machine pronto, returned to the alternate life they had established together. This ugly regression to an old narrative could not be erased fast enough.

He pulled up in front of the carpet distribution warehouse, braking to a hard stop. He opened the door to the backseat with one hand, gesturing with the gun with the other. When she didn't move quickly enough, he pulled her out by her arms, still bound tightly at the wrist.

He propped her up on her feet and poked her forward to the main entrance of the building. He produced a key, opened the door, and urged her inside.

"Where are you taking me?" she sputtered, eyes still glazed over with fear.

"Back in time," he responded. "And you're not going to escape again."

They advanced across the cavernous main space of the warehouse, passing the dark aisles of towering, cobwebbed shelves. Entering the back offices, they moved through the sharp twists and turns of a narrow, windowless hallway.

He pushed her forward into the wardrobe room.

One corner of the room contained piles of opened boxes from the steady stream of mail-order vintage clothing and costumes to feed the time travel. He grabbed a sharp pair of scissors and cut Lisetta's wrists free from the twine. Then he directed her attention to an item on the floor.

"Put it on."

He pointed to the torn wedding dress, which remained in a white heap.

She looked at it, then stared back at him with big eyes.

"Now," he said.

"Please...." she said in a thin whisper.

"Pick it up."

She slowly bent down and picked up the dress. She held it from the top. As it opened in a long flow, gaps were evident in the rips in the fabric.

Danny saw the damage, but concentrated hard on not seeing the flaws, and the dress became pure and unharmed again in his eyes.

Lisetta simply stood there, staring at the wedding dress.

"What's the matter?" said Danny impatiently. "Take off your clothes. Get into that dress. Right now. We have a big scene coming up."

Trembling, she placed the dress on a chair. She looked down at the plain clothes she was currently wearing. With shaking fingers, she started to unbutton her blouse. Then she stopped and turned, shyly, with her back to him.

"Being modest?" said Danny. "That's okay. That's how it should be. I'm not supposed to see the bride get into her wedding dress, right? So, I'm going to step out—for just one minute. I need to get the champagne for our big night. I'll be just down the hall, a few steps away. You do not leave this room, understand?" He gestured with the gun, which had been successful so far in ensuring compliance. "If you try to run—I have this. I will catch up with you, and it won't be good. Say you understand."

She nodded.

"No," he said. "Say it."

"I understand," she said in a small voice.

"Get dressed."

Danny stepped out of the wardrobe room and shut the door. Standing still for a moment, he waited to see if she would try to escape. Listening carefully, he could hear the sounds of shuffling clothing and light whimpering.

Satisfied, Danny moved down the hall to the main office. Inside the office, he walked over to a large refrigerator and opened it.

A green bottle of champagne sat on the top shelf, backlit by the interior bulb, illuminated in a special glow for a special occasion.

"Ah," said Danny, retrieving it.

He admired the chilled bottle in his hands. The biggest moment of his new lifetime was just around the corner. The young newlyweds were going to consummate their love, commencing an exciting life of bliss together, the way it was meant to be.

He knew Lisetta would come around. She still suffered flashbacks and it messed with her mind. But she would rediscover her true feelings for him. This was the life she wanted, too. She would settle in and realize the truth. There was no going back.

Danny shut the refrigerator door.

As he walked the corridor, toward the wardrobe room, he was immediately alarmed to see light emitting from the wardrobe room's open doorway.

He gripped the gun tightly in one hand and the neck of the champagne bottle in the other.

Had she really attempted to flee?

He quickened his pace, reaching the open door.

"Ah, good," he said. She stood in the center of the room in the wedding gown, sad-faced but positively lovely. Danny began to feel a shiver of excitement, but it was replaced by a cold jolt of shock as he stepped inside the room to get closer to his bride.

His son Adam stood next to her.

"Dad," he said. "We need to talk."

"What are you doing here?" Danny felt an instant slam of dizziness, competing worlds colliding for his attention.

"I've been waiting for you." Adam spoke in a steady, measured voice. "I've been here a long time. It's given me the opportunity to check all this out. Dad, you're not well."

"You don't know what you're talking about," Danny said sharply.

Lisetta inched closer to Adam, cowering from Danny.

"Dad, this is *insane*."

"I have discovered the secrets of time travel. I don't expect you to understand."

"Please. You can't continue to go down this path. I saw the van...."

"What are you talking about?" Danny's grip tightened on the gun.

"I was in the garage. The delivery van. The front is all dented up and—"

"*Shut up*." Danny's temper exploded. Adam's words were stabbing him and had to stop entering the airway.

Adam took a deep breath. His eyes locked on Danny's gun, which Danny had lifted to aim into Adam's face. Danny stepped closer to Adam, keeping the weapon steady.

Adam said softly, "You're not going to hurt anybody. We're all going to leave here together."

"Stay away from my bride," said Danny.

"Bride?" said Adam. "I don't think so. She's crying. Leave her alone."

"Those are tears of joy."

"No, it's obvious they're not."

"You're not the author of this story," said Danny. "Now get out or I'll shoot."

Their eyes were level. They nearly stood toe to toe, identical height.

Adam gave him a long, hard stare. "You would really shoot me? I'm your son."

"No," said Danny. "You're not. You're nobody. You don't even exist."

"You can't erase me, Dad. I'm right here in front of you. And, yes, I care about you."

Danny clenched his teeth. He refused to let the moment shift his emotions. He had to remain firm and inside the right timeline.

"*Get out.*"

Adam shook his head with unwavering confidence. He spoke plainly. "No. I'm not leaving. Give me the gun, Dad."

Every time Adam said "Dad," it was another jab to Danny's heart. He couldn't stand it. He wanted to squirm. "You're not getting this gun. I will shoot you. GET OUT."

Danny thrust the gun forward aggressively and Adam responded with an attempt to snatch it from his father's grasp. In the sudden flurry of movement, Danny struck Adam over the head with the champagne bottle, producing a hard *thud*. Adam stumbled backward and then fell to the floor, stunned by the blow. Danny dropped the bottle and used his free hand to grab Lisetta by the wrist.

"Come with me!" he shouted.

Danny hurried out of the room, tugging Lisetta with him, ignoring her pleas. He brought her to a far end of the hall, where he pushed her with him through the black curtain that led to the time machine. Once inside, Danny felt the outside world fade away. He pulled Lisetta through a zigzag of dimly lit corridors, each appearing identical to the other, with long blank stretches of wall interrupted by a sequence of doors of identical design.

When Danny reached the entrance to the desired date in their time travel, he threw open the door. He pushed Lisetta inside with such force that she fell to the floor. He shut the door behind them and locked it with the loud thunk of a sturdy bolt.

Danny announced the destination. He flicked a switch and lit up the room to officially transfer them to the elegant bridal suite of Chicago's downtown Hyatt Hotel, overlooking the nighttime city skyline.

"We made it!" he shouted. "The trip is a success. We have traveled back in time, twenty-three years, eight months, eleven days to our wedding night. The greatest moment in our lives!"

Lisetta responded with a scream.

He rushed over and put his arms around her, trying to console her.

"No, no, honey, no. Forget everything else. Let it all wash away. It's all gone. There is only this. We are going to make it right again. I love you. You love me...."

She pushed him away and screamed again.

He felt an unsettling mixture of sorrow and rage.

"Please stop. Be happy. Be excited. This is a time of great joy."

He tried to pull her up to her feet and she pushed him away with another scream. He fell against the bed, arms flailing, scattering the rose petals until they no longer formed the outline of a heart.

"Don't touch me!" she screamed.

"Where are you?" yelled Adam from somewhere in the maze of time travel sets.

"God damn it!" said Danny. He had failed to stop him for long.

"I'm coming for you!" shouted Adam. His voice was muffled, as if stuck in the walls. Danny could imagine him frantic and lost in the nest of time machine destinations, hearing them but unable to trace their exact location.

"Don't make any more sounds!" Danny told Lisetta.

"Help!" she responded, screaming. "Please *help!*"

Danny waved the gun at her, but it no longer shut her up. He hated the gun. It was totally inappropriate for this scene. It didn't belong in the script.

"I need you to say your lines properly," he told her, trying to speak calmly, but panting nonetheless.

"What lines?"

"We have lines. We worked on them together. Don't you remember? Why can't you just go along with this?"

"I'm not! I won't!"

"Let her go!" shouted Adam, and he sounded closer, but still muffled.

Lisetta screamed, "We're here! In here!"

Adam pounded on a wall. Danny realized Adam was stomping across an adjacent set—disturbing one of his meticulous time travel rooms!

"You're ruining everything!" Danny screamed at him.

"I hear you in there!" said Adam. It sounded like he was moving along the wall, trying to determine their exact location.

"You are interfering with a scientific breakthrough of

enormous magnitude with significant consequence!" Danny told him.

Lisetta cowered in a corner of the bridal suite.

Danny felt the gun go greasy in his grasp, slick with palm sweat. He didn't know where to aim it. He didn't know what to do.

He looked around the room, a carefully constructed set for the ultimate expression of love and union, now playing host to the most ugly, awful scene imaginable.

Danny joined Lisetta in the corner and placed a hand over her mouth. He pointed the gun at her breast. "Sshhh…." he said.

There was a long, tense stretch of silence.

Danny squeezed his eyes shut. He tried to wish Adam away. He imagined Adam fading into nothingness like a disappearing ghost, no longer a reality. He wanted to erase him with his mind.

Then a huge *whack* sounded from the other side of the wall, across the room.

Danny jumped.

Lisetta screamed.

Cockroaches and mice began to race across the floor, startled from beneath the bed, running in circles. Lisetta screamed louder.

The next *whack* shook the entire room.

"Son of a bitch," said Danny. He stared forward at the lengthening cracks spreading across the wall. After the next boom of impact, the tip of an axe blade emerged from the other side.

Adam continued pounding the axe into the wall of the set.

"Don't do it!" screamed Danny, shaking with outrage. "Don't you dare!"

Lisetta screamed again for help.

Adam exploded through a hole in the wall, pushing past large chunks of plasterboard, axe in hand, purple lump on forehead, eyes blazing.

Lisetta ran to him.

Danny aimed the gun at them both but felt helpless to pull the trigger. "Stop!" he implored them, without effect. They didn't believe he would shoot them. Or maybe they didn't care.

As Adam stepped fully into the room through the hole, Danny could see his childhood bedroom behind him. The juxtaposition of time and place made him nauseous. His arm shook and the gun wavered, unsteady. He wanted to cry.

Lisetta threw her arms around Adam, her rescuer.

"Why are you doing this to me?" said Danny, now simply overcome by sorrow.

"I called the police," said Adam, staring at him. "There's no use in fighting. It's over."

"You—you called the police?"

Lisetta continued to clutch Adam tight.

"Dad, who is this girl? Why have you kidnapped her?"

"I haven't kidnapped anybody," said Danny. "That's my wife."

"Your wife? Dad, she's half your age."

"Yes, yes, we both are."

"What do you mean?"

"We traveled back in time."

"Stop it, Dad. Who is this?"

"It's Lisetta."

"No, I'm not!" said the woman in Adam's arms.

Danny grew confused. "What do you mean? Of course you are."

"Who are you?" Adam asked, facing her. "What's your name?"

"Mindy."

Danny felt as though a punch had landed deep inside his gut. "What?"

"Dad, this isn't the woman from before," said Adam. "This isn't the same person you said was your wife at the Christmas table. This is...it looks like her, but she's a lot younger."

"I'm *Mindy*," said the woman forcefully. "Lisetta is my *mother*."

"Wait, no," said Danny, head spinning. In that moment, all fantasy dropped away. The bridal suite became nothing more than a cheap, crude stage set. Adam was unmistakably his son. And the crying woman in Adam's arms....

"You're Mindy," said Danny. "I thought you were...." And

then a sickening blow of realization buckled his knees.

"I killed Lisetta."

"You ran over my mom!" said Mindy sharply, crying.

"I thought it was...you were...."

Mindy shouted at him. "She told me everything! Then you broke into our house! You grabbed me!"

"Oh, dear God." Danny's legs wobbled. He swooned. "My only love in life, and I killed her."

Police sirens could be heard outside the warehouse walls.

"I'm sorry, Dad," said Adam. "I had no choice."

"You really called the police?"

"It's over. You need help. You need a hospital."

"They'll take all this away."

"You've become dangerous to other people. To yourself."

"I didn't mean to hurt anybody. I just wanted to make things right."

The sirens grew louder, nearer.

"I have to get her to safety," said Adam. "I'm going out now... to meet with the police. Are you coming with us?"

Danny looked at Adam and Mindy for a long moment. "No," he said.

Mindy's face was pale. She was shaking, still dressed in the torn wedding gown. "Come on," said Adam. He gently guided her through the opening in the wall and out of the hotel room set.

Standing alone in the center of the bridal suite, Danny watched them go.

His mind flashed back to the car striking Lisetta. Hard. Running her over.

He ached all over. He wiped away the tears spilling from his eyes with his free hand. The other hand continued to hold the gun.

The sound of police sirens became a relentless swarm, like a horrible hornet's nest.

"I'm sorry, Lisetta," he said in a small voice.

Danny walked across the room, trampling the fallen rose petals. He stepped through the hole in the wall.

He entered his childhood bedroom.

He focused hard on his setting. He wrapped himself in the comfort of his boyhood sanctuary. He ignored the cobwebs, the insects, the debris of a broken model airplane, and the gaping hole in the fake wall. He sat on the thick shag carpet, surrounded by his old science fiction paperbacks, vintage comic books, airplane kits and baseball bedspread. He thought about his brother Reed, all-star pitcher. He summoned happiness for his brother, his parents and himself.

Danny shut his eyes and tried to escape into a swirling suction of darkness, wanting to succumb to the time tunnel, but the searing police sirens ruined his meditation and gripped him tighter in the current reality. He tried to beat the sounds out of his head, pounding a fist against the side of his skull.

"Stop," he murmured. "Stop. *Stop.*"

He needed to grab onto something comforting and hold on tight.

"Toby," he said.

Danny wanted to hug his dog, the yellow Labrador retriever he received on his ninth birthday. He wanted to bury his face in the warm softness of his fur.

Danny called out Toby's name.

But Toby didn't magically appear at his side.

Where was Toby?

He cried out for Toby with increasing urgency. Toby was his only remaining friend. Loyal without judgment.

He couldn't lose him again.

Danny jumped to his feet. He hurried out of the bedroom and into the time machine passageway. He instinctively managed the mazelike twists and turns. He pushed through the thick, black curtain, back into the main corridor.

Danny rushed into the office.

He stared down at Toby's small, padded bed, positioned next to water and food bowls. The bed was empty, save for a rubber bone and squeaky toy porcupine.

"Toby?"

Danny rushed back into the corridor. He ran its full length to the doorway that separated the back offices from the main warehouse. The door, which was usually kept closed and locked, was now wide open.

"Toby!"

Danny ran into the cavernous warehouse, shouting out for his dog. His voice echoed off the high ceilings. He cursed Adam for leaving the doors open—what if Toby got loose?

Up ahead, Danny saw Toby.

The yellow Lab stood in the open doorway that led outdoors. He was a dark shape against the incoming sunlight.

"Toby, get back in here!" shouted Danny, running toward him.

Toby bolted out of the building, disappearing into the light.

"Toby, no!"

Danny couldn't bear the thought of Toby swallowed up in the dangers of the big city. What if Toby vanished forever? His blood ran cold with fear. On top of everything else, he couldn't lose Toby a second time.

Danny ran outside, legs pumping hard, immediately blinded by the low glare of the sunset. He pushed forward.

Someone yelled out: "Put down the gun!"

"No!" shouted Danny. He lost sight of Toby. He could only see a blockade of police cars with flashing blue lights. Dazed, he continued running, calling out, "Come back!"

More voices shouted at him to drop the gun, repeating it with increased urgency.

"No!" Danny yelled into the chaos. Still running, he aimed his weapon into the blur of cars and shadowy figures against the piercing sunlight. "You drop *your* guns!"

An immediate crackle of gunfire filled Danny's ears. He felt the shock of multiple bullets searing his flesh. His legs gave way and he toppled forward, hard, into the cement. His gun fell from his grasp and he clutched his wounds, rolling for a moment, experiencing the earth and sky spin around him.

When his body became still, Danny coughed, feeling like the wind had been knocked out of him. In his clenched hands, the front of his shirt grew wet. He didn't want to look but knew it was blood.

Danny shuddered and gasped. It hurt to breathe. He felt

an awful pain in his chest and stomach. After that, he didn't know what to feel. His brain raced with inconclusive thoughts. His eyes stared into blue sky.

Then a big dog head filled his vision.

"Toby!"

The yellow Labrador retriever had returned. He hovered over Danny. He started to lick Danny's face.

Danny laughed with joy.

"Toby. You came back…."

He forgot all about the pain. He felt only happiness, as if everything that was broken in his life had been repaired in one sweeping correction.

"Don't ever leave again…."

Then two people crouched over him, blocking the bright sunlight. He squinted to make out their identities.

"I'm so sorry…." said the young man.

"Is he still alive?" asked the young woman. She wore a white wedding dress.

Danny didn't move, eyes thinning, keeping his gaze on the faces looking down at him.

He recognized them and smiled.

Young Danny. Young Lisetta.

He felt transported, as if leaving his body. He was traveling back in time and fully becoming the youth of his dreams. This was it; this was perfect.

Danny's head tilted away from them as he experienced a departure from his old, broken-down shell. He surrendered to the younger, more hopeful version of himself above.

He stared passively into the pale blue sky. At that moment, an airplane glided into his view, graceful, steady, and unburdened, like a bird. He watched the airplane in awe.

Danny imagined himself soaring in the clouds, far above the earth. He felt everything slip away, but he was not afraid. This, right now, was all he ever needed.

Flight.

TRAVEL LOG:
REVERSAL 31Y 3M 6D

Today I opened my life and made corrections to bring about a happier existence. The time machine is a success. For the first time in as long as I can remember, I feel happy and calm inside. I discovered the contentment and fulfillment of realizing one's dreams. We only get one shot in this world, or so they say. You can't undo what's done. But I am building a new set of tracks. I have realized incredible powers that exceed the limitations of time. Everything around me is falling in place, orderly and perfect, as it should be. I've waited a lifetime for this moment. Finally, at last, I have found peace.

About The Author

BRIAN PINKERTON is a *USA Today* Bestselling Author of fiction in the suspense, thriller, mystery and horror genres. His novels include *Abducted, Vengeance, Killer's Diary, Rough Cut, Bender, Anatomy of Evil, How I Started the Apocalypse,* and *The Gemini Experiment.* Select titles have also been released as audio books and in foreign languages.

Brian's short stories have appeared in anthologies including *Chicago Blues, PULP!,* and *Zombie Zoology.* His screenplays have finished in the top 100 of Project Greenlight and top two percent of the Nicholl Fellowship of the Academy of Motion Picture Arts and Sciences. Brian received his B.A. from the University of Iowa and Master's Degree from Northwestern University.

Curious about other Crossroad Press books?
Stop by our site:
http://store.crossroadpress.com
We offer quality writing
in digital, audio, and print formats.